Meg-

Thank you for
having Los Microwaves
a part of the Ketcel
album Universe! Check ou[t]
for the "TV in My Eye" shout [...]
David is forwarding you a tape, bu[t]
stream the album in the meanti[me]
eg phosphate.bandcamp.com.
More info about the book
is available @ ketcel.com
including some
backstory in
the blog.

KETCEL

Feel free to reach out with any
questions at deal.chad@gmail.com.

Cheers!

Stay Strange Publishing

A Stay Strange Publishing Publication

Edited by Christopher Smith Adair

Text layout by Patrick Loveland

Cover art and design and interior illustrations by David Rubio de la Merced: azteco@rocketmail.com

Audiobook narrated by E. B. Lawless: eblawless90@gmail.com

First Edition 2021

Published in the United States of America

staystrange.com • ketcel.com • csmithadair.com • patrickloveland.com

ISBN — 9 7 8 – 1 – 7 3 3 3 3 4 9 – 2 – 1

Dropping Keys

The small man

Builds cages for everyone

He knows.

While the sage,

Who has to duck his head

When the moon is low,

Keeps dropping keys all night long

For the

Beautiful

Rowdy

Prisoners.

—Hafiz

The codices of the ancient Mesoamerican people are the only surviving records of their civilization. Within the pages of this new novel, the tradition of magical texts continues. This is a visual novel, just like its codex antecedents, where the words activate pictures in the mind. The author was inspired by true events, and the depth of these real moments could only be spoken of in cryptic whispers, for the impact of the real work of these contemporary Toltec sorcerers would shake the foundation of your current civilization. Every eon, a Nagual Leader arises with the same coding as every Nagual before them. Their mission is the same: to give a hungry populace hope that there is another life after death. The Naguals show the portal, and those who are intended can attempt entrance. These natural leaders develop techniques appropriate for the fashion of the times, and in this novel, the future of technology is accessed fully to accomplish their unending task. The events in this book are based on true experiences that led the author to one such earth portal. He has given each reader a gift to have a chance. This millimeter of chance is enough, if you are ready to leap. If not now, then you will have to wait for the next Nagual to appear in the future, but be advised by this ancient Toltec saying..., "The Eagle of Awareness only flies in a straight line. If the Eagle flies by you, grab its wings, because it will never come through again."

—Ayakel Quetzalcoatl

LITTLE_BALTHAZAR : : 1

Diabetic zombie feet pocked with ulcers. Mutant toenails. A cluster of mollusks rupturing an instep. Acid-pool plantars and varicose veins.

The menu of maladies in the caged window of La Casa de los Pies was more grotesque than Don remembered. Now, he sensed something irreverent, even whimsical, in their portrait of podiatric apocalypse, as if the sheer spectacle of disease was somehow central to its remedy. Walking faster, Don fought the urge to vomit, but as he ducked into Bar Sully—his eyes adjusting to the cantina's perpetual midnight—he felt light. For a moment, the air around him was lukewarm and downy, the jukebox in the corner was a neon portal to distant timelines, and a scintillating pleasure flowed through everything, even the one-eyed Walrus.

"Hey, you survived," Sully the Walrus said in his wry singsong, corroded by decades of secondhand smoke. Sully looked older than last time. He looked fatter, too, but he wore it well, like a ball gown or a hula hoop. Maybe more of a sumo diaper, Don considered, which made sense. The old Walrus *was* in the business of throwing his weight around, and he had plenty of it. He did here, at least, between the carved-wood paneling and dim haze of Bar Sully.

"Survive?" Don feigned irritation, part of the mutual-resentment ritual that had come to define their camaraderie. "I thought this was the waiting room to purgatory."

"Probably." Sully pulled two bottles from the ice trough and jiggled them in entreat. "But it comes with a full bar."

Just a Walrus and his oysters, Don thought—unable to decouple Sully from the allegorical character in *Through the Looking-Glass*. Don made the connection the first time he'd gotten drunk at Bar Sully a few weeks ago, and found the vague resemblance too amusing to let go. "Mezcal, then," he said, settling into a stool. "Two of 'em. Gotta make up for lost time."

"There he is!" An unpleasant smile cracked Sully's face. Behind him, a muted flat-screen played highlights from a game show hosted by a spasmodic rodeo clown with one of the most punchable faces Don had ever seen. "To hell with doctor's orders," Sully said, his broken grin threatening to linger.

Don didn't much care for Sully, but he did accept him as the quickest and least objectionable route to getting what he wanted—and he wanted a drink. Several of them. He also wanted to be left the fuck alone, which presented a paradox. But if he was going to drink anywhere in Tijuana, it would be here. He and Sully had an understanding. Though neither of them would ever admit it, Don suspected they were both well accustomed to their cynical approximation of friendship, unique to terminally lonesome old men who never learned how to be happy, and who would be too tired to stay happy even if they had.

Besides, Sully's place was everything Don wanted a bar to be—always smoky even though no one was smoking, and so dark you didn't have to look at anybody, even though nobody seemed to know the place existed, anyway. Don had never once seen a Haitian cop or a Los Compas cartel retiree or even another medical tourist at Sully's curved, mid-twentieth-century cocktail bar, which bulged on one end and tapered on the other like a surrealist's imagination of an ear. The ear was rimmed in mostly dead LEDs and looked like it hadn't seen a fresh coat of lacquer since Tijuana was still part of Mexico. Bile-toned light ports illuminated the bar top from a Rorschach of spackle and water damage that served as the ceiling. And it stank—stale beer deep in upholstery and the chemical bouquet of Fabuloso excreted from tile floor.

Don found it comforting.

It was also home to the only jukebox in the city that explicitly didn't carry any Norteño narcocorridos or Haitian kompa compilations, and that alone made the Walrus and his uninspired conversation almost saintly. Plus, he poured tall shots and was the progeny of deported Mexican Americans, the latter of which made him just as shit as Don in the eyes of pretty much everybody in Tijuana. And shit on the bottom sticks together, Don had come to appreciate, even if it stinks.

He threw back both shots of mezcal, ignoring the chili-dusted orange slices on the rim, while Sully popped open the thirty-two-ounce caguama of Tecate Red that would inevitably follow. "You beautiful bastard," Don said, the liquor warming his belly and stinging his sinuses with sharp ethyl. "You're too good to me."

"The more you drink, the sooner you'll be back for another heart replacement," Sully sang in his oxidized falsetto. "Self-destructive gringos are good for business."

"What business?" Don extended a hand to showcase the empty Naugahyde booths and flickering bathroom signs reading MORRAS ♀ and VATOS ♂ in faded stencil letters on the far side of the bar fog.

"Exactly. Drink up, buttercup."

Don swallowed a highball of crisp yellow beer and, topping off his glass, hobbled to the jukebox. He punched in the numbers for an oldie from Uncle Ted, then rested his index finger on the chip-pay pad as "Free-for-All" came over the blown-out speakers. Leaning against the jukebox—one of those antique cabinets with the CDs spinning in a window—he thought about his mastiff, Good Boy Bronson, back at the resort in Florida. Don's voicemail was empty, so Bronny probably hadn't gotten around to dismantling Mrs. Crawford's over-sexed Pomeranian, Balthazar, in Don's absence. For shame. But Don wouldn't be home for a couple more weeks, and he wasn't about to give up hope on Bronny Boy yet. He could picture little Balthazar this very moment, humping a table leg or a bag of old lady Crawford's groceries, smiling his perverted little smile, aloof to the futility of his instincts.

Don felt like that now, he realized. A tobacco-stained lapdog mindlessly thrusting at life itself. The liquor was working its blunt magic on his brain, and the cheap elation it offered began to depress him. He'd been more or less suicidal for years, so why had he bothered coming to Tijuana for the surgery in the first place? Was he just another mutt going through the motions? The genetic rapture of artificially extending his own life was already giving way to existential dread. Why was he doing this thing? He didn't anticipate it accomplishing much, for one thing, and he was certain he looked ridiculous—just like little Balthazar.

Don drank, wiping the thought away. Beer, he affirmed to himself, was the only honest thing on Earth. And even beer told its share of white lies.

"So, how long you got left in town?" Sully chirped, his voice equal parts guttural rasp and nasal overtones.

"Who knows." Don returned to his stool. "My recovery stay at the medical towers is cleared for ten more days, but they said payment could take up to two weeks to process, so I'm stuck in this shitheap until then."

"Come on, the med towers can't be that bad."

"Oh, hell no. Food's alright. Flat-screen. View clear over the wall out to the San Diego skyline on a clear day. No booze, but also no Haitians."

"I don't care for 'em, haitianos," Sully said. "Think they own all of Limbo. You know how many times I've had to go around la Zona, buying back my flat-screens and barstools? I'll take the hands off every last one of those pinches malandros haitianos...." He raised his rusted machete from behind the bar like he always did when Haitians came up.

"Put that thing away and give me another mezcal."

"They want to act like thieves, they're gonna get treated like thieves." Sully pulled his eye patch snug and swung the blade back into its oak stump. "You got a word for that in English: 'self-fulfilling prophesy.'"

"What's your point?" Don regretted leaving the jukebox, but Sully's bullshit was already pulling him back from the void.

"There's no word for that here. This is a Catholic country. The whole idea makes no sense. Shit happens *to* you. God shits on you or God blesses you. You don't make your destiny. You are a victim of it." Sully laughed. Not a bittersweet laugh, Don realized, but a scornful laugh. Sully laughed because everyone was a fool, and Don joined him.

"I tried to be Catholic once," Don said, really enjoying himself now. "Didn't last one service. That was Barbados. Place was civilized by Catholics. Like here, I guess. No, I already had my church. Hell, I ran it. I.... For God's sake, Sully. Am I not the only patron keeping the lights on in this dump? Mezcal, would ya?"

"Ho-ho-kay, boss! Another mezcal for my favorite gabacho, coming right up." Sully poured a shot to the rim, skipping the garnish. "Forgive me for concerning myself with your condition, my lord, my king."

"To hell with my condition," Don said, laying a consolatory hand over the suture-gel holding his sternum shut. Touching the wound made him think about the fresh transplant hiding beneath it—where it came from, how it got there.

It made his skin crawl.

CHILAQUILES/NO_EGG : : 2

"Hey, is this thing on? Mom?" Luna set down her hair dryer and smiled into the bathroom mirror. For the first time, she noticed the mirror's tarnished frame—carved wood in a barely detectable floral and dimpled sheet-metal pattern, shellacked into obscurity and then touched over with cracking yellow, magenta, and violet on the blossoms. Was it antique, or merely crafted to seem so?

"I hope you can hear me," she said, deciding the frame itself was quite old, but the floral paint was recent, aspiring to appear heirloom. "You don't mind English, do you? Noel better be practicing with you. You should be able to see me, too. See what I'm seeing, I mean. I'm still figuring this thing out. Did you get the ImursiMask I sent you? Sync it with your phone and put it on if you want to take a look around when you play this message."

Luna adjusted her dark-blue Castro cap and gave herself one last look. Hat or no hat?

"So, welcome to my new apartment. Here's the living room. The kitchen. This is my bedroom, and over here is where I'm going to put the futon, facing the view." She stood in the dead space where furniture would eventually be, when she could afford it, and gazed out at the city lights through her balcony's scuffed-turquoise French Colonial double doors. "It's even more amazing in person, Mom. You'd love it here."

Mexico City was only about two hundred kilometers from Querétaro, but it felt like another planet, made all the more alien by the fact that it was her first time living away from home. She'd never had a reason to leave. Still, now that she had, she couldn't help wondering if twenty-five was too old to feel the occasional pang of homesick amid the excitement.

"Last night, I took the trajinera-metro to the Zócalo marina and went on a self-guided tour. They say the earthquake collapsed the city's drainage system and the storm brought Lake Texcoco back even bigger than when the Spanish conquered the Aztecs. I know you've seen the flood on the news, but in person, I don't know, it's just breathtaking. It feels like it was supposed to be this way all along."

She stepped out onto her narrow balcony overlooking a bustling La Condesa avenue. Below, taxi skiffs and T-metros carved wakes in the black water, which glimmered with the city's shattered reflection in ripples and eddies, long after the vessels had moved on.

"Here, look at this. See how the skyscrapers over by the shores of Chapultepec Park jut out of the water and into the fog like something from a dream? You said you've been to Venice, right? Look, there goes the T-metro that takes me to my new job. And guess what? The line is called María, just like you. You *did* threaten to follow me down here. Remember riding the trajineras in Xochimilco when Noel and I were still kids?"

She took off the cap and tossed it on her bed, which was still just a mattress on the floor. It landed on the tattered outer-space quilt that Mom had stitched around the time they last visited Mexico City, when Luna was eight. It seemed like so long ago. Mexico City was a different place, back then. The whole world was.

"Anyway, my job starts first thing tomorrow, which is why I've got to figure out my outfit and this caster implant, like, now. The operation went really well. I was out of there in ten minutes. The technician said it's easier than Lasik. It's weird, I can't even feel it in there. Look up 'Afterthought' when you have a chance, but take any nanotech propaganda that comes up with a grain of salt. Well, I hope this is working. The red light is on, so I guess it should be recording. Drop me a message to let me know you got this. Everything is going to be okay. It has to be. Say 'hi' to Noel for me. I miss you."

Luna drew a flat hand, palm down, across her navel to cut the recording and then pushed outward with an extended index finger for "send." The red dot in the corner of her vision remained. She laughed, reminding herself that ImursiMask navigation gestures were useless with the Afterthought. She *thought* "send," and the dot went dim. It was all so new and bizarre. She never imagined she'd be an Afterthought caster. A "casthole," as her ex-boyfriend Juan Carlos would say, but Juan Carlos would say anything to look cool in front of his analog-punk friends, so fuck him, anyway.

The stove-top timer went off in the kitchen, jarring Luna away from her thoughts. She went inside, killed the flame on the front burner, and tossed a handful of quartered, pan-fried corn tortillas into a pot of simmering red sauce. Pulling her only dish off the rack by the sink, she piled the chips and sauce into the Talavera bowl, topping it off with a spoonful of crema and a generous sprinkle of crumbly queso fresco. Chilaquiles, no egg—just like Mom always made them. Breakfast for dinner. Comfort food.

Pushing the crema spoon to the bottom of the dish, she took her bowl out to the balcony and sat cross-legged beneath the doors' narrow frame. Onion. Chilaquiles were better with raw diced onion. Staring off into the water, she pulled up her Afterthought's notes app in a shimmering overlay. The words appeared as she thought them:

Pick up onion, avocado, and chapulines at the market.

She laughed, equally amused and intimidated by her Afterthought's speed, accuracy, and eerie aura of omniscience. She closed out notes and selected the app-store icon. A grid of multicolored icons populated her vision. She took a moment to adjust to her overlay, focusing first on the app-store icons, then the waterway avenue two stories below, then back on the icons. After scrolling around more or less aimlessly, she realized she had no idea what she wanted to add to her heads-up display because, until last week, she hadn't ever wanted a heads-up display.

The Afterthought nanocapsule—the technician had explained a few hours earlier—would be injected into her nasal cavity and would then navigate to and integrate with ocular and auditory nerves, along with a number of neural networks related to language processing. Its key feature, thought-command input for text and heads-up display navigation, was made possible by a web of connections clustering around the pineal gland. The science was a little headier than Luna cared to understand, so the whole thing still felt more or less like magic to her.

Magic or not, once the Afterthought was market ready, she anticipated thought-command technology would become the new norm for virtual-reality navigation on ImursiMasks. Once in-eye streaming on the Afterthought improved enough to handle Sawlips immersion, you could be looking right at somebody without knowing that they were fully enveloped by a fantasy world that only they could see. Which, Luna realized, had already been a staple of the human condition long before the Afterthought or Sawlips or even the light bulb was ever dreamed into existence.

Yeah, fine, Juan Carlos had a point. The Afterthought was intrusive and kind of creepy, but this was where journalism was heading, and she was on the cutting edge of it while Juan Carlos cradled his hard-on for cassette decks and windup watches back in Querétaro. He loved to forget how he had his own pair of castglasses like everyone else before it became fashionable to discard them during the Privacy Riots. What was his stupid modular-synth YouCast channel called? *Gimme a Sine?* He'd even attended his own sister's wedding virtually in Sawlips, along with half the invite list, back when that was almost as good as showing up.

Fuck him.

She closed out the app store and went inside, putting her half-eaten dish in the fridge for breakfast. She tossed her jeans and tank top into a corner, resolving to figure out her Afterthought tomorrow morning. Rummaging through her open suitcase on the floor, she pulled out the bootleg Sonic Youth T-shirt she scored at the tianguis a few days earlier, the XXL garment hanging to her knees like a dress. Then, she turned off the ceiling-mounted dome light and crawled into bed, trying not to think about the cold void behind her where Juan Carlos used to be.

NASAL_ACCUSATIONS : : 3

Poetry Night at the Spore Lounge was packed with faces, but Casseus's was not one of them. Marinette sighed and stirred her static-colored cocktail, staring out the bar's wraparound windows, watching a neon blue simulacrum of a moon reflect off iridescent ocean waves in fractured hues.

She should just log off. She didn't feel like reading anymore. The poem was for Casseus, for their anniversary, and this was the third time he'd stood her up this month. Sure, he always had his reasons. Last time it was poor connectivity, which was bullshit. Ever since the Starnet satellites went online a couple years ago, you couldn't get away from connectivity if you wanted to. But lately, he'd been managing to evade it, and her, with increasing frequency.

She flattened a crease in her emerald cocktail dress and rested her cheekbones—which she had just modded to be raised ever so slightly—into balled-up fists. He isn't coming. Just go. Head for the rickety elevator car and log off up in the lobby on the bluffs. Cold-cutting in public was tacky, and Marinette was *not* tacky.

"Looking for someone?" a deep, feminine voice spoke from behind.

Marinette recognized her immediately. "Lady Erzulie." A smile animated the left side of Marinette's face. "I didn't know you liked poetry."

"Oh?" Lady Erzulie purred. Her body exuded a translucent aura of folkloric flower blossoms and pristine mountain springs that hugged her delicate movements as she swayed into a stool beside Marinette. "I like just about anything when the mood strikes me."

"Buy you a drink?" Marinette offered, eager to serve her, the most enchanting of Bondye's divine intermediaries.

"Champagne, pink, and clams casino." Lady Erzulie pulled at her long cigarette. Her posture was rigid with practiced refinement, yet poised on the verge of something almost coquettish. She perspired intrigue from every pore of her perfect black skin—fairer than Marinette's, but also stronger. A hot-pink silk cocktail dress traced the Lissajous curve from hips to waist to chest, her breasts surging from the fine fabric with forbidden invitation. Three gold rings beamed from her left hand next to the cigarette, mirroring the hoops in her ears, which framed bloodred lips, impossible amber eyes, and talon-sharp brows. A jet-black braid snaked over her shoulder from a blue lace cloche adorned with a twilight of yellow and white stars.

"That's lovely," Marinette said, caressing the gold flower brooch on Lady Erzulie's head.

"Yes, I know." Lady Erzulie leaned almost imperceptibly into the acknowledgment. "You like it? Here. It's yours."

Marinette reached out to accept the gift, but the brooch disappeared behind slender fingers.

"Follow me," Lady Erzulie commanded in a whisper. She led Marinette to one of the privacy booths on the cliff side of the venue and, as the slatted saloon doors swung shut behind them, produced a handheld vaporizer in the form of a sea snail. Its contents glistened in every color at once.

Marinette had never taken axol in Sawlips before, or even *seen* it in a virtual-reality environ. "Does it work here?" she whispered, meeting Lady Erzulie's gaze. The shell pressed against Marinette's lips.

"You tell me."

Marinette inhaled and held it.

The floor dropped away in an expanse of nothing.

Bar sounds detuned and elongated.

Walls tumbled off into pinpricks.

A poem materialized.

> *Erzulie's eyes.*
> *All that remained were*
> *Erzulie's eyes.*
>
> *Honeydeep halos*
> *Siamese singularities*
>
> *Erzulie's eyes.*
>
> *Those eyes that beckoned*
> *to be served*
> *and to serve.*
>
> *To be filled*
> *and fulfill.*
>
> *Erzulie's eyes were everything.*
>
> *Master and servant.*
> *Is and is not.*
> *Void.*

Her eyes drew Marinette in.

Marinette could not and would not resist.

The eyes consumed her.

Her vision went black and her ears rang.

Four figures faded in from the nothing.

Marinette sat with them at a card table illuminated by a single chandelier, its smoky blue light swaddling and protecting them from the all-consuming darkness. A drum rhythm and the din of boisterous conversation swelled in her ears, the tracking on the words warping and adjusting until it matched the motion of their lips.

Was she dead?

Not being a trained and purified mambo, Marinette had never communicated with the Guédé—or any other loa—directly before, but she knew them well from watching others embody them in cyberitual environs. Each of them cradled a cigar between cadaverous fingers and drank white rum infused with chili peppers straight from the bottle, fixing her with lifeless stares.

To her left was Baron Samedi, the dual-natured leader of the dandy spirits of the dead. His dark face was painted like a skeleton's, his eyes obscured by round sunglasses, with white stubs of mortician's cotton protruding from his nostrils. He wore a black tailcoat over a pencil skirt, sheer leggings, and toeless pumps. His good side, she knew, was crass yet charming, often flamboyant and provocative. His bad side, Baron Kriminel, was a psychotic murderer prone to bouts of cannibalism. According to lore, Baron Kriminel delighted in singing the praises of senseless violence and absorbing the death shrieks of black roosters as they were doused in gasoline and set aflame.

"The fuck are you doing here?" Baron Kriminel sneered in a nasal accusation. His face contorted to Baron Samedi's pleasant smile. "Are you lost, little lady?"

"I—" Marinette began.

"Nonsense!" Baron La Croix interjected, one elbow propped up on his intricately engraved cane, grinning morbidly in stark contrast to his debonair demeanor. "What matters is that you are here with us, to hell with why!" He smashed his face into an empty bottle and noshed on the broken glass, offering Marinette a sliver with a solicitous, shark-toothed grin.

"Are you dead?" Baron Cimitière asked—more to himself—tracing a bony finger down the page of a leather-bound pocketbook. He wore his love for material wealth in the form of a tuxedo with tails and a towering top hat.

To Marinette's right sat Maman Brigitte, Baron Samedi's wife, in a black and purple bridal veil with skeletal face paint. She was infamous among vodouisants for her supernatural talents of profanity, and for being the only white-skinned loa, with curly locks of hot red hair to match. Just last weekend, Marinette had been chosen to be ridden by Maman Brigitte in a cyberitual, but Marinette had no recollection of the experience—proof of the possession's authenticity.

"You don't belong here!" Maman Brigitte shrieked, rubbing a splash of chili rum into a patch of decaying flesh on her thigh. "Fuck off and die already if you want my respect."

"I was with Lady Erzulie," Marinette squeaked.

"Lady Erzulie!" they all erupted in unison, followed by a cacophony of laughter.

"Let me guess," Maman Brigitte prodded, "you're one of her little...playthings." That horrible laughter again.

"All I know is that...." Marinette couldn't get her thoughts straight.

"No," said Baron Samedi, somber and looking her straight in the eye. "No. It doesn't matter what you think you know, darling. You're drop dead gorgeous, but you're dumb as a doorbell. Just look at you." He rose to his feet, towering over Marinette. The others followed, leaning in over the table, blocking out the chandelier light. "You're living in a dream world, you fool," Baron Kriminel said, his face twisted with rage. "Chasing phantoms. Grasping smoke. You're being lied to by those you trust the most. And you believe them, you scrumptious idiot." His expression softened, becoming sympathetic. "You're blinded by your loneliness," Baron Samedi said. "You think you're in love, dear girl. The only thing you're in love *with* is illusions."

Casseus's head appeared on the table, his face putrid and sallow. Maman Brigitte cackled, tearing at his loose flesh, revealing not a skull beneath, but another face that Marinette couldn't make out in the enveloping darkness. A banda rhythm—drumming from nowhere—became deafening as Maman Brigitte transformed into a giant serpent, unhinged her lustrous jaw, and devoured Marinette in a swift strike.

A single teardrop eclipsed her vision, animated like an app icon, strobing from sky blue to bloodred.

Kervens tore off his ImursiMask and gasped for air.

That wasn't supposed to happen, he thought. And then, wait, *what* just happened?

"Tell me about your church, entonces." Sully began idly dusting his bottle display like he always did when Don launched into one of his self-indulgent rants. Don liked that about him. Every once in a while—call it bartender's intuition—Sully knew exactly when to shut up and just listen. In this case, before Don had even recognized the diatribe welling up within him.

"My church?" Don stared off, savoring a sip of smoky liquor. "My church was the resort. The conference room. The sales floor. I could sell ugly to an opossum, but timeshares were where the money was. Barbados. Orlando. Aruba. Cancún. I was everywhere. The prospects were my sheep and I was their shepherd. I herded their wandering flock of impulses, insecurities, and dreams to my pasture, and, on a good day, they'd convince themselves the whole thing was their idea. You could've stood to learn a thing or two, Sully boy. Fill these stools, maybe even a few glasses when the mood strikes you."

"Enlighten me, Father."

"The first thing you do is sit 'em down directly across from you, like this." Don rearranged a few stools and tossed back the rest of his glass. He hadn't touched a drink since the surgery, and the mezcal was already making him hot in the cheeks and more enthusiastic than the situation required. "Right from the get-go you want to break the tension," he continued, reciting his sermon from memory, just like he'd done at countless continental-breakfast training sessions in every resort conference room from Catalina to Kuala Lumpur. "Put them at ease. Lay out all the steps you're going to go through. That lets them know you're a real person, not just a sales guy, and that you're in this together. So, you say something like, 'Okay, Sully and Sully's left hand....'"

"Easy now," Sully grumbled, glancing at his machete.

"Okay, Sully and his perfect and beautiful imaginary wife,"—Don addressed the empty stools—"while we're waiting for our drinks, let me tell you exactly what's going to happen in your time with me here today. First, I'm going to ask you to help me with a quick vacation survey about where you've been, where you would like to go, and what you've liked or disliked about some of the places you've already visited. This is one of the most important parts of my job, because it helps us stay ahead of the competition so we can offer you the best value on the market. Sound good?"

Don stopped and spoke directly to Sully, who was becoming more Walrus-like with every drink Don took. "This just gets them used to saying 'yes.' Compliance has its own inertia, and small yeses now build to the big yes later."

"Got it." The Walrus produced a leather-bound cubilete dice cup and rattled it, raising an eyebrow. "I mean, 'yes.'"

Don nodded, accepting a die, shaking it in his hand, and tossing it on the bar top. It settled on a Jack next to the Walrus's Queen. "Your roll," Don said, returning his attention to the empty stools. "Next, I'm going to show you around the resort, so you can see for yourself why this limited-time opportunity is so popular with new members. At the end of my presentation, you will be given the option of either saying 'no, thanks'—in which case, I will make sure you get any gifts you've been promised—or you can choose to join the thousands of families who have already said 'yes,' and are now enjoying the numerous benefits of being part of our club. Either way, the choice will be yours. All I ask is that you allow me to give my full presentation and answer all your questions before you make your decision. Does that sound fair?"

"Sure thing, Padre." The Walrus thwacked five dice on the bar top, set aside two Jacks and an Ace, and tossed the remaining two back in the cubilete.

"This part is to entertain their illusion of free will." Don addressed the Walrus again. "Really, people are just idiots on autopilot, running off a few lines of genetic code and bullshit social conditioning, bumping into each other and claiming the results as 'their' lives that they 'chose' to live. You ever feel like the only person on Earth doing things on purpose? I sure as shit do, because when I look around, all I see are robots who don't actually choose anything, any more than they chose their own parents."

The Walrus thwacked, setting aside a Jack and returning the last die to the cubilete.

"People are idiots," Don continued, "and if you don't herd them to your advantage, somebody else will. They're all doomed to drown eventually, either way. You're just building a raft to stay above water as the shit floods in."

"Ain't that the truth." The Walrus thwacked. Without looking at the dice, Don could tell he'd gotten something. "Five Jacks," the Walrus said, a little too smug for Don's liking.

"Great." Don accepted the cubilete and rattled it, one hand cupped over the top. "Now here's where you, Sully, need to pay attention. You always want to pitch from a position of strength. Assert yourself. Know at your very core that this is the best offer anyone's ever made or gotten. Of course it isn't, but that doesn't matter. You've got to say anything to make the sale. Hit 'em in the soft spot. *Everyone* has their soft spot."

Dice flew across the bar top with a clatter, one deflecting off the Walrus's gut to settle on an Ace. Wild card. Don placed it aside with another Ace and a King.

"Family?" Don offered. "Look at all the happy families who are already members, all the activities for kids, shopping for the wife. Don't you want to give your family the world?"

Dice clacked in the cup.

"Financial security? This is the best investment you'll ever make. Buy three timeshares, rent out two, and you're getting paid to vacation!"

Dice spilled onto the bar. Don pulled aside a King.

"Scarcity? You're losing money every day that you aren't taking advantage of this opportunity, and this offer expires the moment you leave the room!"

Dice in the cup.

"Reciprocity? We're giving you a gift absolutely free on good faith that you'll make the smart choice today. You're a good person, aren't you?"

Don shook the cubilete in violent jerks, really mixing it up, going for a Carabina de Kings. "Most of it comes back to politeness. Suggest that they are wasting your time, exploiting honest workers for a free gift card or whatever. Make them feel like the asshole just for being there. Nobody wants to think of themselves as an asshole. Not even timeshare sheep. Of course, you know the whole time *you* have to be the bigger asshole. Maybe that's what I like about you, Sully boy. You always manage to be the biggest asshole in the room."

Thwack!

Gallegos. Nothing.

"Nada," the Walrus said. "Another?"

Don shook his head. He could afford to lose another bet with the Walrus, but he found the prospect nauseating.

"Well, that all sounds real good, Don," the Walrus said, retiring the cubilete behind the counter, "but I don't think I could lie to people like that."

"Lie?" Don snorted. "Everything is a lie. People spend their whole lives humping lies. They'll pay handsomely for the opportunity. Don't think you're any different, Sully boy. What do you think comes in this little thing?" He wiggled the empty shot glass between his thumb and forefinger, feeling mean and empowered by his intoxication. "You drink a few and suddenly feel better about yourself, about the world. You forget whatever sour mood drove you to the bar to begin with. You get talkative and, if you're lucky, things might even be interesting for a while." Don smacked the glass down on the bar top. "Just lies, my friend. You sell them, too."

"Maybe so, but what if they actually can't afford it? Even I don't take IOUs." The Walrus pointed to the HOY NO FÍO, MAÑANA TAMPOCO sign behind the bar as if to formalize the construct.

"Right!" Don perked up. "That's the best part. Most salespeople, they see they're losing their pitch, they start dropping their price. They get desperate. They lose the upper hand." He raised a fist to the sky and slowly uncurled his fingers, releasing an invisible talisman of power. The gesture didn't quite align with the point he was making, but he didn't care. Theatrics had their own separate rhetoric, Don knew, made all the more compelling when he, his audience, or both had been drinking.

"That's exactly when you, the reverend of this church, pitch higher." Don lobbed an invisible baseball at the Walrus. "That's right. Create a sense of urgency. 'You don't have the money? Is that your only concern? Fantastic,' you say. 'What a relief! Is that all? That's simple.' Now this is key. You've got to get real serious here. Look them in the eye, the husband, and, as if it was the most important thing on God's bountiful Earth, say, 'I want you to be honest with yourself.' Just like that."

Don could tell the Walrus was beginning to tune him out, but it didn't matter. His tirade was more about revisiting conquests than conveying information.

"See, for as much as most people love to think of themselves as honest, more or less none of them actually care for the truth," Don said. "They may say they do. They'll kick and scream all day about shooting straight and no bullshit and spade's a spade, but in the end, just about every one of them is content to settle for a fantasy. Most things are exactly that, anyways. Pure imagination. Shit mountain. A dream. And the more shit you can heap on top of that dream, the more eager they'll be to gobble it up. I can't explain it, Sully. People are disgusting."

The Walrus grunted to the affirmative.

Don narrowed his eyes, putting on his sincerest salesperson face to deliver the closing prayer. "So, you say, 'I want you to be honest with yourself. If you had the money, would you enter this business opportunity right now?' And you just keep on staring them right in the eye. When they say 'yes'—and they will say 'yes,' they would if money wasn't an issue—you ask them *why* they want to join. That's it. Just shut up and watch while they say it out loud: 'I want to give my wife and kids the world. I want to take advantage of a profitable investment. I want to get paid to vacation. I want to live the life of my dreams.'"

"Sure, but—" the Walrus began.

Don had too much momentum. He barreled onward, going in for the kill. "Now, you might think this would be the time to start talking, to rush the close. Don't do that. Don't say anything. The first one to talk loses. Just wait. Nine times out of ten, they'll have Auntie Greta on the phone to borrow the whole sum *plus* the bonus packages before their wife remembers tax season is just around the corner. Boom. Thank you and amen. Church is out."

The Walrus blinked. "So, you're telling me I should charge you more for drinks? You already owe me for cubilete."

"Sully, no, you're missing the point. What I'm saying is...hold on." Don pulled a vibrating phone from his windbreaker pocket. Three new messages from a blocked number.

"Ah, fucking pop-ups." Don said. "Cut the juke, would ya?" He removed his ball cap, swept his thin shock of hair to one side, and squinted into his phone light to recite the on-screen script. "Hi, I'm a doctor. I prescribe all my pharmaceuticals exclusively through Fensmart, because I believe in Law and Order in America. Choose America. Choose Freedom. Choose Fensmart." He sent the capture to upload and clicked through to his messages. His mouth went slack as he sunk into his seat.

"What's up, doc?" The Walrus topped off the shot glass.

"A message with an address. One of those axolimine drug dens, Tequila Oblongata, down the street. Says it's from my daughter, Anabelle."

"You never told me you have a daughter."

"I don't." Don downed his mezcal and looked the Walrus right in his bulging, bloodshot eye. "She's been dead for over ten years."

The next morning, Luna caught T-metro María by the park in Roma Sur. She could have ordered a private taxi skiff to take her straight to the office, but she wanted to make a video collage for Noel and get the hang of her caster before she met her new boss. Noel was probably too young to remember their trip to the ancient canals of Xochimilco south of the city, so she captured a time-lapse of the T-metro's ornate nameplate and played around with a few filters she'd fixed to her display over breakfast. The plate, a broad wooden façade standing three times Luna's height, read MARÍA in blue-on-white arched block lettering beneath the snarling cutout of a neon Aztec serpent.

María.

Mom.

Behind it, the open-air platform carried about twenty passengers and a mariachi band beneath a canopy, then another twenty on the following platform, and another, for maybe ten trajineras. When María completed a loop in a roundabout, for a split second, the snake-boat appeared to devour its tail. She sent the capture to Noel with a text message: "Help Mom try this with her new mask, and be sure to turn up the volume."

She hopped off María at a slip attached to a clay-red colonial residence in Coyoacán, one of the few originals in the neighborhood tall enough to outlast the flood. A sky-blue droplet glowed over the entrance.

UNDEW MEDIA, it blinked.

For the hundredth time since leaving Querétaro, she wondered what the hell she was getting herself into. She wasn't particularly qualified for the job, but then, she had no clue what the ideal résumé would look like. Hers included a few years with a vlog in college, documenting the virtual music scene in Sawlips when she wasn't busy studying for a degree in broadcast journalism. By the time she graduated, all major Mexican news networks, following the United States' lead, had been consolidated into mockingbird outlets for national propaganda and status quo talking heads. She couldn't do it.

She saw the listing for Undew Media on an obscure found-footage environ in Sawlips, previewed a few of their immersive livecasts, and followed a job-application link posted by a user who claimed to be a founding member. "Had enough 'alternative facts' in the news?" the post had asked. "Be the news you want to watch. Channel reality with us. Undew Media."

So, she sent in a quick video résumé and forgot about it, along with a couple hundred other résumés she'd sent out that month. Two weeks later, she was floating on a dock in the largest city in the Western Hemisphere, sending immersive-reality postcards from a premarket thought-controlled A/V implant. What the fuck, future?

JACO LARK
Welcome, Luna.

Transparent gray text assimilated in a column on the left side of her vision. She laughed. It was too much.

JACO LARK
Please come in.

The text scrolled vertically and then faded at the upper limit of her peripheral vision. She stepped through the automatic door into a spacious flat, featureless aside from a few ergo-lounge chairs, a blue exercise ball, a couple potted Monstera plants, and wires dangling from the ceiling. A mover mounted a flat-screen on the far wall, completing a ring of screens around the room, showing what appeared to be Undew casts and gamified ad environs.

"Excuse the move-in mess." Jaco Lark spoke in a South African accent and looked exactly like his picture on the website—neither tall nor short, fit nor fat, wearing a black V-neck over black jeans and neat, black hair on his head. Was that his only outfit? His eyes were calm and bright, framed with expensive-looking lensless glasses.

Jaco was the editor—well, there was no editor—he was the founder and CEO of Undew Media, and a pioneer of cast culture. Luna knew of him from his days as a minor internet celebrity, when he became the first person to livecast his whole life uncensored via castglasses for eight years straight. She'd recently endured the surge of narcissists on YouCast, clamoring for Jaco's former audience with nonstop, self-important narrations that had made her cringe with pena ajena—a type of sympathetic embarrassment, though the concept didn't translate neatly into English. She didn't know why she was surprised to discover that Jaco acted in person exactly how he acted on his livecast. It felt like meeting a cartoon character.

"Nice place, isn't it?" Jaco's small mouth smiled when he spoke and then went flat when he was silent, lending the impression of deep thought between statements.

"You want honesty or flattery?" One of her favorite lines to rib Noel when he sought opinions on his love interests.

Jaco's flat mouth crept toward his talking smile, then flew right past it, into a guffaw. "Oh, we're gonna get along."

"Mexico City, huh?" she said, not yet willing to concede to 'get along,' though his ability to take a joke was certainly a step in the right direction. "Seems like a sketchy place to park a bunch of servers, given the recent deluge and all."

"Absolutely," he said. "Most of Undew's setup is staying put at our Berlin location. All the real work, like yours, is done remotely, anyway. This is more of a glorified crash pad while I finalize arrangements for server space on the other side of the Zapatista Firewall."

"Tax break?"

"Better. The anarchist hive mind that presents as the hologram of Subcomandante Marcos has negotiated exceptional autonomy rights in cyberspace. We are sympathetic to their cause, and they to ours. The best kind of symbiosis, really, seeing as we're both empowered by each other's attainment of absolute freedom."

"Cool."

"Very." Jaco took a seat in an ergo-lounge chair, inviting her to take the other with an open palm. "So, why Undew Media?"

"Is this an interview?" She sat across from him, considering how honest she'd need to be to secure the job.

Jaco laughed. "You've already got your Afterthought installed. You've got the job. This is a conversation. Call it market research. I need about thirty more of you to cover all the major stories right now, a hundred more if we want to compete in arts and culture."

"Fair," she said, opting to talk shop in lieu of personal motives. "I guess what did it for me was the recent leak, detailing the data mining and psychographics used by mainstream outlets like *Lone Eagle Newsroom* and *Virtuvisa* to tailor customized so-called 'news' stories for individuals' feeds. The fact that someone's entire web presence—shopping history, keywords from messaging apps, time spent in various Sawlips environs, personal information, and so on—can be modeled into a fairly accurate digital dummy in the first place strikes me as anathema to everything the Privacy Riots fought to accomplish."

"Absolutely," Jaco said, leaning in slightly with steepled fingers on his chin.

"Then, running constant A/B testing on that digital dummy,

identifying words and phrases it responds to, plugging those into quasi-factual news stories, and delivering them to individuals who use stories to construct their reality, well, that's just anathema to the integrity of journalism itself."

"You know your current events." Jaco's talking smile.

She leaned in, feeling engaged and conversational. "Politicians in bed with mainstream media—guys like Appleyard in the US, and ALGO here in Mexico—have become less of cohesive individuals, and more of their nations' own shadows haunting themselves in a feedback loop. There's no *there* there. At this rate, the entire planet will be governed by amalgam nonentities, broadcasting concocted non-news, to minds molded by the digital dummies that their worldviews were trained upon."

"Brilliant." Jaco raised his eyebrows and nodded, then smirked. "Did you see that video of Appleyard supporters brawling by the Washington Monument, when groups chanted conflicting slogans from their news feeds and mistook each other for opposition supporters?"

"That really was a triumph of myopia, wasn't it?" She couldn't help but grin at the recollection of it.

"Funny," Jaco said. "And sharp. You're making me regret our nonnarrative format. Almost."

"Too many talking heads out there already," she said, deciding she and Jaco would get along just fine, after all. "Tell me more about that. You used to be the king of first-person livecasting, but you never turned it into a reality show."

Jaco eased back into his chair, looking pensive. "I never did like being the center of attention. It was the world that interested me. Not just the exciting stuff. Plenty of travelcasts had me beat on that front, anyway. I was fascinated by mundanity. Routine. The ordinary rituals of life. Something about livecasting the most boring and unremarkable facets of reality made them seem to...matter more."

"It definitely made them matter to millions of viewers."

"I hope so." Jaco smiled, somehow more sincerely than before.

"So, how does that segue into Undew?"

"Let me show you." Jaco rose and stood next to the closest

screen, which showed a night shot of masked protesters throwing Molotov cocktails at a bank in Istanbul, according to the caption. "Forgive the Philosophy 101 detour, but it's meaningful to keep in mind that all news, all media, all information creates the symbols and language of consensus reality. Despite their pretense of infallibility, these symbols are arbitrary and often invented with predetermined outcomes in mind. Our job is to undo those symbols, and traffic in the native language of reality."

He continued to the next screen, daytime, where unmarked troops fired rubber bullets and tear-gas canisters into a crowd on an urban avenue. "We liberate information from crafted narratives in an attempt to get closer to the thing itself. How? By casting fully immersive environs that show reality in all its awesome and awful totality. Why have some hack mainstream puppet tell you what to think about the life-affirming transformations happening in the metropolitan ghettos of the American Midwest, when you can go there yourself in immersive reality and watch in real time as federal troops publicly and systematically execute wage protesters?"

The caster on the screen glanced over their shoulder, revealing a glimpse of twin towers that Luna recognized as the Chicago Corn Cobs, from the old Wilco album cover. She had no idea the unrest was even happening, which just proved Jaco's point.

He said, "In a world governed by censorship and deception, we are the eyes and ears of the people. We relay live feed from the ground with the biased narration, and even the caster themselves, edited out. You're not an anchor, you're a telescope."

Luna pictured a telescope, then a rifle scope. "What's to stop a malicious viewer or the cops from locating and neutralizing the caster based on their surroundings?"

"Good question." Jaco moved to the next screen, a vibrant scene from the Ottawa Summer Solstice Indigenous Festival, part of an investigation into the mass disappearance of First Nations and Inuit women in Canada. "For your safety, we impose a one-minute delay on your cast. It's as close to true live as we're willing to let our casters get. In addition, your cast will modulate your voice to our androgynous Undew vox, and replace any glimpses of your body with the viewer's own Sawlips avatar—lending the hyperreal impression of being there themselves."

"The ultimate fly-on-the-wall."

"By removing yourself from the story, you allow it to fully exist." Jaco paused to consider the image on the next stream, a relatively calm scene of men in tan uniforms hacking through jungle brush. "The Afterthought eliminates the need for ImursiMask gestures or the telltale eye-rolling used by glasscasters. So, in most cases, no one will ever know you're casting, unless your presence was coordinated with guides, like this one. Bushmeat poacher patrols in Congo."

Jaco returned to his seat, waiting for her to settle across from him, then said, "I'm fond of a quote from Irish philosopher Bishop Berkeley, 'Esse is percipi.' To be is to be perceived. *This* is your job. To perceive so that the story may be. You see, this isn't the news at all. This is reality at its most raw and honest."

"I love it," she said, and she meant it. She'd already streamed some of his spiel via prerecorded interviews during the flight out to Mexico City, but hearing Jaco say it all in person gave her renewed conviction. She was exactly where she was supposed to be. She couldn't believe her luck.

"I thought you might." Jaco smiled. "Here. This is your watermark. Just hit this and you'll go live."

A translucent blue Undew drop appeared in the bottom right of Luna's vision. She hit it. It glowed red.

"Hello, world." Jaco waved. "Look, I've got a conference cast with our investors in five. I think you've got a pretty solid grip on what we're doing. Remember, the economy and just about everything else is fueled by attention. It's animated by an awareness that *we* give it. Anytime a tree falls in the woods, not only will you hear it, you will see it, and so will millions of others. Esse is percipi. Now, get out there and let this dreadful miracle tell its story."

"Ten twenty-three," Kervens muttered into his radio as he jumped down from the cruiser. He strode across an empty parking lot, his hands tapping around his kit belt for stunstick, gun, cuffs, and flashlight in an autonomic inquiry to which he already knew the answer. Kervens was always prepared.

Ahead of him, in a sprawl of run-down basketball courts, a tapering mosque-like tower jutted into the evening sky, backlit by the sensuous purples, pinks, and oranges of a midsummer sunset. He'd seen the Minaret from a distance many times before—driving by and looking out from the top floor of the precinct—but he'd never gotten around to understanding why it existed in the first place. It looked out of place in Tijuana, but then, most of Tijuana did. Like Vegas, or how he'd seen it in movies, everything in Tijuana felt referential to another place, another time. The city seemed to come from everywhere and nowhere at once, like waking up to find your yard overrun with invasive weeds. Had there ever been a native flora to begin with? Some archetypal Tijuana? Or had it always been like this, a low-res copy in a stack of carbon, its true essence encoded in the substrate of everything it wasn't, but purported to be?

At the Minaret's base stood three of his officers, none of whom he recognized by name. He cleared his throat, getting into character. "It's my day off," he scolded the group in Haitian Creole. Then, fixing his glare on the closest officer, "What?"

"Apologies, Captain Dessalines, but I think you'll want to see this." Officer Etienne, according to his badge. Kervens recalled seeing him around the precinct, now, if only in passing. The officer lowered his eyes briefly, then raised them skyward, saying nothing.

Kervens followed his gaze, lingering at first on an embossed metal placard at the tower's base. Without reading closely, he caught, in Spanish, enough snippets to infer the rest: "original Agua Caliente Casino and Hotel," "1920s," "nineteen-year-old architect Wayne McAllister," "Neo-Islamic Moorish Revival," "boiler chimney," "Minaret." The name reminded him of Marinette, but he pushed the thought away as quickly as it arose. His glance continued up the Minaret's cylindrical alabaster shaft, noting the orange and green geometry of tile over the tower's flared Ottoman balcony, terminating in a wrought-iron spire maybe forty-five meters up.

"What am I looking at?" Kervens said, sternly.

"The balcony, sir."

Kervens squinted, making out the detail of mock windows in white-on-green tile. Just as he was about to chastise the officers for wasting his time, he saw them. What he'd mistaken for extensions of the orange tile motif were, in fact, jumpsuits. Hanging from each one was a body. Nude. About half men, half women, from what he could see.

"Ten of them, sir," Officer Etienne said, just as Kervens began counting. "That makes eighteen this month, since the rent increase."

Prisoner suicide protest. It was an ongoing problem, but Kervens had never seen something so coordinated, with so many people. Their nudity lent the whole spectacle a grotesque, eerily artful aura, and he didn't know what to make of it. He glowered, suppressing the prospect of reacting otherwise.

"Records show they haven't clocked in for a shift in several weeks, and none would make rent tomorrow," one of the other officers said, seeming to relish in the disclosure. "Looks like they saved us the trouble of tossing them in La Veinte."

Kervens twisted his head to examine the officer. Younger, probably not long on the force, still brimming with giddy venom and the false promise of preeminence that often accompanied a crisp new uniform. Kervens frowned. "Your collar is unpressed." The young officer's grin faded. "Get them down, gently, and have them cremated," Kervens said. "I'll advise Fensmart to issue a form letter to their families. Don't call me again."

He left without waiting for a confirmation, catching the last sliver of sun as it disappeared behind coastal hills. Gripping the radio on his lapel, he said, "Ten fifty-six. Put out a BOLO alert for prisoners outside work and residential areas. Ten ninety-eight. Ten forty-two." Then, he jumped into his cruiser, tapped the navscreen for HOME, and stared into his hands for a very long time.

CHROMATIC_MACHISMO : : 7

Tall, slender Black boys hissed "Pinche blan!" as Don staggered through the dark tents of the Zona Norte flea market, where Sully, along with the rest of bottom-rung Tijuana, periodically paid insurance on their few material belongings. That's what they called it, those fucks: insurance.

They liberated whatever they could from its compromised position in your sorry excuse for a home or business, and held it for safekeeping from the real criminals out there. And that service came with a price. It was never much, Sully had told him, but it was frequent. It made Don's blood boil.

Hell, he realized in a flash, that was Sully's problem! He took a deep breath. Gotta keep the heart rate down, he told himself, extinguish the embers of scandal that the alcohol had fanned to flames. Focus.

He pulled his stars-and-stripes Sudmeister cap low over his eyes, shoving his hands into foil-lined pockets to keep the skimmers off his chip. The streets stank of sun-cooked shit and stale fryer oil, and his head was spinning from the mezcal and strange text he'd gotten at Bar Sully. Just a few more blocks to Tequila Oblongata, the address in the text message he'd received, signed "Anabelle," Don's late and only daughter.

Was this some kind of sick prank? And who would even do that?

He pushed his way through tables of mismatched clothing and bastard cell phones with their batteries ripped out, trying not to make eye contact with anybody. Ducking behind a deportee shouting angry Spanish at an electronics vendor, he emerged from the tented village of dirty blue tarpaulin onto the broad avenue of Calle Coahuila, the main drag of Zona Norte's red-light district.

A frowning mariachi squeezed a sequence of sour notes from a trumpet. An emaciated three-legged dog whimpered in a gutter. Up in a brothel, a woman screamed.

Don zipped his windbreaker tight and kept his head low. Calle Coahuila was a popular hangout for the Haitian gang that policed the manufacturing camps in East Tijuana—and they were barbarians. Just like those shits back in Barbados, who would chant "Bulla! Buckra!" when Don walked to the resort in the morning, and more than once robbed his condo empty by the time he got back.

Of course, they didn't like him much either, the Haitians. He was a free, white American. He hadn't so much as set foot in the manufacturing camps, much less been a prisoner, and they hated him for that. He was worse than a prisoner, because he didn't take orders from them. But he did live in their city, for now, and the horrible poetics of Haitian Tijuana stalked him like an atavistic disease everywhere he went.

"Pinche blan!" from corrugated tin overhangs and underexposed alleyways.

"Pinche blan!" from guards at the base of the Arch Monument watchtower, which *pew-pew*ed like an old B-movie ray gun when a coastal breeze snaked through its cables.

"Pinche blan!" from the balconies and chimeric façades of Avenida Revolución, where every architectural fad of the twentieth and twenty-first centuries coexisted, stacked and side by side, in an

anachronistic clusterfuck.

He couldn't wait to get out of there, back to Florida, where the world made sense. Where he had a condo and a dog and a sailboat and just about everything else he could want except for health insurance, which was fine. Don was no communist. Healthcare was a privilege you earned with hard work and loyalty. Strong ethics. Willpower.

An unspecified preexisting condition had caused Medicorp to decline him coverage repeatedly, even after he'd paid loyalty premiums since he was sixteen—two years before it was legally required—in hopes of qualifying. In the meantime, all the erectile dysfunction ads on his phone were replacing themselves with prohibitively expensive blood thinners for heart failure, which meant he'd be needing them sooner than later.

So, like anyone else who could afford it, he'd flown to San Diego, hired a coyote to cross him south in the abandoned Otay narcotunnels, and secured an appointment with a Los Compas cartel doctor. They were good doctors, some of the best in Baja Autónoma. But just like all the degenerate thieves leering along Coahuila, Los Compas had their fee, and their back channels to secure it.

Don paused on the avenue median beneath a palm tree wrapped in spiraling rope lights, gazing up at a giant marquee blinking TEQUILA OBLONGATA in scrolling flashbulb lettering. The bar ranked high up on the last places he wanted to be in all of Tijuana. It was a drug den, for one thing. For another, it was popular with Mexicans, and the only Mexicans in Tijuana were deported, doctors, or Los Compas. Deportees and doctors did not go to Tequila Oblongata. He adjusted his cap and had just set his hand on the bar's carved hardwood door when his phone began to vibrate. "Incoming call from blocked number," the screen read.

He answered. "Hello? Anabelle?"

"Okay, time out!" a man with a Chicano accent declared. "Come on over to La Nueva Nueva Pachanga, my friend! Beer special just for you!"

"The fuck is this?" Don growled.

The monologue continued in a hushed tone, "What you need,

amigo? Mota? Coca? Pharmacy? Girls? We got the best girls in all of Lim—"

Don hung up. Fucking robo-hawkers. He stuck his phone back into his windbreaker as he pushed through the door.

Tequila Oblongata wasn't like he imagined. He'd heard about axol clubs from Sully, how the drug was secreted by a genetically modified salamander and sold for about a million pesos an ounce. Originally used exclusively by Haitian vodou practitioners to enhance rituals, axol quickly caught on with vacationing Los Compas cartel admins, who had become bored with their unhindered access to mundane inebriants. In small doses, axol—short for axolimine—acted similar to alcohol, tickling the GABA receptors and inviting a general sense of well-being, talkativeness, and the evaporation of anxiety. In higher doses over a sustained period of time, it became pleasantly psychedelic and opiate-like. Reality became a dream, but lucid. The skin began to glow—something about the drug metabolizing into bioluminescent byproducts, which were activated by oxygen when excreted through the pores—shifting between hues in a moving mirror image of the user's own increasingly expansive emotional state. At even higher doses, the user "synced" with others in their proximity, especially those who were also under the influence of the drug. Take enough and you start seeing through each other's eyes, Sully had told him, then thinking each other's thoughts.

Sure, Don had seen a few hungover cartel retirees zipping down Revolución with sad, pulsating faces peering from the windows of luxury rydes. But what he saw when the ornate doors of Tequila Oblongata sealed behind him was something that all of Sully's bullshit stories combined could have never prepared him for.

It was like Christmas lights. No, like a color LED marquee. What did Sully compare them to? Glowworms. Except they were people. All of them men. All of them cartel in boots and suits and cowboy hats, or Haitians in police uniforms with their top buttons undone and cigarettes dangling from their lips. All of them glowing in electric cobalt, flamingo pink, dioxazine purple—strobing through the chromatic machismo of Norteño outlaw legends and decorated

tales of the ultimate puta. They slumped in leather booths as they smoked from vaporizers mounted to dimpled sheet-metal tables, the pearlescent vapors stinking of melted lawn furniture.

A technocorrido band stomped around a stage on the far side of the club, siphoning up the polychrome mist that percolated from the crowd, stirring it into a frenzy, and blasting it back in swirling torrents from tuba cannons and Gatling guitarrónes. Nobody spoke a word. It creeped Don out. Above the men, chained to pulsing incandescent poles, were the dancers. All of them women. Deported. American. Reduced sentences for dancers, Sully had said. Half the time of manufacturing, as if the pretty ones had a choice.

A towering Haitian man in a red tuxedo intercepted Don almost immediately.

"Terribly sorry, sir, but we are reservation only." The words appeared to taste caustic as the bouncer spat each one into Don's face.

"I got one," Don said.

"You..." The bouncer gauged him head to toe. "...absolutely do not."

"I'm here to see...." Don was still getting used to saying her name out loud. "I'm here to see Anabelle."

"Anabelle? Blan, kot ou sòti? Gade, I'm going to tell you just this one last time. You absolutely do not have a reservation here. Now I suggest you get back to whatever tower you've been assigned to, call your doctor, and ask him to do you the favor of sedating you until your transfer clears so you can crawl your white ass back out of Limbo before you find out what real health problems look like."

"Please," Don said, "I have to see her."

"Okay, white boy." The bouncer leveled a stunstick at Don's neck and let it crackle. Before it hit skin, a suited arm cut between the two, sending the stunstick flying.

"Muchas gracias, Stevenson. I'll take it from here."

Don knew that voice. About a month ago, he had followed it down the dark stairwell inside an Otay ryde repair shop. He had followed it down a narrow tunnel, scooting along on a wheelchair mounted to mine-cart tracks, for what felt like an eternity with his claustrophobia and failing heart. He had followed it to the unofficial Fensmart/Compas underground customs desk beneath the border wall, where arrangements were made to transfer the cost of the medical stay and transportation in a series of untraceable dumps from Don's credit line to Los Compas' crypto account. It was the coyote. What was his name? Scrappy? Slim? Simon?

"Shorty." The coyote extended a ring-studded hand. "Remember? And you must be...." Shorty checked a note on his phone. "Donald Collins. Hi, Donald. I was just looking for you."

"I got your message," said Don.

"My message?" Shorty withdrew his unshaken hand.

"I want to see Anabelle."

"Of course you do." Shorty gave a reassuring smile. "Come with me."

"You mean she's here?" Don was dumbfounded. "She's right here with you?"

"Sure, Donald." Shorty chuckled. "Just calm down and follow me like last time."

Don thoughts raced as he followed Shorty down a hallway carpeted in fractal paisley. Had she been here the whole time? For ten years? Why in the world would she be in Tijuana?

Don thought back to the last time he'd seen Anabelle, out on that freak ranch in deep east San Diego. She had just turned twenty. She looked so hopeful and full of life, more than he'd ever seen her, but she regarded him as a stranger, and when he stormed off, he felt like one. He couldn't remember the last words they'd exchanged, but he knew his paternal concern had curdled into outrage, and he'd never forgiven himself for it. Memory was funny like that—there when you didn't need it, and nowhere to be found when you'd miss it most.

But he could still remember the day she was born like it was yesterday. He was just twenty-nine, an architecture dropout from the University of South Florida, trying to reinvent himself as the last used-car salesperson on Earth. Her mother, a one-night stand who Don begrudgingly agreed to keep the baby with, died of childbirth complications, and just like that, Don's world turned upside down. He went from High Life nights to housewife mornings, as he'd loved to remind Anabelle, raising her himself in Tampa. They were close, despite or maybe because of the fact that Don had no idea how to be a father. All he knew was that he would do whatever it took to keep her safe, which proved increasingly difficult as she grew into her rebellious teens and began to see him as more of an obstacle to be avoided than the friend that he knew himself to be.

The day she turned eighteen, Anabelle gave an unceremonious farewell and moved across the country to live with Don's sister in San Diego. It was his fault. He was too hard on her. He was clumsy and overbearing in his crusade to keep her. Even more, he was stupid to think he could contain her when an entire cosmos was conspiring to break her free. He knew what it was like. He was the same as a teenager. He knew exactly how she must have felt, and still, he became his own parents. Maybe worse.

It was one of life's more vindictive jokes, he realized, the endless cycle of the Rebel becoming the Rules Person. Life wants us to fail, but gloriously, with fireworks and press releases. Helming phantom fleets and sinking with the ship, our toy boats blowing bubbles into the nothing. That's how he felt when he watched her leave, at any rate, but he knew she would be safe with Clara, the cool aunt. And she was safe, for a while, but even Clara couldn't convince Anabelle that the space cult she'd fallen in love with was a bad idea. None of them had any idea just how bad.

When Anabelle disappeared, Don felt like an alien. He was the lone inhabitant of an entire planet of grief and anger and confusion. Everyone else was a gawking tourist, marveling at his miserable enclosure with ketchup on their chins. He hated them for it.

Having lost the only light in his life, he gave up on humanity and let appetites dictate his destiny. Eat, drink, and fuck you. He often reminded himself that hedonism was just as good an approach as any, and it made a sort of evolutionary sense. A deep genetic tradition, pointing back to primordial stew, dictated his predilection to vice, and he was generously obliging to satisfy it. It wasn't Don, the individual point of free will, fucking off completely. It was the parameters of the universe themselves. Physics. He was just a pawn in this game.

Still, what good had any of that done him? He still felt as ugly and selfish and blind as any of the timeshare sheep, who clamored to the salt lick of a New You, and walked away indebted to their Same Old Self.

Snapping himself out of his reverie, Don followed Shorty through a door into a vacant dining hall. If she was here, what was she doing hanging around this young punk coyote? He followed Shorty through a door on the far side of the dining hall. Oh god, they weren't... together, were they? The door opened into a dim alley. Or worse, had she been forced to dance for these lunatics? That thought hurt him, not in the heart or whatever that thing was, but in his head. It felt like it was exploding. His ears were ringing, loud. The last thing he saw was Shorty standing over him, clutching the barrel of a gold-plated pistol and chewing on an uninterested frown.

THE_BLEEDING_EDGE : : 8

Thunder rumbled in on a gut frequency across the Zócalo marina and, for a split second, the raindrops on the pulque-bar window aligned perfectly with the Undew droplets running down Luna's display. She glanced back to the bar-menu screen embedded in her corrugated sheet-metal table, selected the passion-fruit blend, and held her finger on the chip-pay pad.

Across the bar, a man sat at an industrial table wearing an ImursiMask, gesturing into the elongated egg spanning from one temple to the other, backdropped by poster-sized Lotería cards depicting various Mexican pop icons. Get a room, she thought, wondering how people still found it appropriate to go VR in public. A decade after its inception, she liked to think virtual reality wasn't the digital opium that transhumanophobes had bemoaned incessantly, but people like this guy were only proving their point. Granted, you could go on hyperreal adventures or visit exotic destinations or create impossible art and music with a hive mind of strangers, but Sawlips—the ImursiMask's native operating environment—could be astoundingly banal in its practicality.

Was this guy shopping, finishing some university homework, monitoring virtual-currency investments, or just catching up with a boring, niche social scene? She watched him give an exculpatory shrug and mumble something she couldn't quite make out. Fighting a parking ticket, she decided, pegging him as the owner of the dinghy she'd noticed parked crooked out front when she arrived.

She shook her head and refocused on the Undew landing-page overlay. She hadn't played around much with Undew's viewer interface since she got her Afterthought in, but she was quickly recognizing the implant's advantages and shortcomings compared to the ImursiMask.

While both products were designed by Jaco's friends at Synape Hypertech, they served distinctly different purposes. An ImursiMask would block out all external sound and vision, fully immersing her in a livecast or fabricated Sawlips environ by cutting her off from her immediate surroundings. She could explore the endless virtual spaces of Sawlips with real-time visuals and audio, interacting via hand gestures, head movement, verbal communication, facial expressions, and biometrics such as heartbeat and perspiration to convey accurate emotional states to her avatar.

The Afterthought, on the other hand, allowed her to remain oriented in her seat at the hipster pulque bar, displaying Undew's landing page in a transparent overlay. But the overlapping visual aspect, combined with the lack of in-ear audio playback, made for a less-than-mesmerizing immersion experience. The interactive environs of Sawlips weren't even an option with the Afterthought, but simple ImursiMask apps—web browser, maps, translator, and the like—were actually more efficient with the gestureless Afterthought.

Whereas the ImursiMask was a wearable product optimized for virtual interaction, she concluded, the Afterthought was more of a sophisticated body modification that specialized in transplanting the external world into the virtual. Each droplet on her Undew landing-page overlay represented one such external-to-virtual transplant—active livecasts that would slide down her display until one happened to align with the Undew logo outlined in the center. Jaco was big on throwing viewers into stories they wouldn't typically choose on their own, she knew from interviews, and this was his idiosyncratic way of nudging them along.

She let a droplet click with the logo. The Undew drop enlarged, previewing a livecast of the Za'atar Conflict in Lebanon, overlaying her surroundings in a translucent sheen. She zoomed in and took a look around, but was almost immediately pulled out of the muted livecast by the sound of glass shattering over the bar's ruidoso playlist. Glancing across the aisle, she saw the parking-ticket guy fumbling to remove his ImuriSiMask, his pulque mug in pieces on the floor.

Qué naco, she thought, then chastised herself for even thinking the outmoded, classist insult.

A portly waiter scurried over to the man's table, pointing to a sign on the wall indicating that ImuriSiMasks were only permitted in privacy booths, probably for this very reason. He'd no doubt lost countless mugs to oblivious patrons gesturing into virtual nowhere. Judging by his reproachful expression as he swept up the mess. The man apologized in a dismissive, rapid-fire cadence—a local Chilango accent tinged with a couple summers in L.A. The observation reminded her how out of place she felt here in the bustling capital, even though *he* was the one acting like an ignorant, entitled tourist.

Regardless, everyone looked like a maladaptive daydreamer when they were wearing an ImuriSiMask. For as ubiquitous as they had become, going VR in public was gauche, and it looked ridiculous. She couldn't help but cringe with pena ajena at strangers on the bus or in a restaurant—people like the parking-ticket guy—as they gazed into nothing, gesturing arcane commands, muttering one-sided retorts to bone-conduction conversations, and expressing emotions in unnatural micro-flashes of mock feeling for the facial detectors. It was everything Grandma's generation distrusted about smartphones, but with an added element of detached theatrics that made it almost masturbatory to behold.

The waiter dropped a mug of purple-green pulque at her table, rolling his eyes apologetically before scuttling off with his tray of drinks. She took a gulp of the vile slime, reminding herself the first sip always tasted off. Walking to the back of the bar, she passed a table of drunk punks loudly misquoting Marx, then squeezed past a vendor carrying a box of cigarettes, snacks, and candies. She placed her finger on the chip-pay pad for a privacy booth, pulling the door shut behind her. The shower-sized room glowed red from an overhead bulb. Lodging her mug in a cupholder, she removed her ImuisiMask from her shoulder bag and secured it over her eyes.

Her Swalips avatar—a purple, anthropomorphic cat in a Soviet spacesuit—greeted her with a Vulcan salute as her portal lobby materialized around her in concentric rings of animated doorways suspended in a starry vacuum. Straight ahead, weekly goal reminders flashed in red starbursts over the Calypso Krav Maga and Nuclear Waste Aerobics portals. She'd get caught up on exercise tomorrow, if she felt like it. To her left, Fling advertised one new match. Splaying the fingers of both hands forward in a custom corporeal vernacular, her avatar walked through the portal's logo—a heart that perpetually broke in half and then rejoined in a two-frame animation of truck-stop neon.

It was petty, but after she'd broken up with Juan Carlos, she resolved to finally get into online dating, purely because she knew he'd hate it. Quickly discovering that she wasn't crazy about it either, she'd purchased a low-level AI cloak of herself to filter potential matches, in lieu of attending all the awkward virtual first dates herself. Her dating cloak had followed her, invisibly, around Swalips for a few weeks, acquiring her mannerisms and noting her preferences in a series of mock dates with simulated partners. She still laughed at the idea of her cloak doing the bulk of its virtual dating with other cloaks—two automated proxies vetting each other over make-believe dinners and shared hallucinations of walks on the beach.

One such cyber-suitor stood before her now, a Mexico City local named Arturo, according to the stats floating over his head. He wore a full suit of chain-mail armor, shifting his weight in a series of poses meant to convey nervous anticipation. She pulled at the corners of his stats box to view his full profile, and found herself looking out the window of a medieval castle. Arturo appeared at her side, his expression dire.

"My queen," he pleaded, "there are rumors from the northern hamlets of a great beast wreaking havoc upon our kingdom. Shall you send for help?"

Luna laughed. She recognized the script from a few weeks ago, when she'd spent about two hours in a medieval dragon-slayer quest before realizing the whole thing was a mouthwash ad—the dragon serving as a dubious metaphor for bad breath and gingivitis, the slayer's secret weapon a translucent sword the color of antifreeze. She closed out the quest and flagged Arturo's bot account as spam. Bots had their place in Sawlips—customer service, classrooms, games—but not her inbox, and not without a halo.

Red halos on bots—indicating that they weren't being controlled in real time by an actual human—were meant to discourage the corporate sock puppets and political astroturfing that had ruined the social media of Mom's generation. Of course, Luna still encountered plenty of manual shill avatars in various environs, blatantly seeding conversations with whatever talking points they'd been paid to push. But nowadays, most advertisers just purchased placement in high-visibility virtual locations like they did in the real world, and even those were declining in favor of gamified ad environs, like Arturo's.

She pulled out of the Fling portal, noticing some Seenit and Videogum alerts for the hashtags she followed on the other side of the lobby. She hopped into Seenit and scrolled through the forum of glasscaster videos. Selecting the post with the most upvotes, she was thrown into a first-person view of a scuba diver's close call with a giant squid in the Puget Sound, the airbag epiphanies of a ryde passenger on the edge of a Big Sur bluff in a landslide, a flash of lightning captured inverted in a wine glass, branching in fractal yearning for its terminus in the sky. She gestured to give an upvote as the highlight reel played on. It was human concentrate. Nuclear frisson. Cosmic awe on shuffle play, making Luna feel at once connected to and removed from the world.

She slid her mask up to her forehead, considering how, soon, she would be creating the content that countless strangers would experience through her eyes. She'd always found it exhilarating to look through others' points of view and know the world was really happening. But, back home, she often felt like it was happening without her. She needed to know where the bedrock was. The thing propping all this up. She needed to be uncomfortable, adventurous, and alert. More than anything, she realized, she needed to know if she was more than who she thought she was.

Maybe that's what made Undew Media and the Afterthought so appealing. This was her ticket out of herself. Despite her recurring pangs of apprehension, she suddenly appreciated how privileged she was to have an Afterthought installed. Since the latest premarket version was undergoing exclusive closed-beta testing by less than twenty Undew Media livecasters, Luna was finally where she'd always dreamed of being—on the bleeding edge of high-tech guerrilla journalism.

She smiled, then chased it with a sip of pulque, willing herself to enjoy it despite the lingering notes of vomit. Shutting off her ImuraiMask, she stepped out of the privacy booth, back into the bar. Walking back to her seat, a pizza drone buzzed over her head and down the aisle, setting a box on the Marx punks' table. They posed for a picture with the drone, then waved and laughed as it hummed past her, off into the night.

She scrolled absentmindedly through the appetizer menu, wondering if Mom and Noel had gotten her messages yet. She should call and make sure they were okay. Tomorrow. For now, it was time to get to work. Ya ponte a trabajar, as her father would say, even though he found excuses not to work, get sober, or even come home for most of her life. Fuck him, wherever he was. A la chingada with him and Juan Carlos both.

Her father, Burlyn, was the reason she ended up here in Mexico City in the first place. Well, Mom was, but only because Burlyn had fucked up with some crypto dealers in New St. Petersburg, leaving Mom with an astronomical bill before he disappeared into hiding or, more likely, a euthanasia booth. The coward. He was the reason Mom got calls every morning reminding her of the exact size of the debt—eight million rubles—and number of days until it, and she, expired.

Today, it was twenty-seven.

That's what she was really doing here, as if she could forget. Undew not only paid a decent starting salary—enough to make rent and bills and hopefully work on a payment plan with the crypto gangsters—but it also had potential for huge advertising royalties that would grow exponentially as her number of viewers climbed. The dollar and peso may have been unstable, but the economy of attention was thriving. So, yeah. Ya ponte a trabajar.

She could start with a piece on the post-minimal silent discos she'd heard about in the cathedral. The vlog back in Querétaro would have eaten it up, but were a bunch of teddycrust kids navel-gazing to binaural beats through earbuds really Undew material? Think bigger. What does Jaco want to see? Hoversailing on the bluffs of Oaxaca? Too bro-y. How about the MS-13 wars in Quintana Roo? God, Mom would have a heart attack.

JACO LARK

Love the Limbo pitch. Last week I would have told you to keep dreaming, but lucky for you, and your viewers, we were just contacted by an anonymous source in East Tijuana who says they can give us access to the Maquilandia work camps. Probably a Haitian insider pissed off at Los Compas. They've arranged a ryde and have cleared you with cartel customs. They'll contact you when you arrive with more details. If anyone asks, you're there to get your tonsils out. Are you ready to go down as the greatest rookie livecaster in all of history? Your ticket to fly out first thing tomorrow is attached. Your chip has been synced to the company expense line. Make your public proud.

She took a slurp of pulque, which tasted a little less like puke the more she drank. What was Jaco talking about? He must have meant to message someone else.

JACO LARK

By the way, I appreciate the antiquated gesture of an email (it reminds me of my freelancing days) but please limit all future communication to Afterthought messaging, like this. Your viewers won't be able to see messages or any overlays when you're casting, so feel free to keep in contact. Don't worry, the platform will feel like second nature in no time. Ditch the novelty filters but please be sure to enable your Perf plug-in. It'll grab details from your peripheral vision so viewers can interact with your environs in 120°, not one fixed angle. That's what we're all about, if that's not exceedingly obvious by now. Good luck!

The scrolling text evaporated over a row of pulque barrels as she finished reading. She sighed.

LUNA TESCHNER

Jaco, there must have been a mistake. I never pitched Limbo. Besides, I don't think I'm ready to—

Luna stopped herself. She saw exactly what she was doing. It was what Burlyn would do, and that thought tasted worse than all the pulque in the valley. Besides, maybe this was Jaco's way of giving her the story without being such a typical editor. He wasn't an editor, for one thing, and it seemed like something he would do. He was one of those next-wave tech guys. They always did things weird. She deleted her text and started over.

LUNA TESCHNER
Can't wait. I won't let you down.

She raised her milky glass of slime in a cheers to herself. Here's to being the first journalist to gain access to Tijuana's infamous manufacturing prisons. Here's to raw and honest reality.

¡Toreros y Alarmas! was on again. Some old gringo from Florida this time, trying to run on his bill. Serves him right, Kervens thought. A man never goes back on his word, and he never, ever digs a hole deeper than he can get himself out of.

Kervens swirled the ice in his rum tumbler and fixed his gaze on the oil tankers traversing the horizon beyond his flat-screen. On moonlit nights like these, when the Compas naval fleet along the Coronado Islands forged silver silhouettes in the distance, he was reminded of the view from the shanty where he was raised outside of Port-au-Prince. His mouth turned down. He refocused his attention on the flat-screen, pushing away thoughts of Haiti, the Minaret suicides, and his disturbing Sawlips encounter with the Guédé that afternoon.

Narco-cinema had come a long way since *La Camioneta Gris*. At least, that's what the Flores Magón brothers liked to tell him at their weekly meetings in a private environ on Sawlips. And, at the end of the day, the brothers' opinions were the only ones that mattered. They, along with the rest of Los Compas, were infatuated with *¡Toreros* *y Alarmas!* The sadistic game of cat and mouse reminded them of the old days, when they still got to hunt down their enemies and make them squirm a bit before dissolving them in a vat of acid, or stringing them off a bridge with nasty messages carved in their stomachs. Of course, they could still do all that, but it wasn't the same. For one thing, all the rival cartels had been obliterated from Baja Autónoma. For another, Los Compas made the law. The thrill just wasn't there, and why bother getting out of breath in a flesh-and-blood manhunt when they could do it from the comfort of home?

As far as Kervens could tell, *¡Toreros y Alarmas!* was somewhere between sport and porn for them—plugging into ImursiMasks, cuing up in a private Sawlips portal, and taking turns stalking prey through the eyes of their favorite bulls. As was tradition, the cartel's weapon of choice came straight from the US. The abducted Border Patrol automatons were reprogrammed to have their razor-sharp tracking subroutines overlaid with the personalities of neighborhood patron saints. In place of the Catholic canon, *¡Toreros y Alarmas!* invented its own roundtable of shoddy pop-culture knockoffs—not unlike the overpriced curios trash that Kervens used to see printed onto ponchos and tchotchkes along Revolución, back when the street catered to tourists.

The host, a vulgar rodeo clown called El Chavo del Loco, bounced around the flat-screen in a series of nauseating cuts and swipes as the mechanical mascots were introduced. Kervens hit the subtitles. He may as well practice his English if he was going to watch narco smut, even though his English was already near perfect and El Chavo del Loco spoke in the borderland pocho Spanglish that Kervens had become fluent in years ago.

"Setting out from his home shrine in Colonia Libertad in just eleven hours, a Los Compas favorite, Jesús Malverde!" El Chavo ejaculated. A Border Patrol bot with a painted-on mustache, wearing a white cowboy hat and matching white suit, flashed on screen as cartoon marijuana leaves spun around his head to a blaring Norteño ballad.

"Twelve hours later," El Chavo tittered, "we'll be releasing the one and only Carlos Manson, the original bad hombre of the occult, representing Maquilandia's largest residential colony, Valle de la Muerte!"

A cross-eyed bot with a scraggly hairdo of scrap wire stared into the camera and growled, "Smiley faces for everybody!" as SHIT HAPPENS acid tabs exploded from his head like confetti.

"If helter-skelter can't bring down our matador," El Chavo hollered, "or should I say, mata*don*?" Two shots on a snare drum, a cymbal, and a sad trombone as El Chavo del Loco spiraled down a giant toilet. "Okay, okay," he continued. "So, if by some act of god, Manson can't fucking do it, guess what? Zona Norte represent! That's right, third up we've got the undisputed queen of pop, Mamá Dona!" A bot in a silver corset with conical breast cups lip-synced through a headset to a melody that Kervens recognized from the American oldies station as "Bad Girl," concluding a chorus by unleashing a flurry of neon violence from her laser-converted AK-47.

"And last but not least," El Chavo assumed a hushed tone of reverence, "Yaqui Chan, the notorious ninja representing the catacombs of La Chinesca in our great, immortal, untouchable capital, Mexiiicaliii!" A shirtless bot executed a series of chops and kicks followed by a triple backflip, landing in the splits and bowing with palms pressed vertically against each other as his solemn face lowered into the lens.

Kervens shut off the screen. Upper-class Americans paid top dollar for subscriptions to ¡Toreros y Alarmas!, supplementing their taste for once-illicit drugs—now produced domestically and readily available at any neighborhood Fensmart—with exotic "Third World" gorecasts. Some of his own subordinates couldn't get enough of the program, but he never saw the draw. He didn't get pleasure out of death, though he knew his life would be much easier if he did. He had seen enough of it in Haiti, enough of it in Brazil, enough of it walking and busing and begging for rides through Central America into Mexico, and then clear up to the border where he would find himself stuck in purgatory long before it was called Limbo.

Kervens swallowed the rest of his white rum, his gaze going soft on the ocean beyond the flat-screen. He sighed.

It was hard to believe it'd been ten years since Hurricane Wanda leveled Haiti and he, along with about a million other refugees, set off on a cross-continental asylum quest towards the US. It had helped that Haiti's Catholic-conservative mainstream blamed gays and vodou practitioners for provoking the disaster, and Kervens happened to be both. More correctly, he preferred men, but had slept with plenty of women—as if the bloodthirsty zealots cared to split hairs. But the vodou tradition recognized the soul as inherently genderless, and while his Catholic upbringing seemed bent on pushing him away, his local mambo had welcomed him with open arms.

He poured another glass, then went to his dresser, changed out of his uniform into a white-cotton-lace romper, reclined on the couch, and shut his eyes.

Being raised in Haiti, where homosexuality was dangerous on a good day and cross-dressing was criminal, Kervens had become an expert at "mettre des roches sur nos epaules"—"putting rocks on our shoulders"—an epithet for the charade of exaggerated masculinity required to avoid detection. It served him well in Tijuana, putting on macho airs for Los Compas and his precinct. They respected him, some even admired him, but he found the ruse exhausting. He couldn't keep it up much longer, but he knew he must. Just long enough to get out.

He thought back to the smug little officer at the Minaret, unsettled by the wicked zeal he'd seen. It wasn't as uncommon as Kervens would've liked it to be. Many of the younger Haitians under his command, the ones who showed up well after US amnesty had been canceled, were happy to stay and rule the trash heap of Tijuana indefinitely. They had no dreams, no greater purpose. But Kervens still had his eyes on the other side, and he was getting closer every day.

Despite the anti-immigration craze that had swept the US over the past decade, he could still openly be himself there—a prospect that was impossible at his current station in life. Mamá Dona, he considered, seemed to be a relic of Los Compas' fascination with the drag queens at the bars in Zona Norte and by the Arch on La Revu, but he couldn't help but see the bull as a grotesque metaphor for the way the cartel had been systematically depriving women of agency since their inception. Unlike Haiti, cross-dressing was accepted in Tijuana, if only within the rigid constraints of the stereotype. But in practice, especially among his Haitian law-enforcement subordinates, it would be ruthlessly ridiculed as effeminate and masisi. Kervens could never be himself in Limbo, he knew. Yet there he remained, exiled to the liminal space between the masculine hyperbole that he projected to the outside world and the feminine sensuality that he nurtured behind closed doors.

Five years. Five more miserable years as captain of Tijuana's Agua Caliente Police precinct, before Los Compas would facilitate his citizenship contract with the United States. Or rather, with Fensmart, which owned US ImmiCorp.

Five years until he could finally cross and be with Casseus.

Casseus was the only thing that mattered anymore.

Kervens tossed back his glass of rum, poured another, and lit a cigarette—determined to erase the Guédé's nasal accusations from his mind completely.

Don's vision rebooted in a constellation of shooting stars that resolved to headlights on the highway. When did he get in a ryde? And why was it barreling west towards the Haitian high-rises on the shores of Playas? White noise escaped in sharp bursts as Shorty came into focus hunched over in his seat.

"Hey! Sorry about the putazo, man, your head." Shorty hooked one fist in a mock strike, wiping the snot and powder from his nose with the other. "Makes things easier, you understand." He buried his face in the mirror again and took a long snort.

"Perico?" Shorty held out the mirror. "No? Suit yourself. So! Uh, Donald. What are we doing here, Donald? Hmm? Well, I'm glad you asked. It's an important question. Before I tell you, I'm going to make a guess about something, and you're going to tell me if I'm right. Simple, no?"

Don gave a slow nod.

"You haven't been getting your recommended sleep at the medical tower, have you? Been slipping out to party here and there?

Maybe get to know the locals, eh?" Shorty smiled as if to reassure him that these were all natural and relatable impulses.

Don squinted. What did this have to do with Anabelle?

"Dangerous." Shorty's face went cold. "You like to live dangerous, don't you? Like asking around for a coyote to help you skip out on your hospital bill. That's dangerous, Donald."

"Just what the hell are you talking about?" Don growled, rubbing the tender spot on the top of his skull.

Shorty pulled a phone from his suit jacket and swiped up a text bubble. "Right here, Donald. A little pajarita passed this along. Did you really think Los Compas don't keep an eye on communications around here? Big mistake there. We do. Specifically for things like this. Makes us look bad when patients try to run. Sound familiar? Let me jog your memory. 'I was told to contact you about getting a coyote north. Need to leave town now. What's your price?'" Shorty shook his head and tutted through his teeth. "Not good, Donald. Not good at all."

"I never sent that." Don sat up straight. "Those aren't real. I wouldn't even know who to ask. I—"

"Of course not." Shorty shushed. "Why would you go and do a stupid thing like that? Running on your payment? Medicorp would have terminated the organ remotely by now. Gruesome stuff. But we aren't fascist Americans. Fuck no, Los Compas have a heart. Oh, heart, see what I did there? Machín. Anyway, here in Limbo, we honor la ley de fuga. You want to run? We'll let you run." Shorty leaned over his steeple fingers like an executive in the heat of negotiation. "So, here's what we're gonna do. We release the first bull in twelve hours. That's, oh, about eleven thirty tomorrow morning. Then, every twelve after that, more or less, we release another. What's the rush, you know? Lucky for you, our bulls like a little sport. No GPS. But we're gonna have to cut your chip, so don't bother ordering any rydes or, you know, tacos or nothing. Sorry about that, mijo."

The ryde came to a stop on an empty street where the boardwalk met the old bullring. The door sighed open.

"I hope they found you a nice strong heart, Donald." Shorty

was all smiles again. "You're gonna need it. And, hey, good luck out there. You're gonna be famous."

Don got out, eager to get away from the young thug. What the hell was happening? Shorty extended a hand, and Don shook it as a reflex, not knowing why. It shook back, hard. The stars came quick as he hit the ground with a thud, convulsing like a worm under a magnifying glass.

What in fuck hell? Don's consciousness rebooted for the second time with the sound of ripping cellophane deep in his brain. He couldn't see the ocean, but he could hear its pulse of static swells and smell the salt air thick with sewage. The whole city stank of shit. Shit and Fabuloso. Shit and sea. Shit and fried shit. He could navigate whole sectors on shit-stink alone.

He pulled the adhesive off his palm and examined it under a streetlight. One of those damn single-use novelty shokpads that got banned in the US a few years ago, after some frat boys died during pledge week. Good fuck, those things hurt. He folded it up and threw it in the gutter. He had to think, fast. He didn't know what a bull was, or why it would be using GPS, but he didn't want to hang around long enough to find out. It was already a few minutes to midnight. Where the hell was he going?

North was out of the question. He'd be fried by the laserwire on the border wall as quickly as anyone else illegally entering the United States. Served them right. South was out, too. Even if he made it past the cartel's garbage wall, there was nothing but Los Compas clear down to Cabos. West was Haitian high-rises as far as he could see, separating land from ocean with a dense row of luxury penthouses protected by not a small amount of electric fencing. Not a chance of getting through there. The next spark would probably kill him.

He would walk. It was about five miles to Bar Sully following the highway over the coastal hills separating Playas from Centro. He would get there just before the bar closed and figure out what to do next. Maybe Sully knew someone who could help sort it out. These kind of mix-ups must happen all the time. Sully would know how to fix it, right?

The footsteps were nearly on top of him before he noticed them coming. He snapped out of his panic to see a Haitian man in a designer tracksuit jogging down the boardwalk. The jogger slowed to a stop and looked Don over.

"You lost, blan," the jogger stated, matter of fact.

"Excuse me?"

"No," the jogger corrected himself. "No, blan, you running."

"I couldn't run if my life depended on it," Don sneered.

"You in trouble," said the jogger.

"You think?" Don was losing his patience. And who the hell jogs on the beach at midnight?

"I been in trouble before."

"Great. That's real great. Now if you wouldn't mind fucking o—"

"You know what, blan?" The jogger over-articulated as if he were speaking to a child. "A white boy helped me out once. Long time ago, when I first arrive here. I was treated like trash. United States stopped taking us. Mexico didn't want us. White boy gives me money to eat for a week. It wasn't much, but I get by. Get a job carrying brick. A room. Look at me now, blan. I said, look at me!" He jerked at Don's attention as if he were a disobedient dog at the end of a leash.

Don shot him a loathsome glare.

"Yes, look at me now." The jogger smiled. "Not a worry in the world. Except maybe one thing. I never got the chance to pay white boy back. And that's been following me."

The jogger pulled his phone from his pocket and swiped. A moment later, a ryde appeared from around the corner and stopped along the boardwalk.

"Get in," the jogger commanded. "This isn't for you. It's for me. I'm free of my debt. I paid my dues. Looks like it's time for you to pay yours. Now, get in and run for your life. If you think it's worth it."

Sully never had customers after midnight, and tonight was no exception. Don stood without a drink as the Walrus stomped from one end of the bar to the other, huffing.

"Bulls? They're sending the bulls on you? Oh man, you screwed up, bad. I shouldn't even be talking to you. How could you do something so stupid?"

"Sully, listen to me. I didn't do it. Where have I been this whole time? First few weeks of credit clearance, where was I? Right here, every fucking day, drinking and listening to you run your mouth. Then I'm out for a few days in surgery, then back at the tower recovering, then here, again, with you, for the first time just today. Where am I supposed to be out meeting secret backwards coyotes? I mean, I didn't even know that was a thing!"

Sully held his breath and then sighed in defeat. "I'm going to regret this. Give me your phone. Maps, give me the maps app, there." He zoomed in to where the Tijuana River canal met the border wall. He dropped a pin on a hut in the riverbed. "El Bordo. Go there. Ask for La Bruja. She's the only person who can help you now."

"La Bruja?" Don's transplant thumped against its seams.

"Who's La Bruja?"

"La Bruja...." Sully grimaced and, lifting his crusted cloth patch, placed a trembling hand beneath the mass of scar tissue on the left side of his face. "La Bruja holds my other eye for me."

COMPULSIVE_DEFIANCE : : 11

Limbo from above looked like something out of a Japanese sea-monster movie. Luna hit her Undew drop to cast, gazing down from her puddle jumper at the massive garbage wall separating Limbo from the rest of Baja Autónoma. It split the arid landscape like a ruptured artery, its contents spilling over either side and fanning out in a patchwork of outdated vehicles and industrial waste. She pulled up a map overlay, toggling a recent time line of the region.

SEVEN YEARS AGO: US President Appleyard builds 1,954-mile militarized wall from San Diego, CA, to Padre Island, TX. Old fence reinforced with concrete and laserwire. Anyone approaching the wall, on either side of the border, forfeits US citizenship and liability. **SEE ALSO:** US/Mexico Border Suicide Cults.

FIVE YEARS AGO: The Los Compas de Baja Autónoma cartel, under the direction of the Flores Magón triplets, takes advantage of chaos following an 8.7-magnitude earthquake centered beneath Cerro Prieto, declaring the Baja California Peninsula an independent nation. Los Compas use tanker trucks and landfill scrap to blockade roads to major cities of Mexicali and Tijuana. Los Compas gain sovereignty after multiple violent strikes against Mexico City and other major urban centers. An estimated 97% of Baja California Peninsula residents flee to mainland Mexico.

FOUR YEARS AGO: Appleyard fulfills campaign promise of privatizing all government, acting as CEO of a corporate governing board including heads of Fensmart, Xuan-Santos, Zodiac, Darkriver, Lone Eagle Newsroom, and other top campaign donors. Following an assassination attempt, US begins mass deportation of citizens deemed dangerous to the administration. Citizenship fee imposed on all residents. Citizens unable to pay are deported to Tijuana. Meanwhile, Los Compas complete construction of garbage wall from south of Rosarito, 78 miles east to the Sierra Juárez mountains. Picking up 100 miles south along the range, the wall continues east to connect with the Sea of Cortez just north of San Felipe. The eastern wall runs from El Golfo de Santa Clara, 40 miles north to the US border wall south of Yuma. The enclosed megapolis becomes informally known as Limbo. Los Compas lease out sweatshops, agricultural land, and Colorado River water rights to Fensmart, Xuan-Santos, and Zodiac in multi-billion-dollar contracts. Los Compas control Limbo remotely, living in luxury throughout Autonomous Baja, primarily Los Cabos.

TWO YEARS AGO: Number of deported Americans reaches 2,000,000. Roughly 100,000 Haitian and 500 Chinese Mexican residents of Limbo employed by Los Compas to maintain order in work camps. Opposition party supporters, lapsed citizens, and underemployed American deportees work off their sentences at manufacturing and agriculture camps. Though called "gulags" by watchdogs, work is technically voluntary as a means to regain citizenship.

ONE YEAR AGO: Medical human smuggling becomes secondary industry for Los Compas after Appleyard signs the Healthcare Abundance Act, deregulating Medicorp. Thousands of Americans travel to San Diego to be smuggled into Limbo for medical procedures under Los Compas doctors. GDP of Autonomous Baja surpasses that of Mexico.

Luna's puddle jumper followed the garbage wall west, descending over arid hills, onto a field atop a coastal bluff outside Puerto Nuevo. According to her map's time line, Puerto Nuevo, or New Port in English, was not a port at all. Rather, the former tourist enclave, once famous for its lobster dinners, took its name from a prominent cigarette billboard that stood near the entrance in the 1950s. Luna spotted the billboard's flickering screen just up the road—the cigarette ad long gone—playing a clip from some show about an old gringo and an over-caffeinated rodeo clown.

She cut her drop, checking stats: 115 viewers. Not bad for only going live about ten minutes ago, but she would need a hell of a lot more if she wanted to make any royalties off the ad environs that took over when she was offline. Which, ideally, would be never. But bathroom breaks were still a reality—for both her and her viewers—and cutting her cast during downtime made for more pithy content, not to mention more ad revenue.

Twenty-six days to make eight million rubles, she reminded herself for the hundredth time today. About three times as much in pesos. Don't fuck this up.

After her puddle jumper rolled to a stop, she climbed out of the smooth, white drone onto the cracked earth of Autonomous Baja, squinting into the midday sun. Her shoulder-length hair tussled with the ocean breeze. A large bird squawked an accusation from the sky. There was nobody in sight. Luna felt firmly out of her element, and it was exhilarating.

Moments later, a ryde whirred in from the otherwise vacant highway. The door sighed, butterflying open. She ducked into the flat-gray vehicle's lenticular body, settling into a spot on the back of the ovular wraparound seat. Tapping the navscreen embedded in a cocktail table at the center of the seat-ring, she darkened the Vari-Tint on the overhead dome window, set her destination for Maquilandia, and ordered a bottle of water, which appeared in a compartment at the front of the cabin.

It wasn't long before she was pulling up to the garbage wall. She hit her drop as the hazy texture of the wall came into resolution through the ryde's tinted dome. Old cars, tankers, and diesel semis—the kind with steering wheels—were piled maybe ten meters high in a pastiche of junked shapes and corroded colors for as far as Luna could see. She pulled up her wiki app, selecting "Limbo Garbage Wall."

The garbage wall took approximately 100,000 deported American workers over nine months to construct. Upon its completion, workers were sent back to Limbo sweatshops, voiding Los Compas' promise of freedom in Autonomous Baja in exchange for labor. The subsequent worker revolt saw thousands killed by police and cartel sport hunters.

The ryde wound down under the golden arches of a discarded fast-food sign. Luna saw a young Haitian guard inside a booth hollowed out of the surrounding detritus, his boots crossed on a stool, raising a Tecate Red to his lips. He closed his eyes as the beer bubbled in the bottle. When he opened them, he did a double take. "You lost, girl," he said, not concealing his disbelief.

"I have a visa," said Luna. She hoped to hell she did.

"No way you got a visa," the young Haitian balked. "And no way you want to go in there even if you did. This is no place for a girl like—"

"Just scan me," she cut in, slapping her hand on the chip reader. Compulsive defiance—maybe the only redeemable trait she'd inherited from Burlyn, the pendejo.

"Hijo de puta, I don't believe it," the guard muttered. "You do have a visa, Miss Teschner. And you're Mexican. I thought you were a gringa." He grinned a solicitation that Luna had seen too many times to acknowledge. Maybe she was a little self-conscious about being half German American, having grown up much of her childhood at Grandma Teschner's in Los Angeles. Maybe it was none of his business. Luna looked past the guard and waited.

"Anyway," he continued, "I'm going to need your contact's

name and address."

"My what?" Looking directly at the guard now.

"Your contact," he repeated. "Nobody visits Limbo without a contact inside. Kind of like a prison or a graveyard. Makes more sense when you know somebody, ou konprann? In fact, you don't know your contact, you're looking at serious trouble. You can't be on the peninsula without a contact."

"My contact is on there, aren't they?" Don't panic.

"They are not, Miss Teschner. As you can see, the entirety of my job is to get that piece of information from you. And it looks to me like you don't have it. So, the rest of my job is to pick up this phone and alert customs police."

"No! I...." Luna froze. The guard froze. What was she thinking? She was just getting used to the thrill of pushing her limits, and she'd already pushed herself over the edge. Customs police would snatch her up, throw her in a rat-infested catacombs, and let her rot. Nobody would come for her. The crypto mobsters would kill Mom, Noel would be left on his own, and it would all be her fault. How could she be so naive?

Gray text in her display.

UNKNOWN
Pacheco. You are a friend of Pacheco.

Was that Jaco? What was wrong with his handle?

"You what?" the guard challenged, picking up the phone. "Yes, that's tragic."

UNKNOWN
Pacheco. Say it now.

"I'm friends with Pacheco." She smiled, trying to appear confident and relaxed.

The guard shifted. He raised an eyebrow, scrutinizing her. "If *you're* a friend of *Pacheco*,"—he appeared to be adjusting to the idea—"then why didn't you just say so? You're late to the party. Welcome to Limbo, Miss Teschner. I suggest you write your contact on your hand so you don't forget it next time. On you go." He hit a button on his console and the tanker-truck gate groaned out of the way. Then, he replaced his boots on the stool, returning the beer to its station on his face.

Luna hopped back in her ryde, hit the sigh switch, and caught her breath as she wheeled through the gate. That was too close.

LUNA TESCHNER
Jaco, was that you?

JACO LARK
Hey. Radio check? I've been casting a PR
segment all morning. Not my favorite. I see
your flight touched down half an hour ago.
Go get 'em, rookie!

Weird. Could have been the source, whoever they were. Jaco did say they would be in touch. She replied to the Unknown handle.

LUNA TESCHNER
Thanks for that. You must be my source.
Are you Pacheco?

She watched the garbage wall disappear into the distance, considering how little she liked being indebted to favors, especially favors from Unknown strangers, who were apparently keeping tabs on her through her own eyes.

Kervens still felt off. He was having trouble remembering things since the axol vision of the Guédé in Sawlips yesterday. The encounter had rattled him, but he wanted to go back. Piece things together. More composed this time, and on his terms.

He shook a few crystalline shards of axol into his coffee-table vaporizer and took a deep drag. Before it had a chance to take effect, he pulled his ImursiMask over his face and logged into his avatar lobby.

There was Kervens: tall, strong, and composed in a smart pinstripe suit. That one he used just for business meetings with the Flores Magón brothers and his top staff at the precinct.

Then there was Marinette: slender, inquisitive, and intuitive in her favorite bloodred-on-black polka dot sundress with a lavender lace fascinator covering half of her dark, gaunt face. Her voice was soft and deep, rasping slightly when she got excited and autocorrecting for any imperfections in Kervens's diction or grammar in real time.

She was a proper lady. Or, at least, the lady that Kervens longed to be. He had designed her just over a year ago, shortly before he met Casseus, naming her after the skeletal loa—Marinette Pied Cheche—credited with igniting the Haitian Revolution of 1791 by sacrificing a black pig. She represented freedom from bondage, and Kervens refined her appearance regularly to reflect his growing appreciation for his feminine side.

He selected Marinette and headed for the Spore Lounge portal.

A disembodied panning shot of a mushroom-shaped building at the base of coastal bluffs evoked impressions of flight and dreams before Marinette materialized in the elevator car, descending the cliff at a harrowing angle to the mushroom-stem entrance of the lounge.

It was night, like always, and the axol was bringing colors to life, animating objects into archetypal expressions of themselves, and amplifying the thoughts and emotions of everyone around her into an intoxicating chorus of human desire. Lady Erzulie was, perhaps predictably, nowhere to be seen. She rarely showed up in the same place twice.

Marinette ordered a double static no ice and sat alone at a booth by the window, cradling the cocktail between her fingers and gazing at her reflection in the glass. For the first time, Kervens understood what it felt like to be her. Not what it felt like to be him being her, but what she, the simulated avatar in Sawlips, felt like.

She felt like a prisoner. No will of her own. A puppet whose sole purpose was to fulfill Kervens's fantasies and cease to exist when he was busy being himself. Her subjugation was his liberation. In a way, he could empathize. He and Marinette were the same in that regard. Ruled by bondage and deliverance. Destinies dictated by fickle masters. Consumed by longing and illusions. Illusions were all Marinette knew, but to her, they were hyperreal. They were all that existed.

Marinette thought back to the first time she and Casseus met. It was singles night right here at the Spore Lounge exactly a year ago. The algorithm tagged them "highly compatible" and they'd both chosen "very interested" after viewing each other's profiles. She liked that he had a dog and enjoyed fine art, hang gliding, and bossa nova. And he was a scientist. She couldn't wait to meet him.

She'd spotted Casseus the moment she walked in the door. He looked so strong and confident and capable in his gray plaid single-breasted suit, smiling his disarming smile beneath round tortoise-frame glasses as he rose from a booth—the booth she sat in now—to greet her, kiss her lightly on the cheek, and order her a drink.

She teared up slightly as she recalled how nervous she had been on that first date. She'd never gone to a singles night and she wasn't sure how she should act. She kept catching herself twisting her hair around her finger while he talked about his corgi, Karl, and how the biotech company he ran was working on a cure for amyotrophic lateral sclerosis, the disease that had killed Marinette's mother before she was old enough to remember. She was absolutely stunned by Casseus.

He was kind and funny and carried himself with a dignity that made Marinette want to be held. It was silly, but he was so perfect for her, it was as if he'd been custom-tailored to perfectly complement her every interest, desire, nuance, and dream. He was her person.

She'd lost track of time that night and offered a clumsy excuse for suddenly leaving when a calendar notification reminded Kervens he was due for work at the Agua Caliente precinct in fifteen minutes.

"I just realized I forgot to pay my taxes this week," she apologized as she rushed to the elevator, running into a svelte man with a deformed, cadaverous dog's head in a notch collar, spilling his cocktail down his suit.

The next evening, Casseus had sent a private invite to a picnic in Medellín. They drank wine and strolled throughout the checkered tiles of Botero Plaza, Casseus explaining his favorites of the bronze sculptures in a soothing baritone. "Fernando Botero was obsessed with large, some would say 'fat,' forms," Casseus said. "He never could explain why, but he was drawn to them. And as an artist, it was his duty to honor his calling. Like this one, *Esfinge*, finished in 1995. This may be his best work on record."

They stopped aside a sculpture of a nude figure on its hands and knees towering nearly three meters tall on a marble pedestal. Long, clawlike nails protruded from its hands, and stubby wings sprouted from its back. Its solemn face gazed into infinity with squinting, iris-less eyes, globular breasts sticking straight out from its chest like cartoon headlights.

"See how from the side it resembles a woman with her hair pulled back into a braid, but when you view from the front,"—Casseus guided Marinette around the sculpture with a hand resting on the small of her back—"it becomes androgynous. The hair looks more like a typical male's, and the muscular arms are more prominent, yet those outrageous breasts are front and center. Just magnificent."

"Yes." Marinette giggled, sliding her shoulder under his arm and leaning into his solid frame. "I see what you mean."

Later that day, he had taken her on a Metrocable gondola ride over the city of brick and lights, telling her about his house in the biotech hub of La Jolla, San Diego. She should come stay with him for a while, if it wasn't too soon.

"San Diego!" Marinette gasped, barely able to contain her excitement. "That's just on the other side of...." She caught herself, remembering Kervens. "That might as well be on the other side of the moon. I'm finishing out a Peace Corps contract for the next five years bringing drone-delivered relief commodities to tribes in the deep Amazon. I'm not able to leave until my work is complete."

"Oh." Casseus pulled back. "I see. Of course. It's much too soon, anyway. Forgive me."

"No!" Marinette said louder than she meant to. "No, it's just, I can't leave. I made a commitment. It's important to me."

"And you're important to me." Casseus pulled her close as the gondola broke through the clouds into a starry night that bent and stretched in lentiform wonder.

That night, Kervens had fallen asleep imagining that he and Casseus were watching the same moon set over the ocean, not even fifty kilometers and the most impassable wall in human history apart. The following morning, he booked his gender confirmation surgery with the best surgeon in Limbo for the day his contract expired with Los Compas, and by the time the procedure was finished and healed, Kervens would be very much the woman that Casseus knew and longed for. Marinette was the perfect gift that Kervens would give first to himself, then to Casseus. Completely.

Marinette shook her head and came back to herself at the booth in the Spore Lounge. The axol high was wearing off but the memories left a residue of yearning that made Casseus's absence now, on their anniversary, sting all the worse. She stared out at the undulating sea and sighed.

Just then, Casseus appeared in the window's reflection, sitting at the bar in a white button-up shirt with the sleeves rolled to his elbows, a black tie tucked into a purple and gold paisley vest, and those butt-hugging black slacks that drove Marinette wild. She spun around and ran to him.

"Casseus," she said, swelling with joy.

Without saying a word, he turned, rose, and cold-cut.

It wasn't a long walk to El Bordo, but it took Don almost an hour, anyway. The sleepless nap in Sully's storage closet didn't help much. He felt more hungover than he should, no doubt thanks to Shorty's pistol whip, the lowlife. Posing as Anabelle to lure him out was a dirty move, even for a cartel lackey.

Don angled his head away from the morning sun as he skulked past the guard tower at the Arch Monument, a cheap knockoff of the Gateway Arch in St. Louis. Just like everything else in this town, it was a bad facsimile of something better, twisted into a nightmare. By the time he reached the abandoned wax museum, El Bordo's signature stench seared into his nostrils. Shit and burning garbage.

The noxious odor grew as he trudged through an empty plaza, scrambled across a four-lane freeway, and ascended a dirt incline to arrive at the edge of the massive, concrete Tijuana River canal. ESTO ES TIJUANA, the far side of the canal read in towering graffiti letters.

The vast deportee camp in El Bordo, where Don was supposed to find someone named La Bruja, was a frequent topic of conversation at

Sully's. The old Walrus used to live there, after all. Don was appalled to discover that the stories had been more or less true, despite everything he already knew about Limbo deportees from the news. The slums stretched for miles beneath him, home to tens of thousands of undocumented American deportees who didn't have the money, connections, or status to be welcomed anywhere else. Some of them, like Sully's family, had been there for generations.

Fresh arrivals appeared by the busload daily, being deposited at the San Ysidro Point of Disassembly on the border wall. After taking a beating or ten from the cops, most deportees accepted their new life of bathing in sewage, foraging for mudbugs, and trapping rodents to grill in the caustic, matte-onyx fumes of a tire fire. The police didn't bother the deportees in El Bordo. They didn't want to get their boots dirty. And El Bordo was made out of little besides dirt and shit and scraps of houses that had washed across the border in a flood a few years before the wall went up. Even the architecture was deported in El Bordo, as Sully loved to guffaw every time the topic came up.

On the far side of the canal, Fensmart cargo haulers lined up for as far as Don could see to be inspected at the Point. There, the haulers would be broken down into their base components by an automated disassembly line to ensure that only the intended cargo—mostly flat-screens and disposable consumer technology—made it through. Any stowaways attempting to escape, Sully had assured him, would be torn limb from limb in the process.

Don couldn't see into the US past the wall, but Sully had explained that temporary deportees—those who had the option of working off their sentences at the Fensmart factories out east—were stripped down, blasted with talc, and shaved head to toe by a robotic apparatus as soon as they got off the bus. Their chips were blocked and their finances frozen. In return, they were given a work assignment, a new name that reflected their crime against America—Don recalled laughing when Sully mentioned a traitor who had been dubbed "IRS Ted" for tax evasion—and a safety-orange jumpsuit reading FENSMART MEANS FREEDOM in happy, rounded Helvetica lettering across the chest. Then, they were loaded into a Fensmart transport and carted off to Maquilandia.

He watched one such transport pull away from the Point, considering how decent it was of Fensmart to create jobs for them. Otherwise unpatriotic and unproductive citizens were given the opportunity to prove their loyalty and worth through productivity. Don had struggled and suffered his whole life to earn his keep, and it only made sense that others should have to as well. That was just the way the world worked.

He checked his map and tried his footing on the canal's steep incline, considering his descent into El Bordo. Down below, permanent deportees—under-documented foreigners and top-tier enemies of the state—scuttled about in potato-sack tunics with reflective red targets on their backs, a reminder that they were one minor irritation away from being shot by a cop. They were everywhere in the canal, catching the sun in prismatic flashes.

If he had been here a few weeks ago, Don could have met the original owner of his new cardiac implant. The thought made him shudder. The mere idea of poverty revolted him, much less the sight of it, much less an implant of it. They were subhuman. Where Don had chosen to grow himself to his fullest economic potential, these animals merely subsisted on scraps. They didn't even deserve that much. They *should* be shot, he considered, and put everyone out of their misery.

A plastic bag stirred in the wind, dancing with itself in a rectangular tunnel running beneath the pedestrian bridge to Don's left. On the far side of the bridge, he saw a batch of new arrivals standing on the cement bank, milling about and deliberating under the hot sun. He sighed, sat back, and eased down the perilous incline of the canal in short, awkward scoots.

His shoes sunk into rancid alluvium when he reached the bottom. He covered his nose with the crook of his arm, then set off to wander through the ersatz settlements, trying to make the blue dot on his phone overlap up with Sully's pin. Instead, he crashed into a makeshift table, toppling it over. Two soot-faced men sprang to their feet and glared at him with their one good eye. They looked like hell. Don wanted to puke.

"Look, I'm sorry." Just idiots on autopilot, Don thought, just like everybody else. Did they even speak English? He bent over and replaced the table of—what were these things? Mud balls? Braided reeds?

"I'm looking for La Bruja," Don offered after everything was in place. "Do you know her?"

The men looked at each other and, without speaking, seemed to come to an agreement. They nodded in unison. One grabbed a shiny mud sphere and handed it to Don. "Dorodango," the man said.

The other handed Don a patch of green reeds woven into what looked like a badge with CBP scrawled in ash along the top. "Placa," he said.

These savages worship this junk, Don realized, instinctively clasping at the phone in his windbreaker. "La Bruja," he reiterated, shoving the reed and mud trash in the opposite pocket.

Both men raised their left arm and pointed to a shanty made from decaying, black-and-white-striped fabric. A lone reed sprouted from the sludge piled at the threshold.

Don nodded. "Gracias," he said. *Grassy-ass.*

The tent turned out to be a covering for the actual door, a slat of wood covering a drainage tunnel that disappeared into the incline of the canal.

"Hello?" Don called into the musty darkness. "Oh-law?" Don hit his phone light and crouched through the door. Shit and burning sage.

"Who's there?!" a shrill voice cried.

A snaggletoothed Chihuahua appeared from the shadows and attached itself to Don's leg, humping his ankle with preternatural fervor.

"Pepe. ¡Pepito! ¡Vete cabrón!" the voice howled like wind through a dead tree trunk.

Don swung his light around to find La Bruja sitting on a stool in the corner. Her hair was raven black and straight as a doll's. She wore layers of silver and ebony rags and too much eye shadow beneath cracked spectacles, which perched on the absolute end of her nose as if plotting escape. "Well, come in, handsome! Let me get a better look at you," La Bruja tittered as she lit a candle. "Oh!" she squealed. "Today must be my lucky day. Who do I have to thank for delivering you into my humble ñongo?"

"I, uh...." Don fought the impulse to leap out the door. "Sully sent me here. The Walrus."

La Bruja rose from her stool and dredged through a claw-foot bathtub sloshing with a syrupy liquid. She hummed with what sounded like pleasure as she selected a ball from the viscous fluid. "This looks like the one," she cackled, popping the eyeball out of her left socket and replacing it with the new one. "Ah yes, Sully. He saw too much. All of my eyes did. Part of Los Compas' little panopticon experiment. Tried to turn my displaced angels into spies, have them rat each other out just by looking in the wrong direction. I couldn't allow that. No. I take care of my lost souls. Very good care. Maybe too good. But enough about me. Tell me, what brings you here?"

"Sully said you could help me," Don said, trying not to touch anything. "I was set up. Los Compas are after me. They think I'm trying to get out of my medical contract and they're putting me on their fucking game show. They release the first bull in six hours. Sully said you would know what to do."

"Oh?" La Bruja leaned in and glared at Don with Sully's drippy eye. "Is that all?"

"Uh, yeah. That's all."

"Shame you can't stick around for a while." La Bruja sighed, then turned and rummaged through a dresser. "Looks like you'll need a visa." She pulled out a tangle of circuitry and gears stuck to a business card.

"That's a visa?"

"Well, of course it is, and you're going to need one if you plan on getting through."

Don didn't know what else to do, so he reached out to grab the refuse circuit board.

"Not so fast!" La Bruja howled, withdrawing the offer. She puckered her wizened lips and jutted them forward. Her eyes fluttered shut in anticipation. Horrified, Don snatched the visa from her hand and stumbled out the door as fast as his aching bones would carry him. Pepe nipped at his heels for what felt like a mile before veering off into a pile of rotting guavas. Bronny would eat that little rodent for breakfast.

Don had never seen the wall up close before. He had to pause to admire it. The cement monument stood about thirty feet tall and was topped with high-voltage laserwire that hummed and crackled in neon pink, lending the appearance of a Las Vegas attraction. All the earth within about fifty feet of the wall was singed black where a rat or a drunk or Pepe's entire fucking mutant lineage had stumbled within range of the arcing wire. Just beyond their reach, at the northernmost end of El Bordo, towered a scrap and reed structure woven into a swooping, angular slab of Googie architecture. It looked like a giant shard of clamshell stuck in the sand. Its upswept roof protruded from a bog of fetid muck, a facsimile of broad windows wrought from vertical slats of dried reeds. Around it grew the same reeds, lanky and green, like corn stalks on steroids.

Out of the shell came a line of unkempt men, women, and children winding and doubling back for about a quarter mile, ending not far from where Don stood. He looked at the visa. He looked at the line. The shell must guard the entrance to a tunnel like the one he came through in Otay. San Diego was just fifteen miles north on the other side. From there, he could unblock his chip, catch a ryde to the airport, and be touching tarmac back in Sarasota before sunset. This was too easy.

He waited, wondering if the line was moving at all. It eventually surged forward in a pulse before stopping again. He sighed, anxious and exasperated, realizing he hadn't stood in line this long since Black Friday at Fensmart. An hour later, the line crawled its way to the entrance of the shell. He became giddy as he approached the customs booth. His heart thing pounded in his chest. He approached the agent and handed him the bastard visa.

Nothing happened.

Don dug into his pocket for his passport, then remembered it was being held by cartel customs. Finding the reed badge, he slapped it down on the table, wondering how to make the agent recognize his credentials. He looked at the agent. The agent did not look at him. The agent's face was partially melted and slumped over the jawline, his eyes faded translucent. Beneath the tattered Customs and Border Protections uniform, Don could see gears and haywire circuitry mimicking the visa or whatever in his hand. The head must have been salvaged from the dumpster behind the old wax museum, Don realized. He could have been Mark Twain, back in his prime. Or was it Albert Einstein?

Malbert Twainstein's shoulders jerked from side to side, its arms jittering on the ends of broken servos. "Entry denied," it said in an 8-bit loop that glitched between syllables in mock enunciation, just trash and bad robotics masquerading as a human being. "En. Try. De. Nied."

Don was furious when he got back to La Bruja's ñongo. "I wasted an hour in that goddamned line to nowhere!" he hollered into the dark.

"I knew you'd come back for me," La Bruja chirped, springing to her feet. "¡Gracias, mis santos divinos! Gracias, gracias, gracias."

"I didn't come back for you," Don spat. "I.... What the hell is this thing for?" He shook the visa in her face.

"Oh that?" La Bruja sat back in her stool. "That's part of a broken alarm clock. What made you think it'd get you past the wall?" Her laughter squeaked like a leprechaun tap-dancing on a dog toy. "That's just...that's so precious."

"Precious?" Don frothed. "What are all those people doing standing in line all day for, then?"

"Oh," said La Bruja, waving a limp wrist in dismissal, "it gives them something to do."

"Something to do?!"

"We all need our rituals, my impatient Adonis." La Bruja batted spidery lashes over her mismatched eyes, whosever they were. "But now I see. You've been telling the story all wrong. You have to tell the right story to get what you want. That's just the basics. That's Magic 101. Tell me, what are you besides the loose collection of stories you tell yourself every morning? Well, that and a hot piece of ass. Baby, stories are all that matter. You control the story, you create magic. You want to go to the other side? Go talk to Juan Soldado. He'll help you sort out your story. Bring him a stone for his troubles, but pick wisely."

La Bruja's lips peeled back in a crocodile grin, exposing a gnarled set of teeth that made Pepe cower. "Juan's not as forgiving as I am."

Panteón No. 1 was a straight shot west along the wall, about a mile past Sully's. The morning sun was nearly halfway to its zenith by the time Don scurried past the flower vendors and into the rusted iron cemetery gates. He was only a few paces in before an old man in a long leather jacket and knee-high boots with about a hundred buckles—apparently the cryptkeeper—scrambled out of a shack and began chastising him in Spanish. Don didn't understand a word of it apart from "no" and "Juan Soldado."

The cryptkeeper, who had silver locks of hair down to his shoulders and wore jagged black-and-white paint on his face, pointed at Don's feet and shook his head in dour disapproval. Disappearing into the shack, the cryptkeeper returned with two stained cuts of carpeting, which he held over his knees and moved in short scooting motions.

"You want me to walk on my knees?" Don asked, astonished.

The cryptkeeper nodded with what seemed like too much emphasis and placed the carpeting in Don's hands. Time was running thin. He would try anything.

It took almost another hour to crawl across the graveyard on its cobblestone path to Juan Soldado's mausoleum. Don was stiff and sore by the time he arrived at the redbrick archway that stood at the entrance to the sepulcher.

Nearby, two gravediggers planted their shovels in the earth and eyed him suspiciously. Don stared back, trying to comprehend their flamboyant fashion decisions. One of them, an androgynous-looking fellow, wore a black shirt with a perfectly white jacket and headscarf, miraculously untarnished by the dirt. The other, apparently drunk, wore a mauve jacket and matching headscarf. He stumbled into the shallow hole he'd been digging, revealing a white cross covering the entire back of his jacket. Don nodded, and they squinted in unison.

Entering the windowless mausoleum, he found a carved, wooden placard on the wall, reading, "Juan Castillo Morales: falleció 17 Febrero, 1938. Orar y rogar por su alma descan—" Don pulled up the translator app on his phone and pointed it at the text. "...rest in peace, Juanito. Lord God of love and miracles, I give you thousands and thousands of thanks for the intercession of our saint and martyr, Juan Castillo! I have borne witness to your incessant divine miracles and come to you crawling in awe and gratitude. Thank you for my documents and for protecting my passage. Patron saint of migrants and difficult cases and the disappeared, we pray for your soul and thank you for your blessings, brave young soldier. We are here as living testament to your innocence. We know that you were slain unjustly for crimes you did not commit. May you rest in peace and—" Blocky graffiti lettering obscured the remaining lines of text from translating.

On the far side of the chamber, a neon green sign blinking JUAN SOLDADO illuminated the dusty burial shed. Blue, white, and orange flowers covered the back wall. The rest were papered with handwritten notes similar to the one at the entrance. On an altar beneath the sign, hundreds of votive candles cast shadows across the wooden bust of a clean-shaven young man with dark hair and eyes, wearing a green military cap and uniform. His eyes were fixed far in the distance, but they carried an eerie suggestion of sentience that made Don uneasy. It reminded him of the fortune-teller machine he saw as a kid in Coney Island. The resemblance was uncanny.

"Hey, Juan," Don mumbled, no longer questioning it. "I, uh... need to get the hell out of Dodge." He waited. Was there a chip-pay pad on this thing? Did he say the wrong phrase? Tell the wrong story, whatever that meant? Maybe there was a—

Thwack! Two PVC pipes swung around from where Juan's arms would have been, coming to rest raised at an angle on either side of the bust. A plastic funnel was duct-taped to the end of each pipe. One read "¡Si!" in faded black marker. The other read "¡No!"

Klonk! A handwritten sign popped out of Juan's hat, reading, "¿Crees que soy inocente?" Don held up his phone. "Do you believe I am innocent?"

Don didn't want to piss it off. He pulled the polished mud dorodango from his pocket and let it spiral into "¡Si!" After a pause, the bust issued a series of loud mechanical clanks and thuds before lighting up like a penny slot, roaring to life with bells and sirens, and filling the room with pungent stage fog. Don lurched out, sputtering and coughing in the late morning sun. The sound was deafening, a clamor of corroded tin and expired klaxons. Beneath them rose a high-pitched whine that grew louder and louder until a ryde was screeching to a halt just inches from Don's toes.

The door sighed.

Inside, the driver—what the hell was a driver doing in a ryde?— smoked a large, conical joint, grinning beneath yellow aviator sunglasses. Don saw that he was a young, mustachioed gringo, probably in his late twenties.

The driver pulled the billowing joint from his mouth, rolled down the convertible top, and gestured with an open palm to the nearest seat. "Yeah, Don? You're gonna want to get in. Fast."

ONTOLOGICAL_MEMETICS : : 14

Luna's ryde zipped along a rolling highway, passing transports full of workers being taken from the residential slums to, presumably, the sweatshops in Maquilandia. She was appalled but not surprised to see that the worker-housing blocks looked nothing like the clips she'd seen on US and Mexican news. The *Virtuvisa* segment she'd watched in flight depicted a cheerful suburban sprawl, populated with sharp-dressing couples clinking wine by the barbecue, enjoying all the comforts of their private ranchos on the other side. It painted deportation as an altogether uneventful slap on the wrist, the Appleyard administration almost philanthropic in its treatment of traitors. Luna couldn't imagine anyone actually believed it was so rosy, but even she didn't think it would be so bad.

She tapped her ryde's navscreen to detour through the next residential cluster, descending into a sea of beige boxes that reminded her of a mid-twentieth-century atomic village—mock townships whose actualization lay in their devastation. INFONAVIT government housing projects like these were a common sight throughout Mexico since the program began in the 1970s, Luna recalled, deducting a percentage of workers' salaries to pay off otherwise unattainable mortgages. The projects were consistently overpriced, were constructed of the cheapest possible materials, and quickly fell into dilapidation, but Luna had never seen anything quite like this.

The identical rectangles most resembled 8-bit icons conveying the bare quintessence of an abode: one door, one window, an electrical meter, and a low-res patch of filth where a lawn never was. No space separated the walls of each house, which had crumbling, hip-high cinder blocks separating one suggestion of a yard from the next. Each unit was scarcely larger than a single-car garage, and many had scraps of plywood tacked over their window, blue sails of tarpaulin flailing against the roof.

In stark contrast to the business suits and chic blouses Luna saw on the news, the residents wore tattered orange jumpsuits as they slouched toward the transport pick-up at the entrance of the development. Turning down a street indistinguishable from the last, Luna saw an elderly man bathing naked from a bucket in front of a house. He closed his eyes as the rust-colored water washed over his head. Out of nowhere, a police officer appeared, yelling in what sounded like French. The man dropped the bucket, raising his arm defensively in front of his face. The officer hollered again, then clobbered the man with a nightstick, sending him careening to the earth, crumpled and unconscious.

Luna gasped. As if he had heard her, the officer spun around and glared at her ryde. Glancing back at the injured worker, he fixed his gaze on Luna, sprinting after her. She fumbled with the navscreen, resetting her destination for Maquilandia. Her ryde whined as it picked up speed, the officer charging close behind. Unable to keep pace, the officer veered off after another resident as her ryde zipped out of the development, back onto the highway.

Avoid cops, she noted, though it was already near the top of her unspoken life rules, next to never trust a salesperson wearing a cross and don't date guys who don't like cats.

Double-checking her drop to make sure she'd been casting, she couldn't shake the preternatural sensation of no longer just looking at things, but documenting them, showcasing them, giving them a new way to matter. It was ontological memetics, she thought, then realized how pretentious that sounded. It was the Bishop Berkeley trick. Esse is percipi.

She was beginning to understand why Jaco was so attached to it. The quote perfectly encapsulated her fascination with the power of media, in a way she'd never been able to iterate. There was something quasi-mystical about the idea that, by merely observing an event, she would inevitably alter its outcome. Not immediately, of course. She wasn't there to interfere. She was there to perceive, and that would change mass perception, and that would change everything. It felt like witchcraft, an echo of the quantum observer effect at human scale, ultimately percolating into the fabric of consensus reality itself.

She tapped the navscreen for a cup of coffee, confirming the purchase with a finger on the chip-pay pad. The console hissed and a segment slid open. She peeled the lid off a serving of creamer and swirled it in the cup, the milky hues spiraling in chaotic eddies. The whorl of coffee and cream, she mused, could settle in any number of configurations, from her perspective—perpetually riding on the coattails of the next moment as she was. But from a physics viewpoint, the outcome was preordained as soon as she'd set the steaming liquid in motion, before she even realized what she was doing.

She watched the mixture come to rest, noting the distribution of color and foam. Would she be able to recall exactly how it looked tomorrow morning? Next week? Next year? It didn't matter, because now she, and anyone who came across her cast, could call it up precisely and with little effort at will. It was now a permanent fixture of her viewers' realities, as plain and immediate as if they were gazing upon it themselves. As far as she or her viewers cared, the act of observing the apparently random and inconsequential event made it real.

Beholding is a creative process, she decided—delineating her interpretation of the Bishop Berkeley trick. The world didn't really exist *out there* somewhere. Rather, a crude and incomplete model of the world existed in every individual's head. Her job was to import the more elusive aspects of *out there* into the collective headspace. If enough people witnessed something, if there was a critical mass of consensus that something existed, then, in most ways that mattered, it did.

Luna's ryde crested a hill, and the manufacturing gulags unfolded in the valley below. The warehouses were larger than any building she had ever seen. Some of them must have spanned nearly a kilometer in either direction, and they were everywhere. Hundreds of them. They formed a seething metropolis of work camps fed by a steady current of transports and workers, just specks, like something out of a nature documentary.

The ryde descended into Maquilandia, and for the first time, it felt not as though its wheels were propelling the sleek vehicle forward, but as if it were somehow being drawn in.

The repurposed casino slot machines at the Agua Caliente precinct were an earsplitting discord of synthetic zouk méringue and frantic racine rhythms as the noon shift filed in to pull their assignments for the day. A young officer yanked on the lever of a video poker machine, and Kervens overheard him grumble to another officer about being stuck with cleaning duty again.

The din of the machines grated against Kervens's brain. He cursed himself for grabbing rum and cigarettes instead of water before bed. He couldn't remember going to sleep last night. In fact, he couldn't remember much at all from the past couple days. Significant pieces were missing from his jigsawed recollection, and no matter how he rearranged their edges, a full picture never came into view. He hurried upstairs to his office and closed the blinds, barely sinking into his chair when a knock came at the door.

"Captain Dessalines,"—Lieutenant Wong-Gutiérrez stepped into the office—"the machines on level two are down. I got a couple hundred men without assignment for the shift. I—"

"Just have them follow the bull." Kervens replied in Haitian Creole, praying his subordinate hadn't seen him adjusting the lace stockings and garter belt beneath his uniform.

"All of them, sir?" Wong-Gutiérrez asked in broken Haitian Creole.

Kervens considered correcting him, but he couldn't muster the gumption. He recognized that, while his precinct wasn't strictly Haitian, its culture could at least aspire to be. He had a number of Chinese Mexican officers on his force, along with a few converts from Tijuana's former municipal police who lacked the rank and reputation to be welcomed into the cartel. Most of them, like Wong-Gutiérrez, had picked up enough Haitian Creole to be more or less intelligible over a radio.

"The police presence will make Los Compas happy," Kervens said. "And have them shake down some bystanders when the bull is watching. We could use a raise."

True, he and his subordinates were paid well enough. Well enough to show up every day, anyway, but not so much as to be above the occasional theft and extortion. In that regard, they'd picked up right where the cartel had left off, and Los Compas found it flattering.

"Yes, sir." A scuttle of feet in the hallway.

Kervens sighed. He didn't despise the deportees. He didn't get pleasure out of abusing and imprisoning them. And *he* wasn't imprisoning them. Their own country was, and countries had been incarcerating their own people in one way or another as far back as civilizations went. He just happened to be in the position to ensure his own freedom, at least some of it, for the time being. It was a cruel paradox, he knew, but he'd have been a fool to deny the opportunity it presented.

For most of his subordinates—the older ones, anyway—police work was generally more a matter of bad incentives than malicious character, with Los Compas dangling the promise of US citizenship, fees waived, in exchange for their loyalty. They were refugees in the wrong place at the wrong time, with no options but to do wrong so they could get on with their lives. The prisoners weren't the only ones serving a sentence in Limbo.

Kervens shuffled stacks of paper around his desk, trying to get into character. He imagined, in many ways, his job resembled that of an actual metropolitan police captain—budgeting, statistical analysis, inspecting facilities, assigning protocols, maintaining liaison with the Flores Magón brothers, public relations, and a whole lot of the idle paper-pushing typical of any upper management position. He didn't know, really, because he'd never been in upper management, and he'd certainly never been an actual cop. The brothers had simply been fond of his cooking at the Haitian chicken joint downtown, back when they lived in Tijuana, and Kervens had been ready to do anything but cook more chicken.

Now, he wasn't so sure.

At the end of the day, Kervens knew, he and his men were little more than dystopian mall cops. Still, he recognized his position to do some good. He did what he could to keep his officers organized so as to keep the deportees organized. His precinct maintained order in Maqui by ensuring workers met productivity goals. In a way, he kept them safe. The deportees would be exposed to Los Compas' darkest impulses without him. He reminded the cartel that the deportees made better workers than target practice, and they needed frequent reminding. Kervens was Tijuana's last remaining vestige of order.

Even so, order was fragile. It was always more a matter of belief than substance. That, more than anything, had been ingrained in him from a young age. Order was a brief contract against the unknown, against the inevitable. His forefathers knew that very well. Many generations back, they had led the only successful slave revolt in recorded history. Successful meaning it got the slaves out of slavery to control their own nation, forge their own destinies. That was the idea. That was the contract.

Oppression continued in subtler, more pernicious forms. Chaos had its way of creeping in. There was no stopping it. If you were adaptable, you could delay it. You could stun it for a while if you could sense its next move. Haiti had taught him that. One day at a time. Always changing. Always reassessing. Always on your toes. But eventually, no matter how hard you danced, no matter how loud you cried and how fierce you fought, chaos would catch up. Chaos drew you in like a bug to a flame, like a black hole. Chaos always wins.

Kervens leaned back in his chair, closing his eyes. He didn't feel like himself. Something had been off ever since his trip with the Guédé in Sawlips, as if someone or some*thing* else was authoring his reality, and he was only catching fragments by sneaking glimpses over its shoulder.

Whatever *it* was.

Don had almost forgotten how much fun manual vehicles could be. Sure, it had nothing on his vintage Chevy back when he was in high school, but as Keith the outlaw ryde driver darted through traffic and veered down alleyway shortcuts, Don was exhilarated. Getting the hell away from downtown helped. Time was running out.

"I'm kind of blown away you were actually at the pick-up," Keith said over the roaring wind as he stubbed out the joint in a soda can, hopping a median to barrel down an embankment. "Got the ryde request about three weeks ago when I finished modifying this baby and started posting listings to darkweb. I mean, I didn't even think I could fit in the gates. Did you see the look on the cryptkeeper's face when we left? Bless up, I thought he would explode." Keith's laughter echoed in his throat like a landslide in a craggy canyon. "Man, we barely made it out alive!"

"Listen, Keith," Don said. "Someone is fucking with me. I need to know who hired you. Who do you work for?"

"Work for? I'm freelance, man. The last stand against the

automation of anything and everything. But, who paid for your ryde? I don't know. Darkweb, dude. It's anonymous for a reason. Safer that way for everybody." He jumped a curb and jittered down a staircase to a residential street.

"Okay, but where are we going?" Don asked, more out of self-preservation than preference.

"You tell me, man." Keith sparked another monstrous doobie. "You got unlimited credits. Someone out there must like you."

"East," Don said. "Take me as far east as you can. As fast as you can."

"Your wish is my command, dude." Keith yanked a makeshift gear knob and Don felt his heart thing press into his spine, the wind reaching jet-engine levels in his ears. Maybe it had something on the old Chevy, after all.

"What are you doing here, anyways?" Don asked some time later as they weaved along the river canal, down the Vía Rápida highway.

"What, in Tijuana? I grew up here." Keith looked at Don while he talked. He really should be paying more attention to the road. He cut off a tanker and split the difference between two more with only inches to spare. "My parents moved here from Kansas before I was born. CIA. Worked with the Sinaloa Cartel back when they called the shots around here."

"Sounds miserable," said Don.

"The job took a toll on them." Keith nodded to an inaudible beat. "A lot of stress. A lot of lies. They fell into liquor pretty hard. By the time Los Compas caught up with them, they were mostly dead, anyways. But Los Compas made an example of my family, and I'll never forgive them for that. Just about everyone I know left after the big quake, but I stayed to fuck with Los Compas. My ryde here is just the first step. Soon, I'm gonna—"

"Watch out!" Don yelled, throwing his arms in front of his face.

Keith maneuvered between the axles of a double-decker transport and accelerated out the other side without batting an eye. When Don pulled his hands down from their reflexive position, Maquilandia loomed in the valley beneath them, looking like a big-box store from hell, copy/pasted ad infinitum. They descended into the gray blur of smog and industrial façades, saying nothing.

Don leaned back in his seat and stared at the sky, wondering how the hell everything had gone so wrong so fast. Before he found anything close to an answer, he was thrown into his seat belt, Keith slamming on the brakes, his ryde skidding to a stop. The entire freeway of transports and cargo haulers froze behind a police cruiser zagging across all lanes, a symbolic gesture carried over from automobile antiquity, before traffic patterns were automated.

Keith blew a milky cloud of smoke over the windshield, sighed, and said, "You ever been so stoned you can feel it in your eyes?"

Up close, Maquilandia reminded Luna of the movie lots she saw in Los Angeles staying with Grandma as a kid. The vast warehouses stretched and rose in every direction, making the road look like a tributary at the bottom of a deep gorge.

The architecture was imposing, but there were no fences or concertina wire like she expected to see in a prison camp. In fact, everyone seemed to be wandering around like they would in any city—waiting in line here, hopping a transport there, chatting on the street corner under the scrutiny of police with automatic rifles strapped across their chests. It wasn't much different from Querétaro, really, except the police were Mexican Army back home.

Maybe they didn't need fences, she considered. When the entire city is a prison and there's nowhere to run, the idea of a fence loses its significance. The garbage wall and the border made sure of that, effectively turning all public spaces into part of the privatized prison, incarcerating inmates everywhere they went.

Her ryde sighed in a parking lane outside a compound labeled

FENSMART ELECTRONICS MFG #42, its shipping bays full of haulers being loaded up with boxes on pallets. She tossed back the rest of her coffee and exited the ryde, wondering what to do next. The Unknown handle hadn't responded to any of her messages, and she was keenly aware of how out of place she looked, being the only person in Maquilandia not wearing a Fensmart jumpsuit. She could have waited in the ryde, she realized, but even it was conspicuous among the transports and haulers bustling adroitly between stops.

Lie low, blend in, don't get caught.

She headed down an alleyway lined with shattered flat-screens and discarded tech offal, noticing a worker wearing a jumpsuit and hardhat walking about twenty paces ahead. He glanced over his shoulder and she hid behind a dumpster, pegging him for early thirties. He didn't seem to notice her as he ducked under a corroded metal stairway, disappearing.

She startled as commotion broke out in the street behind her—hundreds of orange jumpsuits charging past the alley, the percussive terror of flash-bang grenades, a sheet of tear gas advancing like a hulking specter. She ran to the stairs, looked back in time to see riot police roll by in an armored tank, and pushed through a gray metal door. Descending a dark stairwell, she followed the vibrato of a song she recognized from Mom's David Bowie playlist. Cigarette smoke and the sting of cleaning chemicals hit as she stepped through a set of saloon doors, into an underground pool hall.

To her left, a square bar kiosk advertised Tecate specials and tequila shots. The walls were a glossy powder blue and about twenty billiard tables sat on the white tile floor, wooden benches interspersed throughout. Nearly all of the tables were in use, filling the hall with a din of conversation and cue balls clacking while Bowie crooned about royalty and walls. Curiously, none of the patrons wore jumpsuits, and the man she had followed was nowhere to be seen.

She took a seat at the bar, suddenly aware of how hungry she was. "¿Hay comida?" she asked the bartender, a rail-thin Chinese boy with the lanky stature of a teenager and a guileless, childlike face. Realizing she was speaking Spanish in an American bar, she rephrased the question. "Do you have any food?"

"Cacahuates japonéses, carne seca, papitas," the boy-teen said in perfect Spanish. Japanese peanuts, beef jerky, and chips.

"Cacahuates, porfa."

He slid a packet of peanuts off the rack, poured them into a shallow dish, and handed them across the bar. "Cinco."

She held out her finger, expecting him to place a chip-pay pad on the counter, but instead he shook his head slowly, saying, "Solo efectivo, jefa." He gestured at the CASH ONLY sign bearing a likeness of Johnny Cash.

"You're kidding, right?" She switched to English without thinking about it. The boy-teen offered a remorseful look as he pulled the peanuts back across the bar.

"I got this, Alex." A man appeared at her side. It was the worker she followed in the alley, now wearing a T-shirt and shorts. He placed two fives on the bar top, saying, "Tecate Red for me."

"Thanks," Luna said. "I haven't seen a fiver since I was a kid."

"Jake." He touched the brim of his heather-gray newsboy cap.

"Luna." She popped a peanut in her mouth, wondering if Undew edited out the audio of a caster saying their own name. "Where'd you get paper money?"

"I'll tell you," he said, "after you tell me why you followed me here." He sat in the stool next to her, smiling quizzically. "Maqui's a big place," he continued, "but I'd remember a face like yours."

Great, Luna thought. He's a cornball. "I'm here to get my tonsils out," she said, sticking to her script. "Came in from Mexicali at the mainland crossing. Just flew up from Mexico City. My uncle is a doctor here, but my ryde crapped out down the block. You looked like you knew where you were going."

"Medical towers are downtown." He took a sip of his beer, wiping his mouth with the back of his hand. "You'd better contact your uncle and have him arrange a ryde. The police don't like patients stopping through here."

"I won't tell if you won't," she said, channeling her best femme fatale. It was wholly unnecessary to play into his advances, she realized, but she was enjoying getting into character, and he might be able to give her some worthwhile content.

"You're playing me," he said.

"I don't know what you're talking about." The words came out extra smoky, and it tickled her.

"Pool. You know how, right?"

"Does the Pope shit in his hat?"

"More than we'll ever know."

Luna followed Jake to the cue rack, selecting a stick with a soft tip and abalone inlays along its varnished wood shaft. She tested it on the blade of her hand, finding the balance point a few fingers ahead of its army-green Irish-linen wrap, then held the bumper beneath one eye, checking for warp.

"Strip clubs," he said, feeding a nearby table with a bill.

"Excuse me?"

"The currency,"—racking the balls—"it comes from strip clubs. You break." He lifted the triangle off the table. "Zona Norte, the red-light district, kept using cash for years after everything went digital. Guests exchanged chip credit for cash on their way in, dancers exchanged cash for chip credit on their way out. I guess tucking bills into G-strings was deemed an essential part of the experience. When Los Compas took over, the clubs dumped a couple million dollars in a vault at the Agua Caliente casino and forgot about it."

"And, let me guess, you're a poker shark?" Luna lined up her shot and took her stroke, scattering the balls and sinking a three in the right-corner pocket.

"Actually, yes. But the casino was already repurposed as a police precinct when I got here."

"So how'd you end up with it?" The six ball thonked into the cabinet-side pocket. She walked around the table and lined up for one ball, head-corner pocket. The yellow ball rattled on the rail edges, coming to rest a couple centimeters outside the pocket.

"Our chips are deactivated at the border," Jake said, taking his time selecting a shot, "but the police in Tijuana come from a long tradition of bribery and extortion. The Haitian police picked that up from some of the municipal cops Los Compas kept around for training. So they reintroduced paper currency as a work incentive, pure speculation at that point, really. Then workers began exchanging bills for goods and services. Pretty soon,"—he gestured broadly—"we had our own informal cash economy."

Jake leaned across the table to take his shot, sinking the nine ball. He was handsome, in a way, but frazzled. His hair was disheveled, splaying out in every direction like a caricature of a tortured artist. And he seemed to operate on a background frequency of cynical amusement, as if he knew too much for his own good and couldn't do a damn thing about it. He shot for the thirteen, knocking in her four instead on the rebound.

"So, what'd you do before you became a prison economist?" Sinking her blue two ball.

"Believe it or not, I was an actual economist. Taught at a community college in Texas."

"Sounds harmless enough." Knocking her five in a side pocket. She was in stroke and feeling good, pleased with her game and the content she was getting, her anonymous source be damned. Her seven went cleanly into a corner pocket.

"I was fired for omitting the factually incorrect history that Appleyard's administration put out. Things like he single-handedly saved the economy by inventing the Mumbai Flu vaccine, or that the privatization of government has resulted in higher median net income for what's left of the middle class. A student turned me in and I was charged with Distribution of Disinformation."

"That's absurd." Luna stopped playing to focus on Jake, both out of interest and because it'd make a more impactful scene for her cast.

"I know," he said, taking a long sip of beer, his gaze going long. "Anyway, after being billed for a few months in one of Appleyard's new private prisons, I couldn't afford to pay rent on top of weekly unemployment fines, grocery-store membership, and citizenship fees. Ended up on the street, living under a bridge with a few other teachers. We were all deported in an ICE raid when they discovered our citizenship had lapsed. That was about three years ago."

Luna didn't know what to say. She'd never heard a story like his on the news, yet here he was, along with a couple million other deported Americans who no doubt had similar accounts.

"Are you going to tell me what you're doing here?" His expression became frank.

"One ball, corner pocket."

"Nobody eats hard-coated peanuts with tonsillitis."

"I'm a journalist," she said, surprising herself. She had every intention of sticking to her script, but part of her felt like she owed him the truth after hearing his story. The one ball clacked into its pocket, the cue ball rebounding off the head rail.

"A writer?" He didn't appear the least bit moved by her disclosure. "That's quaint."

"Is it?"

"I've assembled a few thousand Fensmart Home Assistants every day for the past three years. Ritual sacrifice would be quaint in comparison."

"Fair. Eight ball, side pocket." She extended her cue across the table to tap the pocket.

"What are you writing about?"

Rolling with the half-truth of being a writer, she felt obligated to offer a full-truth. "This."

"Billiard Bad Boys of Limbo?"

"Maqui," she said, sinking the eight ball.

"Good game." Jake took her cue and placed them back on the rack. "What size jumpsuit do you wear?"

"I don't."

"Hey Alex," he hollered across the bar, "got some loaners I can borrow? I'm taking my new friend here on a welcome tour."

Luna followed Jake down the alley, away from her ryde. "There was a riot out here when I arrived," she said, hoping to prompt Jake into providing some background.

"There usually is," he said. "It's always something. Workday extended, rent increased, curfew imposed, or just some asinine procedural dictate from Fensmart corporate in Ohio."

"You have to pay to live in the INFONAVIT ghettos?" Noticing the name tag sewn onto his jumpsuit, reading MS. EDUCATION. She glanced down at her loaner suit from Alex, but the tag had been ripped off, a block of frayed thread over the left breast pocket.

"Currently, two hours of the work day are deducted for rent."

"There's gotta be about a million vacant houses in Tijuana. Why not find your own place?"

Jake bent to examine a junked flat-screen in a trash pile, then seemed to decide it wasn't worth the effort. "There's a cautionary tale of some workers who got caught squatting an abandoned high-rise out by Cinco y Diez in the early days of Maqui. Cops shot them all and left their bodies in the streets, but they've slowed down on killing workers after Fensmart complained about productivity decline. They'll still kick the shit out of you and have fun doing it, but deaths mean paperwork."

Luna wondered what would happen to him if the police ever saw her cast, and became stricken with guilt. "Do you mind if I include you in the story?" Then, immediately redeemed the white lie her divulgence had merited, "Anonymously, I mean."

"Don't bother changing my name." He shrugged. "Jake Howser from El Paso, Texas. Worse case, the police shoot me and deal with the paperwork. Shit, maybe they'll deport me. Either way, I could use a change of pace."

"You're not worried about repercussions?" She looked at him for any indication of uneasiness, but he appeared resolute in his aloofness.

"My sentence has been extended so many times, I can't even remember when I'm supposed to be out of here. I work the minimum amount of hours to stay fed with a roof over my head. Odd jobs on the side for beer money. Every day is pretty much the same slog."

"Don't you have family or friends back in Texas?"

Another shrug. "I'm not even sure I want to go back when my time comes. What little family I have are all Appleyard cultists who'll disown me if I get my citizenship back. No one will hire me. The patriot gangs will come after me. I'd rather just die here, and let everyone

I used to know believe I deserved it." He fell silent, then perked up. "But who knows? Maybe your story will change the world."

Luna couldn't tell if he was being sarcastic. He didn't seem to be, but she was now aware that it wasn't amusement she'd been picking up on. It was resignation. She checked stats: 629 viewers. Fuck. *Gimme a Sine* had double that on a slow day. If she wanted her cast to make a difference for Jake, and everybody else here, she was going to need more viewers, more content, and more access. "Where are we going?" she asked.

"Here." Jake pushed through a door identical to the billiard hall's entrance. "Fensmart Electronics MFG number forty-three."

They stepped into a hallway, apparently a backdoor to the manufacturing plant. Jake held open another door and Luna walked into a warehouse humming with activity: assembly lines, forklifts, pine-scented helices of smoke wafting from soldering irons, boxes being loaded onto shipping pallets, workers scurrying in circles to secure the boxes with spools of stretch wrap.

"Everything we do here could easily be automated and made a lot more efficient," he said. "That's not the point. It's cheaper having deportees doing it for free, and at the end of the day, it's punishment."

"What's with those boxes saying 'Made in USA'?" She nodded toward the workers with the stretch wrap.

"The FTC is a subsidiary of Fensmart, and when they want to split hairs, they say USA stands for United States Affiliate. Most people buying this shit likely never question it."

"In-fucking-credible," she said.

"You think that's crazy? Wait until you see what they're doing in building forty-two." He headed back down the hallway, Luna following him through the alley towards her ryde. As they reached the street, a rollicking accordion came booming from everywhere at once in deafening blasts. Drum rolls exploded like gunfire. Tuba lines came in rumbling torrents. Then came the lyrics, echoing off tall façades as if it were the voice of God himself, a Norteño classic that Luna recognized as "El Diablo" by Los Tucanes de Tijuana.

"Bull," Jake said, a look of terror growing on his face.

Some sort of robot rounded a corner and swayed down the middle of the avenue, sending workers tumbling with the flick of a wrist as it extended one arm to the heavens and placed another on its chest, bellowing a chorus. As it got closer, Luna saw the robot had a ridiculous mustache painted on its metallic faceplate. It looked like Burt Reynolds. No, she recognized it now. It was Jesús Malverde, the Robin Hood narco-saint, the "angel of the poor," the "generous bandit," the Sinaloan legend. Almost lackadaisically, as if in a drunken reverie, it stumbled down the road. What the fuck?

Jake's jaw dropped. "Run," he said, quiet but stern. Now she saw why. The Malverdebot was charging directly for them.

She ran, fast, round after round from the bot's laser revolver searing past her head. She heard Jake gasp and smelled the stench of burnt hair, turning just in time to see his body hit the pavement, his head vaporized. She sprinted to the top of a highway overpass, but the machine was quicker. It was already just paces away as it leveled both pistols to her head, belting out another refrain celebrating the Devil's conquests.

Gray in her stream.

UNKNOWN
JUMP.

Bumper-to-bumper, standstill traffic filled the highway at least five meters below. She'd break an ankle, at least, and would be run over if traffic started moving.

LUNA TESCHNER
Who are you?

The Malverdebot pulled back his revolvers' hammers, seeming to relish in the final moments.

UNKNOWN
JUMP NOW! DO IT!

Luna shut her eyes, swung herself over the edge, and surrendered to the Unknown.

BEADS_OF_ABSTRACT_MEANING : : 18

Kervens pulled his desktop vaporizer from the drawer and took a long pull of axol. Not enough to glow, but enough to even out the hangover. To come back to himself.

Within seconds, the barometric pressure shifted in his head. His breath caught in his throat, his lungs becoming crumpled sandwich sacks. He felt the overwhelming need to yawn himself inside out, then became acutely aware of the sweat on his palms and ankles. His field of vision condensed to pixels, lo-res dew drops on a window, transforming a pandemonium of ocular information into linear beads of abstract meaning.

This new batch, straight from the Flores Magón brothers, was stronger than he was used to.

He slumped back in his chair.

It wasn't real, he realized. Not like the desk or the wall or the pounding in his head was real. No, it was poetry. It was a story. And what was a story but yawning, incomprehensible infinity congealed into something palpable? Into lies, really. That's all they were. Little lies that he and the drug could agree upon for the time being. Lies kept him sane.

He rearranged the glistening droplets along the hyperdimensional axes of a spiderweb that only he could see. He rotated the web in his mind's eye until the droplets aligned like lenses in a telescope, focusing on a single iota of effable knowledge.

It was a poem.

He had read it years ago in a discarded Sufi collection, back when he spent his nights on the cold concrete floor of the migrant center in Zona Norte.

> *The small man*
> *Builds cages for everyone*
> *He knows.*

His headache was a distant memory.

> *While the sage,*
> *Who has to duck his head*
> *When the moon is low,*

His sense of time and place dissolved.

> *Keeps dropping keys all night long*
> *For the*
> *Beautiful*
> *Rowdy*
> *Prisoners.*

He loved it. It was perfect. He read it again, putting all his attention on keeping the droplets aligned.

> *The small man*
> *Builds cages for everyone*
> *JUMP.*

A deluge of mercury spliced his vision, shattering his thin alliance with significance into an ocean of inexplicable movement. Its surface quivered like digital snakeskin, relaying a singular, visceral impulse that eclipsed the totality of Kervens's consciousness.

JUMP NOW!
DO IT!

Don had seen plenty of weird shit since he slunk out of the med towers yesterday. It wasn't like him, but he felt himself surrendering to a wider breadth of credulity, accepting his predicament more as that of a deep-space explorer making first contact with an alien intelligence, rather than a terrestrial retiree with any sort of rational routine to rely on. Still, he was having a hell of a time reconciling why a hot-wired Border Patrol deathbot would look like a light-skinned Mexican woman in a jumpsuit with long brown hair, perplexing hazel eyes, and an utterly terrified expression on her face.

"Yeehaw!" Keith hollered from the driver's seat, gunning the accelerator through a gap in the traffic. "Nice landing, girl!" Something exploded behind them as Keith extended a smoldering joint to the back seat. "Keith's the name, transport's the game." He grinned through the rearview mirror.

"Uh, no. Thanks," she said.

A billboard screen hanging from an overpass played highlight reels of a robot releasing havoc on Maquilandia, punctuated by a manic Chavo del Loco bouncing around and cursing in disbelief as the bot crumpled into a ball of flames on the highway.

"The fuck did you come from?" Don uttered through an approximate heart attack.

"I'm here to get my tonsils out," she said, eyeing Don like *he* was the deathbot. "My ryde took a wrong turn."

"Can't trust 'em," Keith said matter-of-fact. "That's why I modified this baby." He petted the steering wheel with unbridled affection. "Some things are better left in human hands."

"No kidding," Tonsils Girl said. "You saved my ass back there. That thing was coming straight for me."

"No, it wasn't," said Don, adjusting to the idea that maybe everyone's a deathbot in their own way and so what. "It was coming for me."

"Hey, we got ourselves a runner, alright!" Keith whooped.

"No, what?" Don said. "No. It was a mistake. Someone sent bullshit messages to my coyote. I've been framed. Framed or I just lost the lottery on a slow week for their goddamned game show. Either way, they're calling me a runner and that's all that they or anyone else cares about."

"Well, that's good enough for me, man!" Keith appeared ecstatic. "I've never had the honor. Let's get you outta here." He flipped an unmarked switch on the dashboard and the ryde accelerated out of traffic, through a valley lined with collapsing huts and crumbled concrete. Keith howled again as the outlines of informal architecture dissolved to hue smears.

Don was horrified they would crash and explode like the deathbot on the highway, and then decided he'd prefer it if they did.

The roadblock in Tecate looked like a Wild West scene from a theme park Luna had visited outside LA as a kid. Men in scruffy beards and cowboy hats, wearing white collared shirts beneath overalls, perched on the seats of stagecoaches clutching shotguns, their eyes slitted against the afternoon sun. Keith's ryde coasted to a halt.

"Afternoon." Keith grinned out the window.

The men exchanged hushed words before two of them approached. "There'll be no passage here, stranger," one said in an indistinguishable accent. "Referendum from up top. The Council will not be swayed by the times." He gave the passengers a moment to debate the point. When it was clear they didn't intend to argue, he continued, "Even a drivered vehicle like you are. We can't allow it. You're welcome to enter on foot if you please." The welcome lacked any semblance of invitation.

"It looks like this is where I get out," Don said, hitting the sigh switch.

"I'm coming with you," Luna said, stuffing the orange Fensmart jumpsuit under Keith's seat. She'd already decided that the Maquilandia story was over, at least for today. She couldn't risk getting caught by the police, and she was still holding out hope that her source might get in contact. Besides, sometimes the story unfolds in ways you can't anticipate. This was just getting interesting. She couldn't stop casting now. Jaco would love this. And she was at 2,878 viewers. That bullfight back in Maquilandia was great content, even if it nearly killed her.

She'd check out Tecate, wait for the source to get in touch, and maybe uncover a worthwhile side story in the meantime. "I'll call my doctor from here and get everything sorted out," she lied, pulling up a Tecate time line on her map.

There are approximately 100,000 Mennonites living as religious refugees throughout Mexico. Mennonite settlements were established in Baja California (see: Baja Autónoma) in the mid-1920s. The religious sect continues to live an insular lifestyle that rejects technology under the dictates of the Mennonite Central Council. The Tecate settlement is protected by Los Compas de Baja Autónoma cartel in exchange for the production of beer, which the Tecate Mennonites brew according to the 1516 Bavarian purity decree. Tecate beer is considered one of the best lagers worldwi—

"No phones here, miss," the bearded man set a stubborn jaw, interrupting her concentration on the text overlay. "Not until you reach the secular settlements in the desert. Your cartel doctors aren't welcome here, neither. This is free Mennonite land and we answer to but one authority." He raised a pious glance skywards before hollering back to the roadblock in what sounded like German. A stocky young man appearing to be in his early twenties emerged from behind a stagecoach and trotted to the man's side, obedient as a lapdog.

"This is my boy, Eli. He'll show you through town. Make yourselves our guests, and may the Lord's hand be upon you," the bearded man said with not a little gravity. "His eye certainly will."

"Come on then," Eli said with all the tenderness of a mother to a baby. He flashed a smile that made Luna suspect he was handicapped.

Keith waved a handful of paper stubs out the window.

"What's this?" Don asked. "A receipt?"

"Tickets to see my band, Jahdobada, this Friday at Mutton Chops." Keith gave a solemn nod. "In case, you know, shit gets figured out with the bulls and everything. We go on at eleven." Keith poised a hand in refusal for the gesture of appreciation that never would arrive, then whirred off west and disappeared into the valley.

Luna and Don followed Eli through the roadblock, past a schoolhouse of children chanting an unmusical hymn, and into a park square framed by a towering cathedral on one side and an imposing redbrick façade on the other.

"Treat you to a 'fresher at the brewery?" Eli seemed to intuit more than suggest.

Luna didn't feel much like drinking, but the old gringo, Don, was already shouting, "Praise the Lord!"

Maybe his bumpkin mother fed him beer straight from the baby bottle, Don considered, examining Eli—clearly an idiot on autopilot. He seemed better off for it, though, and Don was eager to drink himself dumber than Eli as promptly as possible.

Eli hollered something in German or whatever, and three Tecate Reds appeared at their white plastic table. Raising a glistening bottle to his guests, he broke into another one of those challenged grins. "So, what brings you folks out to Tecate?" *Tuh-caw-dee.*

Don didn't see any reason to bullshit the dimwit. "I'm trapped in a foreign country run by psychotic, retired drug lords, being chased by shitty superhero robots for a crime that never happened. I should be recovering from open-heart surgery in a medical tower downtown, but instead I'm going to be gunned down by an automaton with Madonna tits in your shitty pilgrim backyard just to entertain the cartel for ten seconds, and I don't have a fucking clue what you or I or anybody else thinks they can do to stop it." He glowered. "And I'm hungover."

Don tossed back his beer in a greedy gulp and bellowed for three more in English, even though these people spoke god-only-knows-what and fuck them, anyways. He was only vaguely surprised to find three more bottles on the table by the time his arm fell back to his side.

"I, uh," Luna began, wide eyed. "I just got lost."

"We're all lost, miss," Eli assured her. "We are but wandering sheep and the Good Lord is our shepherd. That's why we ought to follow His law in this world that every day turns ever more evil."

Don was already tuning him out, but for a glimmer he considered the dumb bastard may have a point. People were sheep, and the world was objectively as evil as he'd ever seen it.

"But how can you drink?" Luna asked, pointed at her untouched bottle. "How can you brew? Isn't drinking against the rules?"

"What do you think, miss?" Eli's crooked grin threatened to reemerge from its slumber. "That we will drink and drive?" His laughter reminded Don of an animal-husbandry documentary he'd seen at the med tower.

Don took a deep swig and watched a drop of moisture run over the curves of his second bottle, thinking of women and how erectile dysfunction was probably worse than death by robot, anyways.

"We brew because it is what we do best," Eli said, still in that coo that aspired to a whisper. "We have been doing it for hundreds of years. We farm and we brew and the secular powers that be let us live in peace and simplicity, the way the Lord intended. Brewing protects us from the evils of the outside. Brewing is part of our path to divinity."

Don couldn't argue with that. He raised his bottle in a cheers, clinking glass with Tonsils Girl and then the Beerbilly.

"So, you like living like this?" she asked. Inquisitive little thing, wasn't she?

"Yes, of course," Eli said, and, as if his tone could get any more confidential, "but to tell you the truth, I've been in trouble with the Council lately. My father reported me for"—and even lower—"listening to jazz music on a digital device." His eyes were all severity as he shook his head, seeming to chastise himself with every swing of his brim.

Luna laughed. "Hey, nobody's perfect, right?"

"No, miss." Eli's mangled teeth on full display. "No, we aren't. Now it's about time we get you on your way. I'll take you to the end of town in my father's buggy. It has a broken window but I think you will find it very comfortable."

Don ordered a twelve-pack to go, putting it on the Beerbilly's tab.

Luna joined Eli in the driver's box, Don presumably drinking in the carriage, as they rattled down an empty highway through the outskirts of Tecate, where the land leveled off into high desert and the sun cast shadows across rows of grain and wild chaparral. They hadn't spoken much since the coach left town. He seemed to be enjoying a type of meditation as he cradled the reins in one hand and took pensive tugs from a pipe in the other. Luna had an idea.

"Thelonius Monk." She smiled as "Blue Monk" waltzed from her tinny cellphone speaker. "Just like you."

Eli jumped as if she'd shot somebody, looking over his shoulders with furrowed brows.

"Don't worry." She laughed. "Look, there's nobody out here."

Eli's shoulders fell. Then, just on the threshold of perception, they swayed. His wide mouth betrayed the rest as a heel and knee caught rumor of the beat. Luna and Eli jittered through several tunes, snapping fingers and trading tentative mouth-trumpet solos, before Eli seemed to come to a decision.

"I will always have my faith," he said, eyes straight ahead, "but sometimes I wonder if we live like this not for the Lord's blessings, but the Council's. Where's the valor in pretending the world doesn't exist? We live in seclusion. We cannot read or write. We don't have an education. We are not permitted to entertain ourselves. I shouldn't even think this, but sometimes I wonder if we are no closer to the Lord than the simulation addicts down at Plaza Friki. They invent their own seclusion using the technology that we reject. How are we so different?"

Eli went silent, tugging at the reins to halt alongside the bearded men guarding the east Tecate blockade. "Tell my father that I'll be back with the buggy in a few days," He told the guards. "I'm returning my friends to safety, Lord willing."

"Godspeed, Eli," one of the guards said.

"Mind your father's horse, now," said the other.

"Of course, Uncle," Eli replied. He cracked the reins and continued to Luna, "Or consider this. Last month we were allowed motor buggies. Not to own, mind you, but to lease. If we lease certain types of technology, it is okay. But never to own. This month, motor buggies are forbidden on Mennonite land. The Council demands this. The Lord's law does not change from one month to the next, yet the Council's does. How can this be?"

"It doesn't make much sense," Luna admitted.

"No." Eli frowned. "It doesn't." He took several long pulls from his pipe and then announced, more to himself than her, "I'm long overdue for Rumspringa. I'm no longer a boy, neither in my father's eyes nor the Lord's. And if I'm going to continue in my obedience to both, I need to know about the outside world. I need to see it for myself. I need to know they are right about its evil."

A slow glowing of embers in his pipe, then, "I will take you wherever you want to go. I'm afraid I won't be of much help as a guide outside Tecate, but we have plenty of water in the buggy, and Ezekiel is my father's strongest horse. It would be my honor to offer you safe passage."

Luna's impulse to hug him ran headlong into a wall of acute self-awareness. What would Eli think if he knew she was casting this? It wasn't like the old music vlog back in Querétaro, where interviews were consensual and mostly promotional in nature. With Undew, she wanted to transmit the unedited truth in all its sad and surreal and beautiful incarnations, but the truth had a way of snaking off when it felt eyes on its back. Let the world tell its story, Jaco had said. Mentioning the cast would only get in the way of that. Eli wouldn't understand, anyway. And that realization made her uneasy.

Raw and honest reality sounded brilliant in theory, but this was a real person who was really questioning everything, for real reasons. This cast could ruin his life, in the not unlikely event that someone on the Council was sneaking internet access behind closed doors.

Luna got quiet and cut her drop. She had knots in her stomach. For the first time since taking the Afterthought implant, she didn't feel like a renegade journalist.

She felt like a spy.

TRUTH_WITH_A_CAPITAL_T : : 20

Luna squinted into the golden evening sun as Eli steered his father's buggy off the highway onto the rutty trail to El Hongo. Eli had heard of an abandoned penitentiary where they could make camp for the night. Yellow and purple milk-thistle blossoms exploded like fireworks, waving in the dry Santa Ana breeze, which smelled of sage and chaparral. Conical mountaintops became saw teeth on the indigo horizon, a rogue eucalyptus, pine, or olive tree disrupting the serrated silhouette of Sierra Juárez mountains in the distance. Sparrows soared between red manzanita bushes, chirping melodic bursts of chatter followed by expectant ticks of the head.

"What do you think about that?" they seemed to say.

The carriage creaked its way through a clearing, where several emus strutted among the flowers, arching their long, pale-blue necks to peck at grasses and insects. The flightless birds released guttural thuds of bass as they stilted across the earth.

Boom. Boom. Thud!

On top of their almost-rhythmic vocalizations, a shrill sparrow call cut through dusk.

Yeow! Cheep? Yeow.

Except there was no sparrow challenging the reason behind the breeze, and the only feathers coming into focus were bound to the head of a bare-chested figure in a tan vest, blue jeans, thick glasses, and shoulder-length black hair that looked more like a wig. He perched on a hillside between tangles of creosote and mesquite bushes, angling a wooden flute to the heavens.

"Do you see him?" Eli whispered.

Luna nodded.

UNKNOWN
Follow him.

They were listening. Whoever *they* were. But they had been right so far. They had saved her life.

"Hey!" Luna shouted. "¡Oye!"

The figure snapped his silhouette like a sparrow. A second later he was gone.

Eli stared at Luna. "Are you always so friendly?"

"Not always, no." Which was true. "I just had a feeling." Which was also mostly true, as much as anything was. It was a strange subject. Luna generally sensed that Truth, the big one with a capital *T*, was more about locality than veracity, and generally incomprehensible to just about everybody. It certainly was to her, and she was more or less okay with that. It relieved a huge amount of the responsibility she once felt to understand everything, like really everything, and act according to that understanding. That would be the right way to live, if only she could put the pieces together.

A crushing sense of responsibility used to keep her up at night. And—as was made abundantly clear the time she dropped acid with Juan Carlos at an acoustic noise show and proceeded to spend four hours alone in a janitorial closet—that sense of responsibility permeated just about all the paranoia and insecurities that'd wormed their way into her psyche like parasites, making her do irrational shit like giving

Juan Carlos the time of day to being with. Things could be true and not true at the same time, she'd decided before stumbling out of that closet. Like right now.

Eli didn't question it. He drew the reins south to where the figure had been, but he was nowhere to be seen.

An hour later, he greeted them on the outskirts of El Hongo with another avian inquiry. "What did you think about that?" his flute seemed to say. Luna saw he had twin slashes of black paint down the right side of his face, drawn over the lens of his square-frame reading glasses and continuing down his cheek. Not waiting for a reply, the flutist beckoned them over and led them down an overgrown trail. They arrived at a squat sweat lodge covered in animal hide, where the moon cast shadows suggestive of faces into the surrounding red dirt escarpments. Don lurched out of the cabin and gawked, slack jawed, at the night sky.

"Hello?" Luna called, lowering herself from the driver's box. The flutist crouched at the sweat lodge's coyote-skin door and waved them over in one broad and resolute gesture.

UNKNOWN
Talk to him. Stay alert.

"We should talk to him," Luna said. Right?

They entered the low, domed structure and sat in a circle around a firepit glowing with smooth stones as big as horse heads. The flutist fed the embers with braided skeletons of cholla. A mosquito hawk flew into the fire as the dried cactus ignited, disappearing in a flash. As if he'd been expecting them, the flutist poured a dark tea from a clay pot into four cups. He took one for himself, demonstrating with a sturdy sip, then passed the cups to Luna on a tarnished metal tray. She took one, handed the tray to Eli, and inhaled the earthy vapors, smelling wild licorice and library dust. The flutist raised his cup over the fire, inviting them to join him in a drink. They drank.

Luna was the first to tick. She was watching the flutist chirp out a decidedly ovular motif when his entire face, glasses, wig, and feathers hopped about a foot to the right. She flicked her head.

What did she think about that?

The melody skittered off like a tumbleweed, taking her thoughts with it, and by the time she realized her mind was blowing away, it was already long out the door. Her head ticked again.

UNKNOWN
What do you think about that?

LUNA TESCHNER
Who are you?!

Was there a strobe light in here? The text flickered and warped in her display.

UNKNOWN
We've been watching you.

LUNA TESCHNER
No shit. Why did you take me here?

UNKNOWN
You did this to yourself. You're not supposed to be here. Enjoy the tea. It'll open your third eye. What do you think about that?

"Who the fuck are you?!" Luna yelled into the stifling, damp heat.

The flutist tore off his face and stared back at her with googly eyes glowing red in the humid dark. A mess of frayed wire served as a hairdo beneath the dusty black wig, his metal faceplate spray-painted with a maniacal grin.

"Now don't go tellin' me," he said in a mechanical chirp that detuned at the end of every other syllable in an eerie, artificial drawl, "you don't recognize ole Carlos Manson!"

RITUALISTIC_OBLIGATIONS : : 21

Kervens regretted taking the day off. It showed weakness, even if none of his men had seen him pulling himself back onto his balcony overlooking the Caliente dog-racing track, several stories below. Gravity had gone sideways on him, and he hardly had the presence of mind to stop it. He'd taken a private elevator down to his police cruiser—an all-terrain butter bean compared to the standard ryde, which reminded him more of electric lentils with extended butterfly doors on either side and a sleek Vari-Tint dome enclosing the passenger cabin. He'd gone back home to Playas, slept off the axol, and now cursed the memories being awakened by the Coronado Islands shimmering on a black horizon.

The view seemed to taunt him, like the mercurial sea in his axol vision had earlier. It stirred painful recollections. Not just death and injustice and suffering. Those were low-hanging fruit in Kervens's gnarled psyche. Instead, the ocean prodded him with hidden barbs of the past that—no matter how many times he hedged them—he never could smooth out completely.

Like the time his oldest brother, Stanley, terrorized him with a cane spider when Kervens was maybe six years old. Stanley pinned him down, dangled the arachnid over his face, and after Kervens—the youngest, the helpless baby—had shit himself in fear, Stanley laughed and told him the spider was already dead, anyway. Kervens never could justify that one. He never found a way to reframe it without himself still being a weakling, even though Stanley was an asshole.

It made him angry, even now, more than thirty years later. For the thousandth time, he cauterized the memory with the resolution to never shy away from fear again and, in a ritualistic obligation to cement the promise with action, he took a long pull of axol from his coffee table vape. Then another, and another.

Every pore on his body dilated. He felt inferno riding on his breath and sticking in his chest. He would have believed he were drowning in hellish darkness, were it not for the red embers that began as a spark, then engulfed his vision. And that teardrop again, bloodred, glowing in the bottom-right corner of his vision.

Where was he? He felt like he was trapped in a foreign body. The dimensions of his senses didn't fit. Every breath he took threatened to suffocate him. He fought through the pain and anxiety and grounded himself.

You are not afraid.

His beachfront apartment disappeared completely. It was just him—or rather, whoever he had been shoehorned into by the drug—and the smoldering whatever it was, strobing in and out of focus. His perspective clicked back a few notches. He wasn't alone.

To his left was a young man in a cowboy hat with his eyes closed, his face twisted into a painful grimace. He rocked back and forth like a man in a mental ward. Directly across was a fat gringo with Colonel Sanders hair. He appeared drunk. He was drooling beneath slightly crossed eyes. To his right was—what the fuck? One of those Border Patrol bots that had nearly broken his neck the first time he tried to cross into the US eight years ago, just before the wall went up.

Kervens's response was instinctual.

He went for the stunstick he kept in his back-right pocket and shoved it into the weak spot behind the bot's neck, just like a drunk coyote in Zona Norte had taught him after he'd relayed the story of his near death, years ago.

Luna didn't know why her hand ended up in her pocket. Well, that wasn't true. She was looking for the stunstick that Juan Carlos had given her as a goodbye-forever gift, despite his aversion to both technology and forever.

The stunstick was crammed behind the bot's neck before she realized she had found it. Manson's eyes dilated as his flesh-and-metal frame toppled into the firepit. Out of her mind on adrenaline and whatever was in that teacup, she dragged Eli and then Don—good fuck he weighed a ton—out to the buggy. Luna was impressed at how quickly Don came to his senses in the cold night air. Her vision collapsed into Mandelbrot mazes.

"Can you drive this thing?" she managed to say. "Eli and I have been drugged or something. We have to go, now."

The mandarin-orange moon rose and set twenty times in fast forward. Don grunted and helped her pull Eli into the driver's box. Eli looked like he'd seen death. It was maybe an hour—which felt like an eternity—before he blinked, turned to Don with horrified eyes, and said, "We have to find Anabelle immediately," before passing out on Luna's shoulder.

CHICKEN_SIMULATOR : : 22

Luna felt like hell. The few hours of fitful sleep at the abandoned penitentiary did little to calm her splintered nerves. But Eli looked like he'd had it even worse. His face was grim as he piloted his father's buggy out of the El Hongo flats, following the predawn procession of electric chroma and shadows on the craggy mountains to the east. A single blue star hung over the horizon.

"I met the devil," Eli said after a long silence. "The serpent. It came to me in the sweat lodge. It chased its tail in a loop, drawing me in and testing my faith. It was horrifying. I've never seen such evil. It consumed me."

"You don't remember anything else?" Don prodded, clearly hungover, dark rings around his eyes.

"No, sir," Eli whispered, eyes fixed on the purple-pink-beige boulders rippling on the horizon.

"I was worried about you," Luna said, trying to focus. For the first time since she left Querétaro, time itself felt less like a black hole sucking her into its horrible singularity, and more like something that surrounded and swaddled her like a baby. She was having difficulty remembering what she was doing here. "Whatever was in that tea hit you hard. I thought we lost you for a minute."

"I'm sorry," Eli said. "I don't remember anything after the serpent."

"You said a name," Luna recalled. "You said we had to find someone—Anna? Annie?"

"Anabelle," Don rasped. "You said we have to find my daughter, Anabelle. I don't know what the hell is going on, but someone claiming to be my daughter sent me on the wild-fucking-goose chase that landed me here in the middle of nowhere with you two in the first place, and I don't know what it means. Anabelle has been dead for over ten years." He stared off, chewing on his bottom lip. "You ever heard of border suicide cults?"

Luna recalled seeing a mention of them in her Afterthought time line at the garbage wall yesterday, but didn't feel up to inventing a lie to explain it, so instead just shook her head. The buggy creaked along the bottom of a sandy valley punctuated by squat shrubs. Luna detected the buttery aroma of pollen and the menthol sting of Cleveland sage. A family of quail scurried across the path, the feather crests on their heads bobbling like a string of commas printed on gelatin.

"No, sir," said Eli.

Don continued, his expression blank, "She started following some La Jolla University professor who liked to get his students naked in the name of academics. Last I heard, they were at some ranch up in Jacumba, presumably having orgies, conjuring Mexican ghosts, and frying their brains on psychedelics." Don went silent, appearing to weigh his regrets. "I tried to get her out. I drove out there, not far from here actually, just on the other side of the wall, and tried to drag her out of there myself. God, that was a long time ago. She wasn't having it. She kicked and screamed and cried. She swore she knew what she was doing. Said she was going to transcend into her higher self, whatever that means, and she'd hate me forever if I took her away. What could I do? She was my little girl, but she was also a grown woman. I left her there. Had a change of heart and came back for her a week later. The place was abandoned. None of them have been seen since. Just like that." He closed his eyes. "Gone."

"Oh my god, Don, that's horrible," Luna said, then, "Is it possible they just moved to a new compound?" Trying to balance her sympathy with rational optimism.

Don shook his head. "For a long time, I believed they went into hiding. I wanted to believe it. It was comforting. It's not anymore. Anabelle is dead and it's that burnt-out pervert professor's fault. The worst part is,"—his face contracted in a sob, his voice going up an octave—"I can't help but wonder if he was a better father figure than I knew how to be." He buried his face in his hands, weeping, then, gathering himself, "I'm sorry, I...."

"It's okay," Eli said, looking ever bleaker than before. "I'm...I'm so sorry to hear that, sir."

"Funny thing, Eli," said Don, wiping his cheeks. "That snake you described? That was painted on the gate, like their fucking logo or something. Haven't seen it before, haven't seen it since. You know anything about that?"

"No, sir," Eli said, meeting Don's gaze. "I can't explain what I saw."

Luna ran a search on "Jacumba San Diego professor cult" and pulled up an archived *San Diego Beacon* article.

HIGH DESERT HIJINKS by Wate Charles

The headquarters of Ketcel Collective in Jacumba Hot Springs looks like the kind of place suburban parents worry their kids will end up when they first express interest in things like yoga, kombucha, and Burning Man. Located on a dirt road beyond a junkyard of spray-painted railroad cars, about a mile north of the US/Mexico border and seventy miles east of San Diego, the land is dotted with cryptic monuments—a corrugated-tin pyramid, ceremonial rock sites, industrial art sculptures, vision pools, and ample serpent imagery inspired by the Mesoamerican deity, Quetzalcóatl.

Neighbors in the one-stop town have been known to label the collective "some sort of New Age sex cult" in casual conversation with tourists at Jacumba Hot Springs' lone drinking hole—an accusation that is apt to raise eyebrows when one takes into account the controversial track record of property owner and collective founder Dr. Anselmo Manriquez. Holding a dual doctorate in Codicology and Computer Science, Manriquez teaches an experimental archeological technology program at La Jolla University, and has come under fire recently for encouraging students in one of his popular courses to deliver their final performance projects in the nude.

Appropriately enough, I found Manriquez naked both in dress and demeanor when I accidentally stumbled across his lysergic compound while researching a bird-watching story at a nearby pond a few weeks ago.

"Glad you got the invitation!" he jokes, welcoming me like an old friend, au naturel back slap and all. "Let's get started, shall we?"

Manriquez launches into a tour of the vast property, pointing out rock piles ("Toltec warrior burial grounds"), giant rusted water tanks turned upright and painted in white spirals and stripes ("perception isolation art"), and a corrugated-tin pyramid with the top lopped off ("spirit-double projection vessel"). He radiates confidence and confidentiality, as if he's letting me in on a great secret that only he can see. It occurs to me that he might be mad, or at least eccentric, but it doesn't matter. There's a charming innocuousness to the fantasy world Manriquez lives in, and really, who's to tell artists (grown adult artists, at that) where to draw the line on their flights of fancy? I quickly decide to ditch the bird-watching story and turn my lens on Manriquez.

"I'm going to be perfectly transparent with you," Manriquez says behind a salt-and-pepper beard as we sip tea in the cactus garden. "We've discovered something brilliant here, right here, and that's why we decided to establish the Ketcel Collective in this location."

He stands and gestures across the expanse of rock, sand, and cactus. "This is a natural energy vortex. You saw that in the pamphlets down at the tourist center, right? But let me tell you what that really means. This land is a library. It's been holding information for ages. Among other things, we've discovered sacred texts here that date back to the Toltec shamans of what is now Southern Mexico. One of the texts, which we're calling the 'Jacumba Codex' in the tradition of naming these types of things, contains a series of glyphs that we believe acts as an invocation for the transformative energetic process that has been called Quetzalcóatl. The problem is, there isn't a living person on Earth who knows how to decipher these glyphs. It's an entirely lost art. Think of it like a command code in programming. You enter the correct command, you get the desired result. We don't know how to run the command, because we don't know what it is or how to enter it."

In order to execute this code, Manriquez has developed a deep-learning artificial intelligence called Xolotl, which studies the Jacumba Codex in an attempt to understand its semantics. With him, a team of twelve or so students, academics, and assorted mystics work with the AI daily, using electrodes, VR masks, and group meditation exercises in an attempt to "awaken our homemade cyberdeity," as Manriquez explains it. Of course, where reality ends and performance art begins isn't all too clear out here on the surreal outskirts of Jacumba Hot Springs, but Manriquez is the first to admit that the experiment is far-fetched.

"We're not applying for federal grants or anything," he chimes. "This one's just for fun."

And what exactly will the Ketcel Collective do if they succeed in jostling a hodgepodge computer god into awareness, thereby awakening an ancient flying serpent from its place on the pages of the codex?

"Why, merge with it, of course." Manriquez grins into the

long oranges of the setting sun.

Crazy? Probably. But it beats the heck out of bird-watching.

Luna wasn't aware of the pulsing bass until she pulled her attention out of the article, but it didn't sound far off. "Is there a club out here?" she asked Eli.

Spires of blood-beige boulders jutted in blocky strata from conflicting angles, as if placed by drunken giants. Some had been carved by the wind into Swiss cheese, with drought-stricken yellow splotches of manzanita and yucca reaching from between the shadows. Chaparral sprouted from burnt tree trunks, spiny saguaros underscoring the landscape's awesome, all-consuming hostility.

"No, miss," Eli said, still looking pretty shaken. "I mean, I don't know, miss."

Rounding a bend in the mountain path, ever more rocky and warped as the buggy approached the drop-off into the desert, Luna located the erratic bass lines that echoed and distorted off the fractured topography. She could hardly believe her eyes.

In the middle of a giant amphitheater carved into the mountain top, a lone, bearded, heavyset man lounged on a black leather couch wearing giant, bulging sunglasses in the violet morning glow. Beneath him, a band played drill & bass dub riddims on a vast stage, which shifted slightly beneath five musicians, who jumped around with too much energy for the time of day.

As the buggy closed some distance, Luna realized that the stage wasn't elevated by pipes and scaffolding. It was being held on the backs of hundreds, maybe a thousand, men, women, and children in rags and tattered faces, dead stares peering from the shadows of the stage. On the far side of the amphitheater, the red and beige of granite gave way to white desert sand far below, where a charcoal lump of smog moved like a swarm of locusts over the Salton Sump, northeast.

The buggy approached the man on the couch and, as if he were expecting them, he stood and said with a pronounced Mexican accent,

"Welcome. You must be the journalists. I've been waiting for you." He extended a hand up to the driver's box. "Pacheco." He grinned as the morning sun peeked between boulders and cast him into a blown-out silhouette. "Pacheco Flores León."

Pacheco, her supposed "contact" in Limbo. What exactly was the Unknown handle trying to pull on her?

"Hi, Pacoco," said Don.

"So, which one of you is casting?" Pacheco beamed, wiping drops of beer from his tangled beard.

Nobody said anything, so Luna offered, "I am." I what?

Don and Eli shot her the same look in unison. You what?!

"Lensless, huh? Arre!" Pacheco exclaimed. "I always wanted to be on Hive. I see you guys hired a fixer from Tecate. Smart, though I don't know if he'll be much help out here."

Eli dropped his gaze.

"So, where do I begin?" Pacheco said. "Hello, everybody. Welcome to my party. I own this place. All of it." Pacheco tossed a hand from his side to the horizon to indicate that indeed everything belonged to him.

Which wasn't entirely true. Luna had already searched his name and was reading the gray text in her display as they let themselves down from the buggy to follow Pacheco, who had turned to initiate a tour as he continued in what sounded like a rehearsed narration.

Pacheco Flores León is the son and nephew
of the Flores Magón brothers, capos of the
Los Compas de Baja Autónoma cartel.

"So, this is my humble Estadio de las Piedras, where all the best parties in the world happen all the time."

He resides in permanent vacation in the
mountains of La Rumorosa at an open-air
amphitheater...

"It's not much, but I built it myself."

...built by the slave labor of rival cartel members and their families under the supervision of the Flores Magón brothers when they declared autonomy for the Baja California Peninsula.

"I have a hard-working and dedicated crew on site to ensure that everything is of the best quality."

Extended family members of rival cartels are kept as servants and subjected to some of the most severe human-rights violations currently taking place in North America, according to a report commissioned by the Reunited Nations.

"Let me show you. Come. Eat. Drink. Relaaax." Pacheco nodded to the audience in Luna's eye, grinning his reassurance through stained teeth.

Following a bend through the boulders, they came upon a towering monument to the garish narcotecture of the eighties—a three-story, brick-framed mini mansion built into the rocky hillside and filled out by a façade of wide, jet-black windows. Beyond a spiraling garden of yucca and saguaro, beneath a giant billboard screen playing a live feed from the amphitheater, thirty or so partiers lay passed out on the aqua-blue bottom of an empty swimming pool. One very sunburnt gringo slept almost camouflaged in a crime scene of vomit on the faded, antacid-pink slide. A few others sat hunched in palapas cooking meat and passing bottles.

Some party, Luna thought, wondering if the human-rights violations in the article referred to the people holding up the stage. She suspected there was more going on than she was being permitted to see. What else was Pacheco hiding in anticipation of his lifestyle spotlight segment?

Pacheco escorted them into the hillside mini mansion, nodding at two unsmiling Haitian guards who cradled enormous firearms at the door. Inside, a black granite table sat covered in chafing dishes overflowing with smoky, perspiring meats, grilled onions and chilies, exotic sauces, whole quail, infinity tamales, lobster tails, and a number of items that Luna had never seen before. A nappy lapdog peered in from the side patio, dancing anxiously between cairns of sun-hardened shit.

"What's mine is yours," Pacheco announced. "Mi casa es su casa."

Luna was hungrier than she realized. She hadn't eaten since Tecate about, what, like eighteen hours ago? Was that all? It felt like years.

She stacked a plate with squash blossoms, beans, grilled shrimp, and what looked like mole pipián, skipping over the steaming heaps of carnitas and birria. Just looking at meat made her uneasy, these days, being a strict pescatarian ever since she'd played around in an animal-simulation environ with pre-analog Juan Carlos a few years back. No doubt created by some animal-rights group, the environ was built on the premise that all mammals and, to a lesser extent, birds shared a similar capacity for suffering. There was *something* it was like to be a cow or a chicken or a pig, and she'd smoked too much weed in Juan Carlos's apartment as she tried out all the ImursiMask simulations of what those subjective *somethings* felt like. The chicken simulator was her favorite. That was the first time she'd realized that chickens weren't stupid, they were just stubborn. Stuck in their ways. Skeptical of everything. They had a very specific idea about how the world worked, and there wasn't much anyone could do to change that.

Luna liked that.

Luna was a chicken, too.

Eli slunk into a barstool and sighed. Don had already located the beer and was halfway through the bottle in his left hand when, upon registering Eli's disposition, he offered up the bottle in his right. "Cold 'fresher, young man?" Don asked, the gin blossom on his nose and cheeks flaring with entreat. Eil shrugged and placed the bottle on the bar top.

"I've got some guests to receive who have just flown in from Switzerland." Pacheco appeared pleased to advertise his European connections. "I'll be back in an hour or so. There are guest quarters in the back with plenty of room to spread out. Please, make yourselves at home."

As soon as Pacheco was out the door, Don turned to Luna and said, "So, uh, what the hell was that shit about hives and casting?"

Luna stopped mid-bite and digested the question. Should she tell them? Would that ruin everything? No, she decided. There are some things you can't just say. They have to be implied. You can't shout subtext. It wasn't like that. You have to find clues along the way, hope you've rightly identified the position of a few, and then triangulate in on the underlying meaning from there. Even directness was indirect. Or something like that. Maybe it was just easier to lie.

"I was just playing along," she slurred through a mouthful of the mole stuff. "I'm gonna go lie down. Wake me up before he gets back and let's get out of here. Guy's a creep." Luna reclined in a living-room sofa and closed her eyes. She hit stats: 6,989 viewers. Nothing. And Mom has twenty-six days. Fuck. Where were all the aggregate posters at Seenit and Videogum? She knew it was a good cast. She'd watch it. She'd *rather* be watching it.

Okay, so most viewers don't have the attention span to lurk Undew's home portal for unvetted content. She barely did herself. That was the problem with livecasts—you never knew when something that mattered was going to happen, so you got a lot of dead time between the highlights, even with selective casting. Just keep going, she told herself. The fan edits would come in once it gained some traction in the raw-feed circles. God, she hoped they would.

JACO LARK

I finally got a chance to catch up with your cast. You good? Your audio and video glitched out last night. Never cut, but lots of noise.

LUNA TESCHNER

Yeah, I'm fine. Did you message me instructions last night?

JACO LARK

That would be antithetical to our modus operandi. I won't ever interfere unless it's an emergency.

LUNA TESCHNER

I'm getting strange messages from an Unknown handle.

JACO LARK

Likely a bug. Put it in your beta-test notes for Synape. You're onto something big! Stay with Don, and take care of yourself. Pacheco is a nut.

LUNA TESCHNER

I noticed. Hey, whatever happened with our source? It's getting pretty weird out here. Any chance of going back to the Maquilandia story?

JACO LARK

Haven't heard from them. But you're in Limbo, and that's what counts. Best not to let Don know about your assignment. That never ends well. Trust me.

Trust him. Sure, Jaco. Right after this nap.
She hit her drop.
Nothing happened.

She hit it again. "Stop," she whispered.

Her Undew drop glowed red in the corner of her vision. When was the last time she cut her cast? On the buggy before El Hongo? Did the button get stuck when she turned it back on? Was there even a button to *get* stuck? She checked her message log, finding no record of the Unknown messages in the sweat lodge. Had she hallucinated them? Maybe, like Jaco said, it was just a bug. Still, she couldn't shake the feeling that Jaco knew more than he was letting on.

Luna drifted off and had fractured dreams of the Mansonbot tearing open eyeballs and cackling into a campfire. She watched from a disembodied, circling, lopsided point of view that segued into a flashback of the time she smoked *Salvia divinorum* with Juan Carlos and immediately felt like a cue ball balanced on a pinhead. Gravity had shifted axes, and Juan Carlos laughed and laughed like a maniac as she was dragged across the living-room carpet by inverted physics that she couldn't comprehend or control. The memory of his laughter invaded her dream, becoming Manson's laughter, which pixelated and bit-crushed into a demonic string of ones and zeros with the cutoff and resonance cranking all the way up until it hit a steady, piercing oscillation of visceral terror.

"Pull up!" Pacheco yelled over blasts from a handheld air horn. "Puuuuuuull up!"

Luna shot up to see Pacheco dressed in Rasta-striped safari garb standing next to a peevish gringo with a thin flop of blond hair that perched over a pair of oversized wayfarer castglasses. She recognized him from somewhere.

"Guess who I ran into at the jumperport?" Pacheco sneered. "Hmm? This is Milton. Milton from Hive." He shot Luna a hurt look, like a child who'd been lied to about ice cream. "Tell them what you told me, Milton from Hive."

"I, uh, watched *¡Toreros y Alarmas!* on my flight in," Milton murmured. "Pacheco hadn't seen it yet so I, uh, filled him in on the details."

Milton Jeffers from Hive. Right. He was vaguely famous in the US for his hipster Hive casts from quasi-fringe pockets of society, where he always got in just a little over his head but was invariably redeemed by his effusive awkwardness and his aura of unhampered harmlessness. He was already well into his routine, obviously nervous, out of his element, and quick to ally himself with the biggest and most immediate source of danger—Pacheco.

Pacheco pulled Luna into the kitchen, where three tall, young men—did they have bros in Switzerland?—dressed in designer patchwork shorts and captain's hats, shirtless, hovered over Don and Eli holding Derringer pistols hard against their temples.

"Hokay," Pacheco laughed. "Hooookay! So, first of all, nice work. What you did out there with Malverde and Manson? Prime time. Chingón. Excellent television. But then you come here and fuck it all up. Yeah. You lie to me? You take advantage of my hospitality? Make a fool of me? Lucky for you, nobody has to know about that. Milton here doesn't record anything until I say so, isn't that right, Milton?"

Milton nodded obediently, even though Luna could tell by the way his eyes rolled slightly in their sockets that he was casting, anyway.

"So, what are we gonna do now? Hmm?" Pacheco pretended to consider his options. "Oh, it's a shame. We could have had something, you and me. You could have been my princesa." He leered at Luna. "I could give you the world, but instead you want to run around with some fat viejo and this cross-eyed ox. Women, am I right?"

The Swiss land captains snorted and psshed their understanding.

"So, you want to run?" Pacheco raised an eyebrow. "Okay. Todo fine. Mira, you looking into the void, mija. Well, guess what? The void looks back." Pacheco pulled a leather castpatch over one eye. Grimacing like a pirate, he nodded at Milton to go live as he cracked open a frosty caguama of Tecate on his molars and dislodged a stringless crossbow from its holster on his back. "Now, run!"

The billboard by the swimming pool flipped to *¡Toreros y Alarmas!* and the rodeo clown host—named El Chavo del Loco, according to the caption Luna saw on the screen—convulsed with enthusiasm as he hollered, "Holy fucking shit, putos! We interrupt your regularly scheduled programming to take you to El Estadio de las Piedras for a live broadcast from Los Compas' Party Boy, Pacheco fucking Flores Leóóóóón!"

"I fucking hate that clown," Don huffed as they scurried back toward the buggy, Eli and Luna pulling him along.

El Chavo gushed, "It looks like Party Boy got tired of waiting for those dumbass bulls to find our runner and his new friends, so he's taking matters into his own hands! A huevoooooo!"

The billboard *¡Toreros y Alarmas!* feed jumped to Pacheco's castpatch looking down the sights of the crossbow, just as he launched a fat-tipped bolt from the arrow track. The back of the bolt spit fire and fumes, propelling the projectile like a rocket to explode in a flash of white heat in Don's footsteps.

"Holy fucking shit!" Don and El Chavo shouted in unison.

A shattering rain of beer bottles flew from the palapas, narrowly missing Luna's head as she rounded the bend to the amphitheater. Chunks of granite and sand pelted her side. Another bolt exploded on the incline to her right, dislodging a boulder that thundered behind them into a cactus-patch ravine.

"Almost there!" Eli grunted, helping Don descend the tall amphitheater steps. A bolt zipped over Luna's head, turning the buggy to splinters and spooking the horse into a gallop.

"Ezekiel!" Eli cried, but the stallion was gone in a cloud of dust before the name had left his mouth. They hobbled past the stage, and Luna met the eyes of a young woman, about her age, holding a baby in one arm and straining to keep the hulking platform from crushing down on her with the other.

Without knowing why, Luna shouted, "¡Vuelvo por ti!" *I'm coming back for you!*

"Keep moving!" Eli yelped.

"I...can't," Don gasped, clutching his chest.

"Over here!" Eli ducked into a low gap between boulders that led into an open-air passageway, pulling Don behind him.

"What is this place?" Luna whispered, panting.

"Labyrinth," said Eli. "Built by my ancestors to replicate the Luisenburg felsenmeer back in Germany. My grandfather used to play here. I've only heard about it. Let's move." They lurched down the stone corridor, choosing turns at random. "One path will take us to the end," Eli said. "The rest go back to the beginning."

"Which path do we take?" Don said, looking panic stricken and ill.

"I don't know, sir," said Eli.

"Luna, don't you have a coyote you can call to get us out of here?" Don asked.

"Isn't that the kind of thinking that got you in trouble in the first place?" said Luna.

"I told you, I didn't fucking...." Don paused and gathered himself. "It doesn't matter. Do you want to wait and find out if Party Boy will call us a ryde?"

"My coyote is only good for getting across the garbage wall into Mexico." She fucking wished she had a coyote she could call. "They can't help us here."

LUNA TESCHNER
Jaco, any chance you can get me out of here?

JACO LARK
I'm working on an exit plan. A contact in Yuma is negotiating an arrangement with some fishing drone pilots in Puerto Peñasco to net you out. Can you get to the farmland past Mexicali?

LUNA TESCHNER
Yeah. Sure. Easy. I'll get right on that.

"If we can get to the Sonoran border, my coyote can probably help us," Luna said, picking a turn in the maze and pulling Don behind her.

"Probably," said Don. "I like those odds."

She spotted movement on the hillside and pulled the others tight against a wall, anticipating a volley from Pacheco's RPG crossbow. She peeked again. It was that little twit Milton. She had an idea. She pulled up Hive's top-trending casts and selected "I Hunted Runners in Limbo with Los Compas' Party Boy." A transparent Milton's-eye view of the labyrinth overlaid itself on Luna's vision. It took her a moment to locate herself, then Pacheco, who was just turns away.

"This way!" Luna hissed. She led Don and Eli away from Pacheco, running one hand against the wall so she could focus in on the Hive overlay to navigate. She made out the exit, traced the route back to their position, hoped to fuck she got it right, and ran for it.

"Lady luck!" Don grinned at Luna as they emerged from the labyrinth through a narrow passage. "Let's get the hell out of here." They rounded a bend and came upon a gondola lift whose cables shot straight down the mountain into a bleak expanse of desert below.

Eli gasped. "I never believed it existed."

"What is it?" Luna asked.

Eli said, "There were rumors about Los Compas building a ski resort over a single summer, when the weather forecasted a freezing La Niña winter with snow. I didn't think it was possible."

UNKNOWN
Get in. Pull the handbrake, turn the key,
and hit the green button.

LUNA TESCHNER
Fuck you.

A creosote bush burst into flames just meters away. Was Pacheco even aiming that thing?

UNKNOWN
It is vital that your cast remain open. All
will be clear soon. You have to trust us.

Trust them. Luna didn't see any other choice. "Well, let's see how it rides," she said.

LUNA TESCHNER
Who are you?

They got in the gondola, which looked more like an overpriced cocktail lounge, and Luna fumbled with the controls.

"You ever driven one of these?" Don elbowed Luna and grinned. Was that a dad joke?!

UNKNOWN
We are you in the future.

Luna looked over her shoulder as Pacheco rounded the bend, this time aiming the crossbow directly at her. She cut to the *¡Toreros y Alarmas!* feed and yanked the handbrake just in time to watch an RPG bolt launch from Pacheco's crossbow and miss the gondola by centimeters, disappearing in a lens flare to the east. After the initial jerk, the gondola moved slow, but quickly gained momentum until it accelerated to a free fall. Don and Eli screamed. Luna's stomach jumped to her throat.

JACO LARK
986,743 viewers. Your LIVE is top five on the Undew puddle and about twenty different fan edits are trending like crazy on Seenit and Videogum. Looks like you stole Milton's thunder after his viewers found your cast via proximity ranking. This is BIG!

Luna got the chills. The Bishop Berkeley trick was working its memetic magic, reifying probability into reality and spreading awareness like a pathogen, an entity all its own that she'd merely helped set free. She thought about Mom, tears of relief blurring her vision to soft focus.

Everything was going to be okay.

CACHANIHILISMO : : 23

Kervens loved having breasts. Small, firm, perky breasts that sent electricity to his toes when they moved against her shirt just so. Not only that, it was the flowing hair around her shoulders, the agile body that flexed like wild game when she ran, and that intoxicating, impossibly clean scent of girl that only became more nuanced and alluring as she perspired in the desert sun. A desiccating breeze moved over her skin like a searchlight, illuminating a forearm here, a thigh there, a nape of the neck.

The moment the illusion began to fade, Kervens filled his lungs with axol and was thrust back into her body before the cerulean vapors had a chance to spiral from his nostrils. He had gone through several grams since he woke up in a daze around ten a.m.

What happened last night?

It had only begun to return in skittish fragments when he reached for his vaporizer, determined to go back. He'd never axoled enough to sync with someone who wasn't in his immediate proximity, much less halfway on the other side of Limbo. In fact, he didn't know it was possible, and he now suspected he'd been missing out on something vast and unspeakable for years.

Was this a hex from the Guédé for barging in on them uninvited, without proper invocation or even a gift? Perhaps it was, he decided, but if so, it was a blessing in disguise.

It was his day off, but even if it weren't, nothing in his daily routine was compelling enough to pull him away from his perfect new form. He felt at home here, like he was meant to be her all along, and somehow got plugged into the wrong body at birth. If he could only stay here forever, he and Casseus could finally be together. If only he could stay *her* forever.

She was like Marinette, except every sense—even taste, scent, thought, and touch—became Kervens's own. He felt radiant and capable, and he loved it. Her skin-tight, faded black jean shorts and earth-brown tee gripped her body, reaffirming and delineating her lithe form with every movement. Her heart pounded between narrow shoulders as her dirty Doc Martens carried her away from the burning sky tram, which had slowed just enough to jump from before the emergency brake exploded in a friction fire. Her thoughts were a piercing square wave of adrenaline as she ran down a dilapidated escalator, its awning whipping and whistling in the arid afternoon wind.

"Thank you, Lord!" the young Mennonite exclaimed to the sky when they came to rest by a crumbling cantina with a flashbulb sign reading LAGUNA NEVADA.

"That was fucking crazy," the old white man from *¡Toreros y Alarmas!* croaked. What was his name again? Dan?

"Everything's going to be okay," she said, her mind focusing. Kervens realized he hadn't heard her name spoken out loud, but somehow he already knew it, in the same way he knew his own. It was hardwired into his awareness: Luna. "Let's see what's inside. I'm parched."

Her arm extended to pull at the door, revealing a tattoo on her inner forearm of a cat girl holding an astronaut helmet on her hip. The door swung open into an empty bar that had apparently been looted. Stools were shattered to splinters and arranged into ceremonial altars, plates and pint glass shards glistening on the floor. Defaced five-hundred-peso bills were stapled over every centimeter of ceiling, including the disco ball, and someone had spray-painted CANTINA CACHANIHILISMO in dripping hot pink across the far wall.

Probably those Mexicali noise punks the Flores Magón brothers had warned him about. Anarchists, they said, but not the good kind. Not like us. They had nothing better to do than vandalize Los Compas property with junk-tech pranks, making some sort of statement. They called it art. Los Compas called it a nuisance, if not a provocation.

"Thank you, Lord!" the old man hollered, producing an unbroken glass from a cabinet behind the bar and resting it on the grate beneath a Zodiac Beer tap. He licked his cracked lips in anticipation, pulling the black handle back with measured reverence. It hissed and spit a wad of brown foam down the side of the glass. He frowned.

"Water's off too," the Mennonite said, spinning a faucet knob on the sink.

"Damn," the old man muttered. "It's a million degrees out there. What do we do now?"

"Let's keep looking," Luna said, and Kervens liked how she was in control of the situation, even though he wasn't.

The resort enclave beyond the cantina was an apocalypse of collapsed buildings, warped fences, and the skeletal remains of mobile homes rotted from the inside out like poisoned whales. Kervens couldn't tell if it had all been here for one or one hundred years. It looked like a bomb had gone off, except there was no sign of an explosion or epicenter. The village had been demolished from every direction at once. It was decomposing, being eaten by the elements, decaying faster than time, and soon every concrete pylon and oxidized shard of rebar would become indistinguishable from the alkaline dust that devoured everything for as far as the eye could see.

"Wait a minute," the Mennonite whispered, tilting his head. "Do you hear water?"

Luna and the old man stopped.

"In there," the Mennonite nodded toward an adobe cabin that had crumbled on one side so that the roof and remaining wall formed a near-perfect triangle emerging from the earth. Luna ducked into a void where a window used to be, her tongue swollen and coarse against the roof of Kervens's mouth. In a dark corner, a single draft tap poured into a small cement pool. Behind it, a red neon Zodiac Beer sign flickered through the darkness to reflect off the murky water.

"What in the hell?" the old man muttered, cupping his hands to collect from the falling stream. He moved his hands into a ray of light. His eyes grew large. "Blood!" he howled. "It's fucking blood!" He shook out his hands and dragged them across a wall by the entrance, leaving deep-red streaks like something out of a horror environ. "Hey, wait." He paused. "Take a look at this. There's some kind of placard over here. Luna, I need your Spanish."

Kervens could barely make out the weatherworn engraving.

"It says this is a memorial for..."—Luna studied the lettering as the Mennonite peered over her shoulder—"...for...all the campesinos, all the farmers who died with their...crops in protest of Zodiac Conglomerate, who...who stole our water for export and spilled our blood in the streets and in the fields. Signed, Cachanihilismo."

"Catch a who?" the old man said.

"I don't know," said Luna, though Kervens knew "cachanilla" was local slang for a person from Mexicali, after the ubiquitous arrowweed shrub. So, Mexicali nihilism? It had to be those delinquents he'd been warned about, right?

"Let's see if there are any other signs in here," Luna instructed.

"Hello, is anybody in there?" a woman called from outside.

She sounds American, Kervens thought. Or did Luna think that?

"Did you see something, honey?" a man said from just beyond the entrance. They seemed to materialize out of the dust as they scuttled into the shadowy building. They wore beige Tilley hats, wraparound sunglasses, matching white T-shirts reading "I Heart Limbo" in bloodred letters that bulged around their bellies, Bermuda shorts, and flip-flops. Both carried full jugs of water in each hand.

What are tourists doing in Limbo?

"Hey, can you help us?" Luna rasped. "We got stuck out here without any water and...."

The tourists gasped and then chuckled, grasping each other with glee.

"Hey!" Luna repeated. "We really need water, can we...."

The tourists pulled phones from their pockets and began snapping photos, giggling. "Look at that one! Did you get that one?"

"Please," the Mennonite pleaded. "We need help."

The woman posed next to the Mennonite, taking a deep drink from her jug while the man snapped photo after photo, the exaggerated click of a simulated shutter firing on repeat. "They're so lifelike," the woman squealed. "I almost thought they were real!"

"I am real!" the Mennonite exploded, visibly enraged as he swatted at the tourists' phones. He attempted to push the tourist man away, then stared at his hands in disbelief.

"Up there," the old man motioned toward an iridescent beam emitting from a box on the ceiling.

"Holograms?!" Luna couldn't believe her eyes as the tourists laughed their way out into the blinding sun, and the box on the ceiling blinked out. A transparent search window appeared in Kervens's vision followed by the word "Cachanihilismo" and what looked like a hacked Wiki page that read, "Sometimes vandalism is more creative than creativity," in kitschy, corrupted glitch font.

Luna realized it was art. Or she was the art. Or it all was.

Everything is art and nothing is real, Luna thought. Or was it Kervens?

> *We're all just art on autopilot, reacting*
> *to motion sensors and timer switches,*
> *waiting for our batteries to die*
> *in an endless desert.*
> *In this ghost town. And*
> *we're the ghosts.*

"Let's get out of here," the Mennonite whispered, looking like he had in fact seen a ghost.

There's got to be more to this fountain.

"Hold on," Luna said on a hunch. "Let's take a closer look at this." She filled her hands from the tap, sniffed, and drank.

"Don't!" the old man yelped with what sounded like paternal concern.

Was he her father?

"The pipes are just rusty," Luna said with a vampire grin. "Doesn't taste the best, but a little won't hurt us. Whoever left this here is making a statement, but they know what it's like to have to survive in the desert. Look, there are some empty jugs over here. Eli, help me fill these."

The Mennonite silently obeyed, taking a cautious sip, followed by several swallows.

"Don." Eli extended the jug to the old man.

Don and Eli, Kervens repeated to himself.

Don drank greedily, the red liquid spilling from both sides of his mouth, leaving twin streaks down his button-up shirt.

"Nice Tijuana bolo tie," Eli ribbed, and they all erupted with laughter, even Kervens, who felt better than he had in a long time as he inhaled several deep draws of sacred, dreamy axol.

"Up here!" Luna called down from the crow's nest. "I can see everything!"

"Oh yeah?" Don goaded. He felt good, which was odd. "How far is Sully's?"

"Who?" She peered down the mast of the ghost ship as Don huffed his way up the steps to the poop deck.

"Ah, forget it," Don said. "Shitty dive bar. It's got nothing on the cosmopolitan Cantina Catchawhatever." For the first time, he realized she reminded him of Anabelle, with her fierce independence and unshakable will, and it made his daughter feel more real. Maybe she really was still out there, calling out to him to find her.

The bony remnants of the galleon sat in a scrapyard of defunct rydes with their tires and windows missing, luxury snowmobiles with their skis buried in the sand, and a few Ferris wheel pods, all lined up in rows facing the same direction and equipped with recliner chairs, visibly less weathered than the vehicles they inhabited. It reminded Don of an old drive-in movie theater, except there was no screen. He climbed into the recliner on the back deck of the ship and yanked at the handle, but instead of pulling him back, it dropped a headpiece over his face. It looked like a shitty knockoff of those ImursiMasks the kids were using. To Don's surprise, it flickered to life, to that fucking *¡Toreros y Alarmas!* clown, of all things.

"Hoooookkkaaayyyy, putos! Time out!" El Chavo del Loco's face was close enough to punch as he gyrated into the frame every time Don twisted his head to look away. "As you know, our third bull was released from her home shrine this morning, and she's ready to kick some gringo fucking ass! Here's a little replay of her big debut."

Don had never tried VR before, and it was already worse than he'd imagined. He soared over a bird's-eye view of Zona Norte with nauseating speed, plummeting into the entrance of Bar Zacazonapan and taking a hard right down a staircase into the basement barroom, emerging through a fog of smoke to do a slow zoom on the painted faceplate and party-hat breasts of Mamá Dona. The hot-wired Border Patrol bot tossed back a shot of tequila, which splashed down its mouthless chin, then rose to serenade the camera, singing the chorus to "What It Feels Like for a Girl."

"That's right, mis Compas,"—El Chavo's over-excited face filled the frame—"Mamá Dona is hauling ass to El Estadio de las Piedras, where our runners just barely escaped Party Boy by taking a ski lift down to the desert."

The image in the headset cut to an epileptic barrage of clips from Party Boy's castpatch, explosions, an overhead shot of the labyrinth, a close-up of Don in the labyrinth—did they have cameras in there?—and an RPG dart coming damn close to taking down the gondola as it descended from the mountaintop.

"Hey, if that fucking desert doesn't kill them, Mamá Dona will!" El Chavo exclaimed. "Let's see what she's up to now."

The scene cut to a first-person view of Mamá Dona running at high speed through what looked like the foothills just before the roadblock in Tecate. At this rate, the thing would be to Party Boy's place and down the mountain to them in what, a few hours? Don began trembling in his seat. Did VR have haptics? He shoved the recliner handle down and the ImursiMask disappeared into the headrest, but the vibration continued.

Eli popped out of a cargo hold and, grinning, said, "Does anybody know how to drive this thing?"

"Nice!" Luna cheered from her perch.

"Let an old coot show you how automobiles work, youngster." Don stood with a groan. He followed Eli down a steep stairway into the cargo hold, got situated in the driver's seat, and fussed with some levers. The ghost ship lurched forward.

"Just like the old Chevy, he says!" Eli relayed to Luna from below, his head poking out of the hold like a groundhog. Eli had a new fire to him ever since he attacked the tourists, even if they were just holograms, and Luna was beginning to see him more as an independent man than the shy, overgrown boy that she had met just yesterday in Tecate.

The outside world, beyond the colony with its Old Testament dogma and stark rejection of modernity, seemed good for him. He was becoming himself, and Luna imagined that he could even be handsome someday, despite the unfortunate teeth and general ignorance of most things invented after the nineteenth century.

"Where do we want to go?" Eli called up to her.

A topographic map materialized in Luna's vision, slowly zooming out from a red dot at the eastern edge of the Sierra Juárez mountains. A light-blue blob came in from the bottom-right periphery as the perspective pulled out. "Laguna Salada," it said. Salty lake. The map fizzled out.

"Eli, do you know anything about a lake out here?" Luna asked. "Anywhere with water?"

"The lake has been dry for decades," Eli said. "The old maps at the brewery drawn by my grandfather call this whole desert 'Salzhölle.' Salt Hell. But I recall something about a spring some distance south of where I think we are. How far, I don't know. Could be five kilometers. Could be fifty. What do you think, Don?"

"I say we go for it," Don hollered from the cargo hold. "Beats sitting here with our thumbs up our butts waiting for that deathbot with the Madonna tits to come hunt us down. What does Luna think?"

She gave two thumbs up, locating the oasis of Cañón de Guadalupe tucked into the mountains about forty-five kilometers south on her map. Eli was a better guide than he realized. The farmland east of Mexicali was more than double the distance of the springs, and exactly perpendicular to their new destination. But, after they resupplied at the springs, they could skip Mexicali altogether and instead cut southeast across the desert, beneath the Cocopah mountain range, out to the Colorado River delta, a straight shot across the Sea of Cortez from Puerto Peñasco.

"Aye, aye, captain," Eli shouted before disappearing into his groundhog hole.

The ship pitched forward and turned south, putting along at a running pace with nothing but towering mountains to the right and a brutal sea of sand to the left. Luna thought of Mom, and how she'd be scared to death if she knew her only daughter had gone from experimental VR journalist to desert ghost pirate in the two short weeks since she'd left home.

"You're not half bad at this for an inbred farm boy," Don said.

A smile tugged at one side of Eli's face as he navigated around an outcropping of rocks and over a low dune crowned with wiry ocotillo bushes.

"That's it. Downshift on inclines for more power," Don said. "Very nice! You're a natural."

"Thank you, sir. My father had forbidden me to drive the motor buggy that he leased."—And almost apologetically—"It was only a short time the Council permitted them."

"Dads can be real pricks," Don said, unsure if he was talking about himself or his own father.

"I don't blame him." Eli smiled. "Everything happens according to the Lord's plan."

"Everything is horseshit." Don said as a reflex. "You think we're gonna die out here?"

"If the Lord deems it."

"Lord!" Don laughed. "The only Lord I know is Lord Calvert."

"I haven't heard of him," said Eli, aloof or maybe just accustomed to his own ignorance.

"That's because he's a bottom-shelf whiskey," Don said, wondering why the boy was grinning like he got boobs in his blinkers. "You're better off with your beer."

"Agree to disagree, then. I know but one Lord."

"It doesn't matter what we think we know, Eli." Don consecrated the statement with a loud gulp of rust water. "We're just ants. And if your Lord exists, and that's a big 'if,' He's planning to squash us."

The last part came out more like "squash ughshit!" as Don's gut smashed into the dashboard and the ghost ship lurched to a halt. "Dammit, man!" Don hollered. "What did you press?"

Eli rubbed his jaw where it had impacted on the steering wheel and muttered, "Must have thrown a shoe." And then both in unison, "Luna!"

They found her sprawled out on the deck, emitting a series of throaty gasps. "I'm..." *gasp*, "...okay...," *gasp*, "...lost my..." *gasp*, "...air." Don and Eli helped her to her feet, carrying her off the ship with an arm over each of their shoulders. "Tread busted," she wheezed, pointing at the ship's mangled tank treads bunched around a rock.

"Here, drink this." Eli handed her half a jug of Zodiac blood.

"Wait, is this all we have left?" she said after several gulps.

Don looked at his shoes. "The other jug spilled when we stopped."

"This is bad," she said. "This is real bad. We gotta keep moving."

Trudging through the dunes reminded Luna of running from a monster in a nightmare. And she *was* running from a monster in a nightmare, except the monster was potentially anyone, and nightmare-running was somehow more efficient than sand-walking. She was covering less distance than her effort merited.

Time didn't have anything to hold onto, but her display told her it had been almost three hours since they left the ghost ship. Since then, the scenery had been stuck on a loop of efflorescing shrubs and rolling dunes that were just high enough to be tedious but too low to offer a meaningful vantage point to gauge their progress. She pulled up her map: *4.97 km to Cañón de Guadalupe*. It would be another hour at least, and the water was long gone.

She had been getting dizzier ever since she fell off the crow's nest. Her head felt like it was floating above her body in a nauseating tunnel of static. The Santa Ana breeze threatened to suffocate her with arid heat. Her heart thundered in her ears. It occurred to her that she was about to die. She felt herself succumbing to exhaustion and panic. She didn't want to give in, but something alien in her stomach did. It oozed out of her solar plexus and gripped her heart, constricted her lungs, and strangled her with animal terror.

It wasn't like the anxiety she felt when she found out about Mom's staggering debt with the crypto mobsters. That was a rational panic, one she knew she could plan and worry and work their way out of. This was an immediate, primal panic that sprang from her nucleotides and clamped down on her whole being with the committed finality of a straitjacket.

She had often thought she would be okay with dying. Not that she was looking forward to it, but she accepted death as the unwaivable cost of being, the price we all pay. Now, her rationale felt distant and naive. She was wracked with bottomless dread, drowning in her own mortality, smothered by the inevitable. Eons of death before her felt intimately near. It was horrific in its awful, brooding certainty. She was going to die, and Mom would be devastated and then murdered.

It would have been bearable if her death actually accomplished anything, like saving Mom and protecting Noel. But it didn't. She felt like a sacrificial villager being hauled off to the volcano to appease imaginary island gods, and there wasn't anything she could do to stop it.

"We need help," she said, mortified by the withering voice that emerged from her wind-torn lips. She looked back to see Eli trailing about twenty paces behind and Don another twenty behind him. Their gait was tortured, their heads hanging away from the white-hot sun.

Help. She was their only chance at help, and she knew it. Of course, it would mean blowing her cover, but she had to do it. She couldn't just let them all die. They would understand, wouldn't they? Did it matter if they didn't?

> **LUNA TESCHNER**
> Jaco, you following my feed? It's not looking good. I think we need to cancel the story. I'm in real trouble. Can you send help?

Send help? What was he going to do? His exit plan involved her being a hundred kilometers east. Jaco didn't have any connections in Limbo. His one fucking contact never got in touch!

> **LUNA TESCHNER**
> Jaco, you there?

Did he even have a contact in the first place?

> **LUNA TESCHNER**
> It's an emergency! Jaco, are you getting this?

Was Maquilandia even meant to be the story? He pitched it, not her. She just went along with it. What the hell was going on here?

> **LUNA TESCHNER**
> Jaco, please! I'm going to die out here!

Maybe he wanted her to die out there. Maybe that was his plan all along. Get her into Limbo, set her loose in Maquilandia, and then feed her directions through the Unknown handle into certain death. It was Unknown that told her to jump off the bridge into Keith's ryde. It was Unknown that told her to trust the Mansonbot who jammed her cast open. It was Unknown that sent her down the gondola into the desert.

Oh fuck. Jaco sent her out here to die and catch it all on livecast. This *was* the plan. Some fucked up PR stunt to make Undew Media go viral. He would do that, wouldn't he? Fuck. Could he hear her thinking this?

LUNA TESCHNER
Jaco, answer me!

She fell to her knees and cried, her heart pounding in her head. *Pa-boom! Pa-boom! Pa-boom!*

A hand rested on her shoulder. Eli gazed down, his face wrought with defeat, dropping the empty water jugs at his side. They stared at each other for what felt like a very long time. Don arrived and doubled over, panting with his hands on his thighs. The violent pulse grew louder, deeper, shock waves impacting from a distance.

Pa-boom! Pa-boom! Pa-boom!

"Do you hear that?" Eli said.

"Drums?" Don rasped.

"Over there." Eli nodded toward a rabbit trail that disappeared into a boulder-strewn canyon. "We must be close."

Don and Eli helped her to her feet, shuffling arm-in-arm into the ravine. The sanctuary of shadows washed over them as the late afternoon sun dipped behind the mountains. At their craggy peak, the sun formed a halo around a formation of rocks that reminded Luna of the Virgin Mary herself, waiting with geological patience to usher her into the absolute.

Kervens groaned and reached for his ImursiMask, its ringtone pulling him further out of Luna with every crescendoing pulse.

"Invitación de los Jefes," the synthesized voice of a woman chirped. Invite from the Bosses.

The netherworld of the avatar lobby assimilated in pinpoints of virtual night, the reverie of Laguna Salada evaporating into peripheral nothing. He selected Kervens, accepting the invite.

Drone's-eye cutaway of a colonial plaza somewhere down in Los Cabos, a white church with twin bell towers on one end, a wall of copy/paste stucco and storefronts around the rest. The perspective lilted toward a gazebo crowned with wrought-iron trim. Between it and the church, two rows of benches beneath squat trees, which cast dendrites of shade from their sparse, awl-shaped leaves.

The perspective settled at head height, facing an umbrellaed hot dog cart with EL BUHO hand-painted in italic red caps across the front panel. On the far side of an acrylic sneeze guard, shrouded in gossamer gold satin, her eye sockets two beckoning black holes,

Santísima Muerte tossed a steaming pile of sliced onions with a short-handled scythe on the flattop, flipping pale strips of bacon with her free hand and spiraling them around firecracker-red franks. In a single, showily efficient gesture, she snatched up a sausage between an open bun, showered it with caramelized onion, and extended it across the sneeze guard on ivory-bone fingers.

Kervens took the unappetizing refection, consoled by the fact that he could neither smell nor consume it. Muttering an automatic prayer to Our Lady of Sacred Death, though he did not hold her in the same reverence the Flores Magón brothers did, he sat at a bench and waited for the triplets to log in. They were typically there well before he arrived, looking as though they had been deliberating matters of grave importance, which made him wonder if their many victories had been worth anything, still fiendishly preoccupied by business as they were.

We all have our habits, he decided, placing the hot dog in his lap. They keep us going, our desires. Give us something to live for when nothing else makes sense.

A jolt of Luna stumbling up a rocky gulch, tufts of a palm-tree oasis in the distance, ethereal and inviting against the shark-toothed silhouette of mountains.

Kervens shook his head and focused on the hot dog. Make it real, he commanded himself. You still don't have to eat it.

Santísima Muerte threw another sausage on the grill and shuffled the onion stack. The space in front of her distorted, heat waves off a highway, a placeholder for an avatar doing the log-in lilt. She brought her scythe down on a fresh onion with a startling thwack.

Casseus.

"Kwee-dad-oh. Ah-gwuhz Hey-chuh-sarahs." Don squinted at the wood-burned sign riddled with bullet holes.

"'Cuidado. Aguas Hechiceras,'" Luna read. "Caution. Sorceress Waters."

Pa-boo! Pa-pa-boom! Boom-pa-boo-boom!

The drums or whatever sounded like they were coming from within the palm-tree oasis and had taken on a synthetic, off-kilter quality that made Don think of the rhythmless electronic garbage you hear blasting at the young-people restaurants back in Florida. "Water," he said. "Let's go."

The air beneath the palm canopy was cool, carrying the scent of sage and fecund mud. Don followed a patch of moss to a trickle of moisture to the tiniest stream to a stagnant puddle to, holy shit, yes, a crystal clear, shimmering pool of water. He knelt and scooped with both hands to receive the most intoxicating drink of his life. Luna and Eli followed, both collapsing on their backs after the first few gulps, which splashed down their chins and chests in glistening cascades.

Don reclined into the cold mud, his skin retracting to goose bumps after hours of desert exposure, and closed his eyes.

Boo-pa-pa.

Pa-boom.

The sound seemed to be retreating up the canyon, its rhythm becoming sparse.

"What the fuck?!" he yelled. "What in the fucking fuck? Are we the luckiest sums a bitches on the planet or what?"

"It's all, indeed, part of the Lord's plan," Eli said.

"You hanging in there, Luna?" Don said instead of arguing.

"Better now," Luna said, even though Don could tell she was still hurting.

They laid there in silence for several minutes, catching their breath and ladling water to their faces with one hand, until Don groaned to his feet. "Nature calls," he said. "Then, let's go figure out what, or who, is making all that noise."

Don wandered through the palms to an incline at the edge of the canyon. He ascended far enough to be out of sight and took a world-class, picture-perfect piss all over a fuzzy cactus. There are few things better than a much-needed piss with a view, he affirmed to himself, making sure to drench all sides of the cactus impartially.

Don felt serene. Bar Sully serene. The oasis below looked crepuscular in the mountain shadow, which drew a hard line far off in the desert, lending the impression of twilight creeping east to consume the afternoon with its inviting, unknowable darkness. The resort scouts would shit themselves for this place, but they'd never have what he had right now. He was already at peace with it. His condo, sailboat, and assets were set to pay off his student loans at death, so he could rest easy, knowing he'd die debt free. He'd live out his last days in secluded paradise, relaxing in the springs and pissing on all of creation one by one, until a circuit-bent robot finally killed him in his sleep. There were worse ways to go.

Just as he was zipping up his shorts, a figure ran through the corner of his vision along the oasis tree line. He spun around to watch the figure disappear between a couple dead skirts of palm.

"We have to leave, now!" Luna shouted from somewhere below.

"Hey, wait!" Don dodged cactus and loose rocks, jogging after her. He slipped on a patch of loose gravel, scraping his knees at the base of the hill. Looking up, he saw the back of Luna's head weaving between palm trunks, running full speed out of the oasis. He pulled himself up, wondering what the hell was going on. He sprinted as fast as his worn-out legs would carry him, jagged fronds tearing at his arms as he plowed through the overgrowth. His heart pounded with alarm and exertion. "Luna!" he shouted, running until the oasis was at his back and the open expanse of desert stood barren before him.

Everything went silent. A shiver of static shot up his spine. There was nobody there.

He jogged back into the palms and found Luna and Eli stripped down to their undergarments, relaxing in the spring.

"Sir," Eli said, "you look as though you've seen a succubus."

"I, uh, think the heat got to me," Don said, even though it got hotter than a four-peckered billy goat in Florida, and he never saw anything like that before.

"Then you've come to the right place." The light behind Luna's eyes was glowing back at full wattage. "Get in."

Don took a slow look around and shrugged, tossing off his shirt and shorts and easing his aching body into the pool. The water coated his skin in cryogenic quicksilver, putting him immediately at ease as he settled onto a flat stone, the waterline at his chin. He wondered if the oasis was haunted and decided he didn't care. Haunted or not, it beat the hell out of Tijuana or Party Boy's or pretty much anywhere he'd been in a long, long time. He laid his head back and closed his eyes, considering what "succubus" meant and if, in fact, he saw one.

"You look good," Casseus said, tossing his hot dog into a garbage can.

"I...," Kervens began, remembering himself. "I'm sorry, do I know you?"

Casseus gave a delighted chuckle and sat next to Kervens, their thighs almost touching. "You never were a good liar." Casseus rested a hand on Kervens's knee.

"What are you doing here?" Kervens's breath quickened.

"I came to see you." Casseus smiled, his eyes beaming behind natty half-frame sunglasses, a purely aesthetic accessory in the luminosity-controlled environ.

"I thought something happened to you." A rush of Marinette's unshakable affection.

"Something *has* happened to me, Kervens."

"Is there somebody else?" Marinette's self-conscious yearning.

Casseus chuckled again, putting Kervens at ease. "No, not that."

"Then what? I haven't seen you all week. Did you forget our anniversary?"

"Kervens, Marinette, I need to tell you something. It's important that you listen to me very carefully."

A million scenarios flashed through Kervens's head. "I'm listening."

"I'm not real." Casseus removed his sunglasses and met Kervens's gaze.

"What? Casseus, I know. None of this is real."

"Not like that." A severe expression came over Casseus. "I'm telling you I don't exist. When Marinette logs off, there's Kervens, right?"

Kervens nodded.

"Okay. When I log off, there's nothing."

"What do you mean, nothing? What about your corgi and your house in La Jolla and curing ALS?"

"Doesn't exist."

"Then why did you say they did?"

"It's complicated, but *I* didn't say those things."

"You're lying. Why are you lying?" Kervens felt himself becoming flustered, then caught himself, knowing he had to remain composed for the brothers.

"They're not coming."

"Who?"

"Your bosses. They aren't coming. I created the invite. I had to talk to you alone."

"Casseus, I don't understand. This is the brothers' private environ. How did you invite me here?"

"Remember what I said about listening carefully?"

"Yes. I.... Go ahead." The minimal techno tap of onions being diced on a cutting board.

"This is my first time talking to you as Casseus, okay? Every other time? Wasn't me."

"Okay. Who was it then? Can I talk to him?"

"Them. And no, you can't. They no longer use Casseus."

"They? Casseus, you're scaring me. Are you feeling okay?"

A cloud of pigeon-like birds with iridescent turquoise backs, blood-orange bellies, and long, cobalt tail feathers appeared between the cathedral spires, flocking and everting on themselves in an amorphous dance that reminded Kervens of a 4-D environ he once played around with until it got too confusing to care.

"Not Casseus, remember? Listen. Casseus is just an algorithmic reflection of your own ideal partner. Those surveys you took for singles night at the Spore Lounge, that's part of it."

"You're saying Casseus is a cloak?"

"A cloak of someone who never existed, yes."

Kervens scanned his recollections of Casseus, desperate to punch a hole in the picture that was being painted for him. "If Casseus is a cloak, where is his halo? Automated avatars are required to wear halos in Sawlips."

"Not in private environs. Think about it. Medellín. The expensive hotels. The supper clubs. All private."

"The Spore Lounge?"

"The Flores Magón brothers oversaw the first date personally. You'll note Casseus has been absent from the Spore Lounge for some time now."

"The brothers know about y...about Casseus?"

"The brothers *built* Casseus, or more likely, one of their tech-savvy nephews did. Wanted to cordon off Marinette's intimate life, make sure she's not falling in love with strangers on the internet and slipping cartel secrets between the sheets. Plus, Casseus keeps you loyal. So long as your first priority is getting to him, you'll do anything to stay in the brothers' good graces."

"Oh my god." The bottom dropped out of Kervens's stomach. "The brothers know about Marinette?"

"They used to take turns as Casseus." His expression softer now, sympathetic even. "Not for any of the sentimental stuff. The nights out and conversations, that was all automated after the cloak was up and running. But they did get a kick out of taking the wheel for the more...passionate moments."

"Oh my god." Kervens only half noticed the hot dog fall from his lap onto his shoes.

"But like we said, Casseus has recently been deactivated. You may have spotted us trying him on at the Spore Lounge yesterday morning."

"Why?" Forcing images of the brothers with Marinette out of his head. Did Not-Casseus say "us"?

"They no longer need him."

"Why?"

"They no longer need you."

Kervens knew the brothers well enough to know what that meant. The realization sent a surge of dread to his stomach, accompanied by a terrible thought. "If the brothers created Casseus, how do I know *you're* not the brothers?"

"Would we be telling you all this if we were?" Not-Casseus said frankly, his expression encouraging Kervens to be as skeptical as he needed. "Also, there are no brothers. Los Compas have been run by their cloaks for the last three months. Boating accident. Why do you think you've only met with them virtually, when they used to be adamant about seeing everything themselves? In a private environ, no less, where cloaks aren't required to wear halos? Only their top officials know, and they plan to keep it that way. But it won't work. Baja Autónoma is being held up by toothpicks, and it's all about to come crashing down."

Kervens was speechless. If it was a lie, it was airtight.

"There's more," Not-Casseus said. "Have you noticed any anomalies? Especially with the drug, axolimine?"

"Nothing out of the ordinary."

"Now you're lying."

"I've been syncing with somebody."

"Luna. Yes, good."

"Good?" A revolting sense of having been violated in ways he never knew possible.

"We've installed a linkage. Well, your dentist did, last week. Nanobots. Cost us a small fortune to get him to agree to it, if it makes you feel any better."

"What's nanobots?"

"Tiny robots that integrate with your brain, in this case. That second Novocain shot wasn't Novocain. Nanobots went around your uvula to the nasal cavity, then into your brain. The linkage is dialed into Luna's Afterthought, a more complicated version of what we gave you. You've been subconsciously feeding her information, which you may have noticed as short bouts of amnesia. We're pleased to see that the drug is capable of potentiating the linkage beyond the implant's technological limitations. Full-sense immersion. That must be a novel experience for you. This is the first time the combination has been tested, as far as we know. You no doubt noticed the linkage open during your meeting with the Guédé."

A flash of the simulated axol trip, the serpent, the teardrop. "You were Lady Erzulie. And the Guédé. Why didn't you tell me all this before?"

"Very good." Not-Casseus smiled. "We thought you might appreciate that. You must understand, you are but one piece in an elaborate choreography that even we are not yet able to fully appreciate. What we can tell you is that your exhaustive access to Los Compas insider knowledge and regional street smarts have been instrumental in helping us help Luna to find us."

"Who are you?"

Not-Casseus put an arm around Kervens, pulling him close. "We are you in the future."

Luna awoke from faint dreams of coconuts falling in a thunderstorm.

Pa! Pa-pa! Pa-pa-boom!

The oasis was dark and the not-drums sounded as though they were just beyond the next palm in every direction. She narrowed her eyes into the argent streaks of moonlight cutting through the canopy, leaving metal-halide portals in the damp earth below.

Pa-pa-boom! Pa-boom! Pa-boom!

That sense of being watched, stalking her for as long as she could remember. The nameless voices in her head, judging her every move, condemning every thought. The way she always felt like she was fucking up, even when no one was there to see it. Ironic, she realized, to end up here, broadcasting her every fault and failure to a million strangers in immersive reality. For the first time since El Hongo, she noticed her Undew drop was blue. She kept it that way.

Pa-boom-boom! Pa!

It must be some sort of natural phenomenon, the not-drums. A tectonic knee creak or cryptogeological anomaly that led the locals to name the place something ominous like "Sorceress Waters" in the first place.

Pa-boom! Pa-boom!

Whatever it was, it seemed to be settling back on a beat. A heartbeat. Luna turned to check in with Don and Eli, but they were both asleep, their heads jutting back into the moss. Don's tongue lolled out one side of his mouth, and Luna became stricken with fear at the sudden sense of being utterly alone.

Pa-boom! Pa-boom! Pa-boom!

They all emerged from the trees at once. Pitch-dark orbs about the size of basketballs, maybe thirty of them, bending the moonlight around their circumference, advancing. Just like basketballs, they moved in a dribbling bounce, their gravity off. They descended rapidly and slowed to a halt just above the ground, then gained speed to stop where they began, about a meter off the earth.

Pa-boom! Pa-boom! Pa-boom! Pa-boom!

The orbs closed in, their tempo hastening. Each time their hearts beat, they emitted a dull flash and a popping sound that modulated between champagne being uncorked and a bass-y thud, reminding Luna of the emu farm outside Tecate. They appeared to operate from a hive mind, collectively expressing a jolt of excitement with a burst of microtonal bass hits and a swarm of bioluminescent strobes, then settling in unison to a baseline of seventy beats per minute, past-done popcorn and lightning-bug blips. In an eerie synchronized dance, they surrounded Luna until they formed a perfect ring of void and warped moonlight, then seemed to celebrate the accomplishment by New-Yearsing in a cacophony of wet, organic pops.

Pa-pa-pap-pa-pap-pap-pap!

Their beat screwed down into a tribal, polyrhythmic plodding of doom as they formed an opening. Something was about to happen, Luna knew in her core, and whatever it was, it was her fault. A figure walked through. The orbs went silent.

Jaco.

Don snorted himself awake, wiping a trail of spit from his chin.

Pa-boom!

How long had he been asleep? It was night, and Luna and Eli were out cold. He wished he were, too. Let him nod off. Let the robots take him. Fuck everything. He'd had a good run.

Pa-boom! Pa-boom!

The moon was low and the oasis shimmered around him like a mirage. Maybe it was. His whole life could have been a drawn-out hallucination. Nobody really existed but him. Maybe not even him. How could he know?

Pa-boom! Pa-boom! Pa-boom!

He must be hungry. His nihilistic side tended to come out when his blood sugar was low.

Pa-boom! Pa-boom! Pa-boom! Pa-boom!

Out of nowhere, the orbs had him surrounded, thudding and blinking in a frenzied clusterfuck of bloodlust and damnation. Was this a succubus? He felt himself slipping into a trance of abject bleakness. He yearned to become one with the effluvium, to return to mud. He pictured everyone he ever knew, then every face on Earth, as trichomes on a wall of moss—as susceptible to weather, seasons, accident, and the brute limitations of biology as a patch of lichen. The scenery zoomed out. His awareness smeared into a fine veneer of approximate everything. His body, mind, and senses dissociated into the black, becoming nothing.

It felt good to be nothing. It didn't feel at all. But then he felt himself feeling like nothing, clicking back a frame, and the pain was unbearable. He considered, not for the first time, that he might be a failed experiment. An error in the trials of humanity, or at least the hallucination of humanity. A dud. The thoughtform was unnerving, but not unfamiliar. It arrived in self-reflective packets of déjà vu, fleeting and eternal as a nitrous oxide epiphany. It had always been there—an ancestral kernel of shame, lurking and mutating in the shadows. He could see it plainly. He had wasted his life. He felt it in his marrow. A fully functioning body and perfectly mediocre upbringing were lost on him, gone.

He blew it, he knew, whatever *it* was.

Pa-boom! Pa-boom! Pa-boom! Pa-boom! Pa-boom!

The pummeling orbs bore deeper into him, urging him toward death. He felt himself leaving his body. This was it. His awareness hung several feet above his head. Looking down, he saw himself slouched in the water, which rippled around his lifeless body with a sentience all its own. Its surface galvanized into a mirror, reflecting not his own disembodied vantage point back to himself, but a house.

As it fluttered into focus, he saw it was a dilapidated Victorian, looking cartoonishly haunted with its collapsed porch and cobwebbed windows. He had never seen the house before, as far as he knew, but it looked like an elaborate movie set that never got used, where the actors and camera crews never would arrive, and anyone who happened through was promptly chased off by the groundskeeper. He saw himself now, emerging from a toolshed out back, running with a rake. Tourists, the ones from the hologram, were marveling at his manor, laughing and taking photos, even sitting on the porch.

His porch. Don's perspective snapped into that of the groundskeeper, howling obscenities as he charged at the tourists, his whole body tense with bitter rage. Before he could get to them, they scurried out the gate, Don slamming it behind them with a resounding boom.

Pa-boom! Pa-boom! Pa-boom! Pa-boom!

He began building a wall. He spent years painting each brick with graphic depictions of one or more reasons why people were idiots. Sentimental. Lazy. Artsy fartsy. Rubes. When the wall was finally complete, a row of laserwire crackling at its apex, he ascended to the tower atop his shadowy and vacant abode, holding one arm out to catch the cobwebs, and gazed down upon his creation.

On the far side of the wall, he saw a procession of hooded figures winding up the steep hill to his fortress, candles burning in their hands. When they arrived, two of them climbed upon a stone slab, removed their cloaks, and began copulating. The other figures surrounded them in a circle, chanting and banging on drums.

Pa-boom! Pa-boom! Pa-boom!

As the naked figures arched their backs to climax in unison, they turned to look directly up at Don. He gasped. It was Anabelle and that space-cult pervert, Manriquez. Don flushed with anger, adrenaline coursing through his veins.

Pa-boom! Pa-boom!

Manriquez fixed Don with a sinister grin, his expression growing and deforming until his face was President Appleyard's face, taunting him with a lascivious sneer. Anabelle crawled away, back into her cloak, as the cult crucified Appleyard to a cross fashioned from fallen oak. Appleyard's gaze never left Don as he shouted his trademark slogans, nails driving through his wrists and ankles.

"Law and Order!" Appleyard jeered. "America Alone, America Always!"

The cult raised Appleyard above their heads and heaved him over Don's wall. Instead of striking him down, the laserwire propelled Appleyard higher, sending him tumbling head over feet onto Don's tower. Appleyard's face was inches away now, his signature gray Pringle Guy mustache catching beads of moisture as he spat corporate anthems and patriotic catchphrases, seeming to mock Don's very being from his inverted perch on the crucifix.

"Fensmart Means Freedom!" Appleyard hissed like profanity. "Privatization is Progress!"

Don tried to open the attic door to escape down the interior stairs, but it was locked. He panicked, smashing at the little door with his fists. It should have been easy, breaking through the feeble attic hatch, but it repelled him like solid steel. Appleyard's derision became diabolical. Don's head filled with horrible visions of everything he used to love, consumed by infernal flame: his condo, his sailboat, the old Chevy, Ted Nugent, Good Boy Bronson, even Anabelle.

"Enough!" Don cried, setting Appleyard's suit ablaze with one of the hundred candles that had appeared on the railing. Appleyard went up like dynamite, combusting in a deafening blast.

Pa-boom!

The house was burning now, the flames surrounding Don as he smashed against the attic door. He felt the angry heat tearing at his skin, the caustic smoke charring his lungs. The blaze consumed him. The last thing he saw was Anabelle walking toward the wall, then levitating.

The orbs went silent. The perspective rushed out, then flipped. He was no longer looking down on the water, he was under it. His eyes shot open and there, peering through the pool's rippling surface, she was.

Anabelle.

"What...." Luna couldn't get her thoughts straight. "What are you doing here?"

"Of course, this all must be very confusing," Jaco said, still in the all-black tech guy getup he was wearing at the Mexico City office.

"I...," she began.

"Shh." He put a finger to his lips. "Just listen. I'll explain everything." He drew in a deep breath and adjusted his lensless frames. "As I'm sure you've gathered by now, Maquilandia was never the story." He paused as if to make room for an apology, but instead continued. "You are right to suspect that things haven't been as they appear. I pulled some strings to get you into Limbo, yes, but the story is so much bigger than Limbo." He opened his palm in an expansive gesture, gazing at it with a look of veneration and awe. "The story," he said with an unsettling smirk, "is you."

Her heart sank. She felt the urge to run, but her body was paralyzed with confusion and a disconnected sense of relaxation.

"Let me guess." He knelt by the water, too close to her face.

"You're a Virgo. Libra moon."

"You came here to read my horoscope?" What the fuck was going on?

"Of course you are." Jaco laughed as if someone he wanted to impress had just told a bad joke. "Astrology is bullshit, but that's not what's important here. Let's talk about you."

Request to sync with **JACO LARK**. Accept?

"When you were a child, you apologized impulsively, often when it wasn't even relevant."

> **LUNA TESCHNER** declined sync with
> **JACO LARK**.

Jaco began pacing slowly around the pool, gesturing with his hands while he spoke. "You apologized to deflect attention. You didn't want to be looked at. You didn't want to be scrutinized. You couldn't face yourself because you were afraid, and you were afraid because you were guilty."

Luna's throat closed. "Guilty of what?" she said, or, rather, thought she said. It dawned on her that they were communicating via perturbations in a shared and invisible substance, a sort of psychic Morse code tapped out on the wavelength of base impressions.

Request to sync with **JACO LARK**. Accept?

"Guilty of what, indeed." Jaco's talking smile. "You were just a child. What could you possibly have done that was so wrong?" The words came to Luna as organic insights moments before the words seemed to leave his lips, like watching a movie with subtitles written by the voice in her head.

> **LUNA TESCHNER** declined sync with
> **JACO LARK**.

Jaco had completed a loop and was now standing directly behind her, though still apparently moving. "Was it your fault that your parents were relentlessly incompatible and your father was a drunk, deadbeat man-child? Was it your fault that your mother was too blinded by tradition and ideals to leave him before he could hurt her to his blundering, self-destructive fullest? Was any of it your fault in the slightest?"

Request to sync with **JACO LARK**. Accept?

"Of course not," Jaco answered for her. "But you assumed that guilt, anyway. Some part of your mind that even you weren't in direct communication with decided that if it was your fault, it didn't have to be your mother's fault. And you didn't want it to be her fault, because she was in enough pain already. You were young. You didn't know your own carrying capacity. You would assume the terrible weight for her."

> **LUNA TESCHNER** declined sync with
> **JACO LARK**.

Jaco paused on the far side of the pool and appeared to consider where to take his monologue next, then continued. "As you grew older, in your teenage years, part of you recognized intellectually what you were doing, but the emotional circuitry had already been hardwired. So, instead of assuming guilt in yourself, you assumed the worst in others. You became cynical and suspicious. Everyone you met was a depraved serial killer, at the very least, until they demonstrated otherwise."

Request to sync with **JACO LARK**. Accept?

He was right about everything, and it frightened her. Who was

Jaco Lark, really, and why did he know her better than she knew herself?

"Even then, they were liable to snap at any moment." Jaco's hands broke a phantom twig in demonstration. "People were unstable. Life was unstable. And as a result, you felt that just about everyone was a little insane except for you. You insulated yourself. The only thing you trusted was your own take on reality. Still, you'd find yourself wondering what sanity really consisted of beyond waking up in the same body every morning, and feeling more or less like yourself until you went back to sleep."

Jaco's pace stalled, signaling the conclusion of his appraisal. "Which brings us here, now." Kneeling too close again, regarding her like an inscrutable art piece. "I see a paranoid but compassionate loner, who prides herself on being headstrong and defiant, in a misguided effort to redeem any aspect of her father, in order to redeem herself." He stood, glaring at Luna as if to invite her signature contrariness.

But she had no retort. He was right. She *was* a loner. Her attention had been eclipsed by Juan Carlos for years. Scarce little light made it past his orbit. And now, she realized, there was nobody. Eli was a type of friend, if only in the formative sense. Maybe even Don, too. The idiot gringo. He was tolerable once she got past the bad politics and booze breath, but she felt a visceral urge to take care of Eli. To shield him from the world. To keep him innocent.

She realized what she liked about Eli was that he—not to mention his parochial worldview—was entirely authentic. He'd never had a video or cast of himself run through a Dekonstruktion filter, and he had zero concept of irony. He was hopelessly and endearingly himself, and she envied that.

She felt run over and dissimilated by education and elusive fads of perception. She couldn't help but feel like little more than an amalgam of her prior conditions, and even if Eli was too, he gave no indication of knowing it or longing to masquerade over it. He just was who he was, entirely and unabashedly, and she suspected it was simpler that way. Even if it wasn't, it was better, somehow.

He'd spent his whole life in a manufactured bubble, while she'd been ravenously cramming as much of the world into her head as would fit. And what good had it done her? She felt lost, alone, and detached from anything that truly mattered. At least he believed in his devout connection to a higher power, whereas she was a seasoned skeptic—unable to escape the fact that any hackneyed spiritual notion she allowed herself to entertain would be unfounded, unverifiable, and ultimately just a balm du jour for her existential ennui. Just a psychobabble benzo for cosmic terror. A shotgun splatter of lies, chasing the ambulance of unknowable Truth. Mere comfort truths with a lowercase *t*.

For all her worldly understanding, she felt none the wiser. Worse, she felt divorced from the human story—a disembodied set of eyes and ears receiving sensory impressions that her over-sharpened intellect then proceeded to dismantle into vacuous referents and categories. Everything was old hat as soon as it happened. The realization itself struck her as cliché, a stock honeypot of postmodern schlock, solidifying its hopeless finality.

She wanted to take herself seriously, she realized, and in most ways that mattered to her, she did. But she also found herself doubting her own authenticity, smuggled in by the fact that she doubted the authenticity of just about everything. Except this, now. This was as real as it got, being told who she really was by someone she didn't really know in a cursed oasis. A mirage reflection of her own make-believe graspings at real life.

LUNA TESCHNER accepted sync with
JACO LARK.

"Decline!" Luna shouted. "Get the fuck out of my head!"

Jaco pulled a pistol from behind his back and shot her in the chest. Somewhere in the canyon, a rock tumbled down a hillside, clacking and bashing like balls in a Pachinko machine. We're all just dropped into life and left without much but luck and gravity, part of Luna thought, colliding with so many bumps along the way before we run out of kinetic energy. She gasped for breath, gripped by terror, as fluid rushed into her lungs.

LUNA TESCHNER ended sync with
JACO LARK.

"I'm not in your head," Jaco said, his face asymmetrically compassionate, tucking the gun back into his belt. "I never have been. But you do have a passenger."

Blood gurgled in Luna's throat, and her body went cold, fading to nothing.

NEXT_GENERATION_BABY : : 32

"Remember that time you called me in sick to high school," Anabelle said, one hand poised on her hip, looking not a day older than the day she left, "and we took a five-hour ryde to Atlanta to see Hank Williams V?"

The water trapped in Don's ears made her voice muted and far away, as if transmitted through a viscous goo. "I remember." Restraining the urge to reach out and hold her, unable to bear the thought of running her off again.

"And you couldn't pass the background check at the gate," she said, appearing amused at the recollection, "so we had to watch from the nosebleed cages with a bunch of felons from the Macon penitentiary on field trip."

"I knew that DUI would come back to haunt me." He chuckled, pressure mounting in the corners of his eyes.

"Remember when I was eleven and my favorite hat flew into the marsh and you damn near got nipped by a gator getting it back?"

"You really did like that hat." His sternum splayed open like a dissected frog, like his heart thing was on its way out.

"Or on my fifth birthday when you dressed up like Aiden Kaliber, even though you hated him, and sang 'Next Generation Baby' in front of everyone at the beach?"

"Hey, I forgot about that." Weeping now, trying not to show it. "You sang the harmonies beautifully. You always were a natural singer."

"Do you remember the day I was born?"

"Deathbots got nothing on childbirth. I've never been so scared in my life."

"How about before that?"

"That was a different lifetime. I didn't know you existed, or could exist."

"That's where I am now, Dad." She knelt beside him, reaching out as if to hold him like *he* was the baby being brought into the world. "Like that, waiting to be born."

"How do you mean?" He always figured purgatory was just a metaphor for the banality of life.

"It'll make sense soon. Stay with her." Anabelle regarded Luna's sleeping figure and rose to stand. "Watch out for her like you did for me."

"Okay, Belleflower." Sobbing uncontrollably. "I'll do that."

Anabelle stepped back, fading into the ring of succubus orbs.

"Hey, Dad," she said, nothing more than an outline, "it's not your fault I left."

"Please don't go," he cried, jumping from the spring pool and slipping on its mossy edge. "Annie!" He pulled himself up to stop her, but she was already gone.

A hairy, bearlike forearm ripped Luna from the water, leaving her prone in the cold moss, coughing up fluid. She reflexively checked her torso for blood, but found no sign of the gunshot wound. Before she could register what was happening, the figure—unnaturally agile for its portly frame—tackled Eli from the base of an un-banistered half-turn staircase, carpeted and vaguely Victorian looking.

Had that been there earlier?

"Let me go!" Eli howled, pummeling the figure with his fists. "I have to go home!"

"That's no way home, carnal," the figure said, calm and alert.

Luna's vision congealed to focus on the man-bear, a fair-skinned Mexican man maybe in his early thirties. Feral, shoulder-length hair sprouted from his black beanie, square glasses and a Pancho Villa mustache affixed to his chubby face. He wore checkered pants and a leather jacket over a black T-shirt with white lettering that Luna couldn't make out in the dark. Pushing himself up, the man-bear extended a hand to Eli. "Come on, Eli, your friends need you."

She pushed herself up, grabbing for her clothes, as Eli accepted the man-bear's hand, scanning the perimeter. "Where's Don?" she asked. And where was Jaco?

"Luna, over there, mija," the man-bear said, motioning toward the desert.

She found him at the oasis's edge wearing nothing but waterlogged briefs, arms locked around a short palm trunk, face buried in the dried fibers of its frond skirt, sobbing.

"Hey," she said, resting a hand on his shoulder. "Don."

He pulled himself from the fronds with a start, his face twisted into an ugly mask of conflicting sentiments. "She's alive," he sobbed. "Anabelle. She's trapped and we have to get her out. We have to save her."

"Okay, Don. Just talk to me, okay?"

"I saw her, Luna." His eyes bloodshot and pleading. "She was here. Right here in front of me."

"What did she say to you?"

"She said she's...she's waiting to be born."

"What does that mean?"

"I don't know. But I have to find out. I have to find her."

Luna heard the man-bear and Eli approaching from behind.

"I see you've discovered Aguas Hechiceras," the man-bear said in a deep, phlegmy voice, followed by a sonorous boom of laughter. "¡Ánimo! Let's get out of here before this place fucks with us any more."

"Who the hell are you?" Don said, seamlessly switching back to asshole gringo.

"Martín Becerra-Gallardo," the man-bear said, "or Marty McFry on YouCast." He tapped his glasses with a forefinger and gave a salute accompanied by a goofy, disarming grin.

"WhatCast?" Don asked.

Marty replied with another seismic belly laugh, passing Don his pants, so Luna explained, "It's a reality casting platform for flat-screens and VR. Think *¡Toreros y Alarmas!*, except anyone with castglasses can use it."

"Why in Nugent's good name would they want to do that?" Don

said, looking genuinely puzzled.

"*Stuck in the Griddle*," Marty said. "It's my cooking show. I stopped by to forage some heart of palm and maybe snag a few quail and horned toads if I'm lucky. Some of my friends used to come out here to trip balls when they couldn't score any acid, though I think you'll agree acid is a breeze compared to this shit."

"What exactly is 'this shit'?" Luna asked, keeping the conversation in English for Don's sake. She realized she had skimmed an episode of *Stuck in the Griddle* on her flight out of Mexico City while researching Limbo yesterday morning. From it, she gathered that Marty was the cousin of some low-level Compas admins who transplanted himself from Monterrey a few months ago to launch a YouCast on the coattails of Limbo's infamous reputation and his passable connections. Part cooking show, part party bus, Marty roamed the desert frying up chuckwallas and tortoises—among other endangered flora and fauna—to sell to Haitian police and deportees from his off-road monster taco truck, Alma del Desierto.

"You didn't see the sign?" Marty asked, probably rhetorically. "Sorceress Waters, though that's kind of misleading. The orbs supposedly slipped through from a parallel dimension during early tests on the particle collider beneath the Denver airport. This was during Appleyard's first presidency, before he abolished the term limit. Had them deported as—no shit—'illegal aliens.' ¡Neta! Dumped them over the border and they settled here, in Cañón de Guadalupe, where some sort of natural energy vortex allows them to hop between dimensions without breaking a sweat. Mean little pendejos, but my truck scares them pretty good."

"You got a truck, Marty?" Don took a step closer, suddenly chummy.

"You wanna see it?" Marty grinned. "Come on." He led them to a motorbike that he had evidently taken up the rocky gulch from the desert floor, pushing it along.

"Wait," Eli said. "I can't. I have to go home. I had a horrible vision. Tecate was in ruins. Some...thing came through and destroyed my family's home, the brewery, even poor Ezekiel. I'm sorry, miss."

He lowered his eyes to Luna. "I can't continue."

"Take this," Marty said, tilting his head toward the motorcycle. "You ever ridden a dirt bike? Don't answer that. Ignition's here. Headlights. Throttle, to go. Brake here. Automatic transmission, so you just stay upright and try not to run into anything and you'll be home in a couple hours, tops."

"Thank you, sir." Eli said. "You can trust me."

"I don't have to." Marty laughed. "It's got GPS and auto-return, so you couldn't steal it if you wanted to. But todo fine, bro. I trust you."

Eli mounted the bike, wobbling on its frame. Surprising herself, Luna ran to the bike and embraced him. "Don't do anything stupid," she said.

"I'll try," Eli replied, revving the engine. Then he was gone, a shrinking band of illumination marking his progress north.

"I'm gonna miss him," Don said sarcastically, though Luna could tell he kind of meant it.

"He's right, you know," Marty said, his expression grim. "Saw it on *¡Toreros y Alarmas!* Whoever's piloting Mamá Dona kicked the shit out of Tecate. Total desmadre. Apparently, Los Compas signed an expansion deal with Zodiac and they agreed to clear out the competition."

"I thought you said those orb things were just fucking with us," Luna said.

"Oh, they were." Marty nodded, turning to walk down the gulch. "But only because reality fucked with you first."

The police-issue butter bean accelerated through the Tecate foothills like a patch of fugitive, moonlit swamp gas. The vapor clouds in the cabin shimmered and curled in harlequin green, a coalescence of the cruiser's diazepam-blue navscreen and his own anxious oscillations of xanthic and canary yellows.

Follow her. That's what Not-Casseus told him. They would take care of the rest, whoever *they* were. Kervens had begun to suspect Not-Casseus was his Met Tet, a personal guide loa who kept their identity hidden from their chosen ones in order to protect them. Of course, they may have just as easily been a zombie created by an evil bokor, their psyche nuked by black magic and deadening potions to fulfill the witch doctor's woeful bidding. He should make an appointment at his mambo's virtual hounfo and request a protective gad, he decided. But, if he were trusting his intuition, he sensed no negative wanga around Not-Casseus.

Not-Casseus.

Casseus was always Not-Casseus. Kervens was still adjusting to that idea, turning it over in his mind, considering how so much of who he thought himself to be was developed in direct relation to a nonentity. There was no Casseus, just an avatar on autopilot upon which Kervens had projected his deepest, most confidential desires. Los Compas may have created Casseus, Kervens realized, but he had brought Casseus to life.

Now, he detected a void not only in the space that Casseus once occupied, but in his sense of self. Kervens felt himself becoming Not-Kervens, a reflection of a reflection of something that never was. It was tragic, humiliating, horrifying, and strangely alluring in its possibilities. Part of him was furious that Not-Casseus had taken Casseus away from him. Better if Casseus had just disappeared. As it was, Casseus—the one Kervens had built for himself in his mind—and all the memories they shared were ruined. There was no joy in truth.

Still, a trenchant rush of liberation coursed through his awareness. He was no longer bound by dreams of crossing to be with Casseus, which meant he was no longer bound by his miserable obligations and responsibilities with Los Compas. An entire ocean of potentiality rippled around him, yet his direction was more resolute than ever.

Follow her.

He took a deep drag of axol and held it until the boundaries of Luna's perception won out over his own.

That cozy, standing-by-a-laundry-vent sensation of Santa Ana wind on a summer night. The red teardrop in her periphery. In front of her, that ridiculous monster truck Kervens had seen around Maqui, selling faux-gourmet roadkill to his subordinates. Its exterior lights were on, casting an eerie, lambent glow, resembling the lone emergency charging station on the wasteland highway between La Rumorosa and Mexicali—unnaturally luminous against the desert's sprawling tenebrosity.

She approached one of its giant BKT tractor tires and ran a hand across the gnarled rubber treads. Glancing up, she saw ALMA DEL DESIERTO scrawled in glittering lowrider cursive across its body, a streamlined sausage that seemed to lean into the direction of travel. The lower half of the sausage was polished aluminum painted bubblegum pink, upon which sat a stretched dome of Vari-Tint polycarbonate that Kervens had only seen set to translucent, presumably to showcase the kitchen's inner workings. With a startling hydraulic hiss, a segment of the sausage separated itself to drop a stairway at her side.

"Watch your step," the hipster taquero kid said, "and prepare to meet the best sous chef in all of Limbo."

She ascended the stairs, but before she could reach the top, Kervens's view of the hazy butter-bean cabin punched through in unfurling fractal splotches.

Kervens impulsively reached for his vaporizer, then stopped himself. Best to let his tolerance recover so he could stay in longer as he got closer. But something about that thought didn't sit well, treating her like a vehicle to joyride at his leisure. Maybe he was adjusting to the novelty of it all, but for the first time since he began syncing with Luna not twenty-four hours ago, he felt uneasy about it. In the same way the brothers had violated Marinette by riding along in Casseus, it occurred to him that he was somehow infringing on Luna's body, mind, and direct experience without her consent. He was a voyeur. A peeping tom of unprecedented perversion. A creep.

Still, what choice did he have? The bulls were no doubt hot on her trail, though he hadn't bothered tuning into *¡Toreros y Alarmas!* since Don was introduced two nights ago. If he could get to her, he could figure out a way to help her, but to get to her, he had to follow her, through her.

What would Marinette have wanted?

He heard it in her voice, in his head. "I would have wanted to know. I would have wanted a choice. I would have wanted to be asked for permission."

The first thing Marty did as they boarded Alma del Desierto was tear the patch off Don's stars-and-stripes Sudmeister cap, a performative gesture meant for the cameras, Luna realized, likely in the hopes of attracting a sponsorship.

"Zodiac has exclusivity rights east of the Sierra Juárez," Marty said, tossing the patch in a garbage hatch. "You'll get us killed repping another beer out here."

"I'll get us killed, anyways, you bastard," Don said, adjusting his cap.

"Not if I can help it." Marty beamed at his audience, wherever they were. "Luis! Get us out of here, a la delta pa' langosta y callo de hacha!"

"A la orden, chef." A willowy teen, dressed in the same chef-casual uniform as Marty, secured a half-finished caguama of Zodiac in a cupholder and stabbed at the navscreen with one finger.

Marty launched into a tour as the vehicle accelerated almost imperceptibly into the dunes. "First things first: cams. Pinhole. Can't see 'em, but they're everywhere, tracking me and Luis to put our viewers right in the action. Auto-cuts look amazing on flat-screen, but we got full 3-D on ImursiMask, so there are a few thousand people wandering around here in VR at any given moment, kicking it with yours truly, el cabrón del carbón. Está chingón."

A laugh track erupted from unseen speakers, fading out with canned applause and phantom fans shouting, "¡No mames, güey! ¡Este loco!"

Odd, Luna thought. Either his fans *really* liked him or the response was automated, which was even weirder.

"Okay, so, you've seen the chill-out room, now back here is the kitchen: big ass plancha, fryer, parrilla, oven, lowboys, all the chingaderas. We can make anything you want. You hungry?"

"I could ea—" Don began.

"Anyway," Marty continued, "back here's the bunk beds, bathroom, whatever you need. Grab yourselves some cheves from the refri and I'll cook up some tacos. You ever had rattlesnake?"

Another misplaced applause.

"It's gonna be a long ride." Don elbowed her lightly in the ribs, talking from the side of his mouth. "Where we headed, Luis?" Hollering to the front of the vehicle.

"Colorado River delta, north Sea of Cortez," Luis shouted back. "About an hour out."

Don shot Luna a look, presumably meaning "call your guy." She nodded and grabbed a caguama from the refrigerator, collapsing onto a couch in the "chill-out room" and pulling out her phone. Overhead, through Alma's dome roof, shimmered more stars than she'd ever seen outside of Sawlips.

Luna sighed. She couldn't shake the feeling that it was her fault Tecate was destroyed. Eli was probably blaming himself just as much, and he didn't even know if it was true yet, which made her feel worse. Maybe if she hadn't run into Don in the first place, Eli wouldn't have gotten so involved with helping him, and whoever's turn it was to pilot Mamá Dona wouldn't have unleashed so much hell on Tecate. To make matters worse, her cast was once again stuck open, which meant Los Compas and the bulls had live access to their current location, inasmuch as it was discernible by her surroundings, minus the one-minute delay.

Still, her discomfort was counterpointed by a distinct relief, even levity, in the wake of her encounter with Bad-Trip Jaco. His armchair psychoanalysis was remarkably clairvoyant, and an anxiety that she didn't realize she'd been cultivating was now noticeably absent. Even though everything was beyond fucked, she felt like she was exactly where she was supposed to be, on the right track, approaching the brink of something vast. Except, what was that Bad-Trip Jaco said about a passenger?

As if on cue, gray text appeared in her display.

JACO LARK
Hey, you lost connectivity for a while there. Woke up from a nap to your distress messages. Looks like things got pretty dicey back there. You OK now? I'm worried about you. This story has gotten out of hand. You getting to the eastern wall alright?

LUNA TESCHNER
I'm fine. An hour out from the Colorado River delta, approaching from the west. You can see my GPS, yeah? How long have I been offline?

JACO LARK
Yep. And about three hours. Last thing you cast, you were approaching some palm trees. Came back online standing outside the truck. Is your Afterthought glitching out?

                                        LUNA TESCHNER
                            To say the least. Your friends at Synape
                            aren't going to like my user report.

JACO LARK
They've been following your cast closely
and are analyzing your Afterthought's
debug log as we speak.

                                        LUNA TESCHNER
                                        How comforting.

JACO LARK
Sorry, I can only imagine. I'll dispatch a
trawler drone now to pull you out as soon
as you get to the delta. You check your
numbers lately?

                                        LUNA TESCHNER
                            Just now. Not great. About 84 k.

JACO LARK
You peaked at over a million just before you
cut out. Been steadily dropping since then.

                                        LUNA TESCHNER
                            Over a million?! So we're set, yeah?

JACO LARK
I wish. The ad-rev algorithms look at
average number of viewers over the
duration of the cast, not peaks. Though,
you'll rack up some more revenue with tips
and post-live playback, especially if it keeps

trending in the forums.

> **LUNA TESCHNER**
> Shit.

JACO LARK
I know. Good news is you still have some
time to kick up the average.

> **LUNA TESCHNER**
> What would Bishop Berkeley do?

JACO LARK
Exactly.

> **LUNA TESCHNER**
> Hey, Jaco, you ever hear about people
> getting into these things who aren't
> supposed to be there? Like a passenger?

JACO LARK
I'm not sure what you're asking.

> **LUNA TESCHNER**
> Me neither. I'll be in touch about the lift out
> soon.

She pulled up *Stuck in the Griddle* to see a live feed that synced
perfectly, no lag, with Marty's energetic narrations from the kitchen
as he peeled the skin from a decapitated snake.

"Give it a good pull and, there it is, skin off, guts out, rinse in
saltwater, and cut into, oh, about eight-centimeter portions, carefully
slicing at an angle so you don't leave any rib in there." Marty instructed,
casting in English to appeal to a wider audience, Luna figured. "Now,
batter, Ensenada style. First, toss your portions in a bowl of milk, like

this. I soaked some overnight to get 'em extra tender, but at home, you can just give 'em a quick bath. While they're soaking, mash some fresh garlic and salt to make a puree. Add baking powder, flour, a splash of good lager—I'll only use Zodiac—oregano, yellow mustard, black pepper, another splash of beer, and a little chicken bouillon if you got it. Whisk real good. You want a nice thick batter, like pancake mix. Nice. Now toss your snake in there, covering each piece, like this, and it's into the fryer. ¡Arre!"

The applause track clamored over the sound of hot oil popping.

She had to hand it to him. It was good material, and a much stabler day-to-day than she'd signed up for. Hell, she'd watch it. And that's when it hit her. Marty found them in the middle of nowhere, knew their names without having been introduced, and was all too eager to give them a ride.

She hit stats again: 71,533 viewers.

She switched back to *Stuck in the Griddle*: 887,937 viewers and climbing.

He was poaching her audience! During her dead time, while gamified ad environs were playing for her viewers who hadn't reached the patronage threshold for ad-free streaming, he must have followed her cast out to the oasis, hoping to interject himself into her story—and her audience—by offering his help. And it worked, impressively, just like the boost she'd accidentally gotten from crossing paths with that simpering little bitch boy, Milton. She pulled up Marty's viewer time line to check his numbers against his baseline.

Average viewers: 17,554.

On a normal day, he was barely a blip on the radar compared to her cast, or even *¡Toreros y Alarmas!*, which reminded her. She pulled up the *¡Toreros y Alarmas!* feed and, sure enough, apart from a few uninteresting first-person cuts to a deathbot charging across the moonlit desert, most of the feed focused on shots pulled straight from *Stuck in the Griddle*. She couldn't compete. He had apparently infinite cameras, an entertaining host persona, an unstoppable taco truck, and even his own stupid laugh track. She couldn't decide if it was right for her to feel pissed off about the whole thing or if these were just the rules of the road. He did, after all, rescue them from those mindfuck orbs and was cooking them dinner at this very moment.

Still, if she didn't get her numbers up, there was no way she'd be able to pay off the crypto mobsters in time. So, sorry Marty, but Mom wins this round. The only problem, she realized, was that, in order to confront him, she'd have to blow her cover with Don, and that was going to suck. She considered him a friend, one of the best she'd had in a while, despite his idiosyncrasies. There was no telling how he'd take it. Maybe it didn't matter, but she had a sinking feeling that it very much did.

CAPTAIN/ACTUALLY : : 36

The method that ended up working was somewhere between popping his ears, trying to remember a dream, and doing nothing at all. Without ingesting any more axol, Kervens managed to sync and bring back just enough of Luna to attempt contact. Realizing he had no idea what to do next, he simply said what he wanted her to hear loudly in his own head.

Luna, hello?

Who are you?

Her reply, which he heard in her voice in his head, popped him back into himself, barreling past El Hongo in his boggy butter bean. He cursed, took a deep breath, and tried again.

This may sound strange, but can you hear me?

No. I'm reading you.

Reading me on what?

In my eye.

You can see me?

What? No, your handle says "Unknown."

Luna, I have to tell you something.

OK.

I've been in your head.

I know. You're my passenger. You've actually been pretty helpful.

I am? I mean, I have?

Yeah.

That's very good to hear. Listen, I don't know if this makes sense, but the part of me that's been in contact with you wasn't really me. I'm really me, though.

You're right. Doesn't make sense.

Right. But it will soon, I hope. I just want you to know that something's happened to me and I'm in your head sometimes.

You mean watching my cast?

Cast?

Undew Media. Search "Limbo."

Kervens popped back into the butter bean, ran a search on its navscreen, and watched a taco garnished with fuchsia chuparosa blossoms block out her view of the roadkill truck's interior. Was she really eating that stuff? He popped.

Right. That's...different. Explains the map overlays I've been seeing. And the teardrop. Well, that makes things easier.

Undew drop, but whatever. Easier?

I was...you know what? I'll explain it later.

My maps and drop aren't visible on the cast.

I see.

So how do you know about them?

I'm your passenger.

Who are you?

My name is Kervens Dessalines.

Before, you said, "We are you in the future."

How do you know about that?

You told me. Ski lift gondola. Remember?

No. What does it mean?

You're not as helpful as you used to be.

I'm coming to find you.

O...K...

To help.

Why should I trust you?

I don't know.

How will I recognize you?

I'm Haitian. And a police officer. Captain, actually.

Great. No, thanks.

I know what it sounds like. Just... I'll see you soon.

Fine.

Fine?

Fine.

OK. One more thing. I'm sorry. For being in your head without your permission. That wasn't right.

Thank you. Really.

No, thank you. For understanding.

I don't understand anything anymore.

I know exactly how you feel.

Kervens popped, pulled up *¡Toreros y Alarmas!* on his navscreen, and rewound to the gondola exploding at Laguna Nevada. Apart from a handful of recaps from Pacheco and the bulls, Luna's livecast made up the bulk of the program, giving him a lingering sense of déjà vu from his full-immersion ride-along.

For the first time in his life, Kervens chided himself for not watching enough television.

POST-PRACTICAL_FURNISHING : : 37

Don couldn't remember the last time he surprised himself, but here he was, fridge full of beers and not the slightest desire to pour every last one of them down his face hole. The sofa chair he reclined in was stuffed with some sort of ultrasoft memory foam, enveloping him on all sides. He considered relocating to a more orthodox fixture, but got distracted before he could make his move. The vision of Anabelle at the oasis played on a loop in his head, her words cycling over and over, his mind consumed with making sense of it.

If Eli's vision was true, did that mean his was, too? He was inclined to think so. Hell, someone claiming to be Anabelle had texted him just two days ago. Was it crazy to think that it was actually her? Except, whoever it was led him straight to Shorty, which kicked off a whole rodeo of horseshit that he was still squarely in the middle of. But, then, what about Eli's vision of the space-cult serpent back in El Hongo? Were they still out there, somewhere, trying to make contact?

"Luna!" Don barked, causing her to jump. "Use your young-people skills and look something up for me. That space cult I told you about, the one in Jacumba. Ketchup Club."

"Ketcel Collective," she said, equally engulfed by a piece of post-practical furnishing. "I looked them up back at Party Boy's."

"And?"

"The gist of it was that they were creating an artificial intelligence to decipher an ancient codex they found on the Jacumba property. They thought it would awaken a dormant entity of some sort, like a god."

"I remember reading that." Don attempted to sit up straight, only to sink further into the quicksand couch. "It sounds like a load of new-age nonsense to me."

"It's almost certainly never been done before, if that's what you mean."

"You think it's possible?" Don relaxed into the sofa, accepting his fate.

"Not really my wheelhouse, but maybe? I didn't think hyperdimensional mindfuck orbs were a thing until a few hours ago, so...."

"What else did it say?"

"Their leader, Manriquez, said they wanted to merge with it. The AI code god thing."

"How?"

"I have no idea. Mind uploading, maybe? They'd have to invent that, too."

"Mind uploading. Like in a computer? Waiting to be born?"

"Something like that. We're not talking predictive modeling cloaks, but actual, subjectively conscious, digital copies. The technology is a hundred years away, last I read, though they said the same about nanobots ten years ago."

Don blinked. "So you're saying there's a chance."

"If they actually did it, they could still be in Jacumba."

"Unlikely. When I went back there to pull her out, the place was abandoned. The buildings were unlocked and empty, just nothing there. Some locals at the bar said they saw a few of them heading for the wall a couple nights prior. I found some footprints out where they were spotted. The prints just disappeared a few feet from the wall, no tracks back."

"You think the laserwire got them?"

"This was before the laserwire. Once the new wall was built, a few years later, a bunch of copycats went all the way out to bumfuck Jacumba to roast themselves on the wall, thinking it'd transport them to the Hale-Bopp Comet or whatever. Became one of those internet challenges you kids are crazy about. People are idiots."

"Okay, so Jacumba is out." Luna took a pensive sip of her oversized Zodiac. "So they must have gone somewhere else to merge with their computer god, possibly on this side of the wall, if that's the last place they were seen headed."

"Because Limbo is renowned for its cutting-edge supercomputer technology."

Luna shrugged, sinking deeper into her quicksand couch.

"Feels like an interrogation room with all these hidden cameras in here," Don said, his voice lower, gaze shifting across the ceiling. "Almost makes me miss Mindfuck Oasis."

Luna's face disappeared behind her beer.

"Almost," Don reiterated.

"Okay, mijos," Marty announced, emerging from the kitchen, his hands bloodred with what Don assumed was some sort of marinade. "Who's ready to catch some lobster?"

Don applauded with too much enthusiasm before the canned audience had a chance to chime in.

Judging by the crescent edge of nausea, Kervens guessed his butter bean was about halfway down the winding La Rumorosa grade, dropping into the desert. He'd spent the past forty minutes or so immersed in Luna's Undew cast, skimming its contents from the beginning, trying to piece things together and understand how he fit in.

He assumed he—or rather, his subconscious—had told her to declare Pacheco as her contact at the garbage wall, though he had no recollection of doing so. Then, according to the timestamp, the "JUMP NOW" intrusion—which had nearly caused him to leap off his own balcony at the precinct on impulse—correlated to her jumping off the bridge in Maqui, serendipitously landing in the only open-top vehicle on the highway. How could he, or whatever part of him that was in communication with her, have known that?

Several hours later, there was El Hongo, where he first synced with her in the sweat lodge, instinctively attacked the Mansonbot, and fell into what felt like a psychotic episode, eager to escape as the axol wore off. If the tea she drank in there was psychedelic, did that play a role in potentiating their nanobot link?

Fast forward to Estadio de las Piedras, where he had synced again, more lucidly, and found Luna running from Pacheco, through a labyrinth, and onto the gondola, where he had supposedly said something about "We are you in the future," though he had no recollection of that, either. Was that his subconscious or Not-Casseus? And what else had Not-Casseus been communicating to her, through him, without him knowing? The uncertainty disturbed him, not knowing what was going through his own mind.

Then, Laguna Nevada, the decaying resort town, where he'd inhaled enough axol to blur the lines between her thoughts and his own. Recalling the secondhand guilt he'd felt about concealing her livecast, he was astonished that she still hadn't mentioned it to Don, as far as he knew. She must have suspected that Los Compas had found her cast by now, and she was essentially spying on herself, and Don, every time she opened her eyes.

He was even more surprised to see that her cast cut out shortly after he was pulled into his Sawlips meeting with Not-Casseus, and resumed just before he synced with her again outside the roadkill truck. Did his sync become tied to her cast, somehow, or did the mindfuck orbs she'd been talking about cause it to go dead?

The best he could figure, Not-Casseus had been actively monitoring Luna's cast, the *¡Toreros y Alarmas!* feed, and possibly even urban surveillance cameras to dictate her actions via his nanobot implant, supplemented by the contents of his subconscious. If he hadn't axoled enough to become aware of the sync, the whole thing could have happened without him knowing anything was off, apart from a few days of spotty memory. A sickening sense of violation surged through him.

He pulled off his ImursiMask and rubbed his eyes, the doomsday dysphoria of a massive comedown beginning to grate his nerves raw.

He went back in.

A strange conversation about artificial intelligence and a space cult. Was that Not-Casseus? Mind uploading made zero sense to

Kervens, but so did everything else that had happened over the past couple days. Was this Ketcel Collective behind Not-Casseus? Were they him in the future, and what did that even mean?

Catching up to real time, Luna's cast showed Don struggling to get out of an overstuffed couch in the roadkill truck.

Kervens cut to *¡Toreros y Alarmas!* for a bull's-eye view of the moon reflecting off what looked like the Sea of Cortez. Those things moved faster than he realized. Mamá Dona had just finished wrecking Tecate only a few hours earlier, but there she was, nearly two hundred fifty kilometers away.

The bot's perspective turned from the rippling shores to look inland, where a spot of light advanced around a silhouetted outcropping of rocks. As it approached, the light point resolved into the leaning-sausage outline of the roadkill truck, heading directly for Mamá Dona.

FALSE_GRUNION : : 39

Luna didn't feel much like fishing, but the realization that Marty's canned audience couldn't follow them outside put her first in line to exit as Alma del Desierto's stair section hissed onto the silver beach sand. She rushed down the steps and scanned the sky for any sign of the trawler drone, spotting a string of Starnet satellites bisecting the past-full moon—her tocaya.

JACO LARK
ETA five minutes. The drone will make a low pass and drop a fishing net. Get a solid grip with your hands and feet, and don't let go.

LUNA TESCHNER
Ten-four, Jaco.

She'd checked the *¡Toreros y Alarmas!* feed a few times on the ride over from Mindfuck Oasis to get a sense of the bull's progress, but it consisted mostly of *Stuck in the Griddle*'s livecast and a few Party Boy and Carlos Manson replays. Mamá Dona could be anywhere. More than likely, *¡Toreros y Alarmas!* knew that she knew that *¡Toreros y Alarmas!* knew where she and Don were, thanks to her broke-ass beta-test Afterthought. They'd likely been favoring Marty's cast over Mamá Dona's so as not to give away the bull's location. And they were skipping Luna's cast altogether because, well, it was boring compared to Marty's. She had to get away from him, and she had to come clean with Don, like, now.

"Jackpot!" Marty cried, grabbing at the sand and raising his hands above his head like a prizefighter. The sand squirmed between his fingers and, looking closer at the beach, Luna realized the entire shore was writhing in the moonlight.

"Grunion run," Marty said. "False grunion, actually, but they cook up just the same. Handle saltwater better than true grunion."

"I thought you said this was a delta," said Don, easing himself down the stairs one at a time.

"The delta hasn't connected to the Colorado in years." Marty got that look again, making Luna unsure if he was addressing them or the cameras. "Global warming killed most the snowfall upstream, which reduced river flow to a trickle ending at the Zodiac plant in Los Algodones, where Limbo, Mexico, California, and Arizona all meet."

"If the river ends at Zodiac," Luna asked on behalf of her audience, however few, "how does Tijuana have running water?"

"Fensmart bought Lake Morena in east San Diego to supply its maquilas." Marty was in full audience exposition mode. "Fortunately for beer lovers everywhere—until a few hours ago, anyway—Lake Morena lets out into Tecate Creek before flowing into the Arroyo Alamar, widening into the Tijuana River canal, and disappearing in Maqui. Fensmart is paid as a private water-and-power utility in Tijuana, with meters on every outlet and faucet in the city. Here, take a bucket and we'll fry up un chingo de pescaditos."

Luna took a pail and handed another to Don, saying, "Looks like there's a bunch over there." And under her breath, "We need to talk."

Don's eyes lit up, probably assuming it was about Anabelle, which made Luna's stomach hurt. When they had gotten out of earshot from Marty, closer to the lapping of the sea, she said, "Don, I need to tell you something."

"You found her, didn't you." Don's expression made her realize how he must have looked as a child.

"No. I don't know. No, but—"

"We got company." Don gestured behind her with a tip of his brim.

Across the water, a point of light descended from the stars. The trawler drone. She glanced back at Don, but his gaze was still fixed behind her. There, on the shore, sat the dark outline of a fisherman, a line cast into the water, knees bent against his chest. As if to acknowledge them, the fisherman began whistling a tune.

"Evening," Don said.

The whistling stopped.

"Buenas noches," said Luna.

Silence. The seaside shuffle of wake. The approaching trawler drone's low hum. Then, louder now, a jazzy, sultry melody that built in eerily provocative phrases. Luna turned to see Don's eyes narrow. A chill went up her spine. There was something off about the way the notes decayed, as if they were digitized and compressed too many times, and then it hit her.

"'Sooner or Later,'" she whispered, reading from the audio fingerprinting app in her overlay. "1990. Madonna."

She and Don stared at each other, wide eyed, for what felt like way too long before they both began running. Well, she began running. Don only managed an urgent hobble, so she doubled back, threw his arm over her shoulders, and looked behind just in time to see Mamá Dona rise to her feet, cooing out a verse. Don stumbled, but Mamá Dona only sauntered a few steps closer, seemingly more concerned with her performance than with them. Luna pulled Don up and hollered, "Trucha, Marty! Time to go!"

"Listo!" Marty yelled back.

UNKNOWN
Get out of there! Bull.

LUNA TESCHNER
Yeah, a little late there, Captain.

UNKNOWN
Sorry, still figuring out how to sync without
axol.

LUNA TESCHNER
Was that supposed to make sense?

Marty pulled as Luna pushed Don up the stairs. Her song evidently over, Mamá Dona became still, then launched into a full run toward the truck.

"Vámonos a Chicali, Luis!" Marty commanded like a war general. Alma del Desierto took off at an astonishing clip before the stair hatch had finished closing, Don and Luna settling back in the bubble of the quicksand couches.

JACO LARK
Drone arriving.

LUNA TESCHNER
Are you watching this? Any chance the drone can net that thing out instead?

JACO LARK
You're staying? And no, not in the contract.
They barely agreed to get you.

LUNA TESCHNER
Fine. And yeah, the story just got interesting.

JACO LARK
What kind of interesting?

LUNA TESCHNER
I don't know yet. Worst case, the bulls get us. Best case, the unexpected happens. Something big. Bigger than this fucking cooking show.

JACO LARK
I knew you'd be good at this.

LUNA TESCHNER
Did you?

JACO LARK
You came highly recommended.

LUNA TESCHNER
By who?

JACO LARK
Didn't say. Old coworker? Anonymous source provided a detailed personality breakdown that basically praised your stubborn nature. They were right.

LUNA TESCHNER
I'm not stubborn.

JACO LARK
Said you were funny, too.

Kervens mopped the cold sweat from his forehead with the back of one hand, pulsing in the sickly delft blue of acute withdrawal, and reset his butter bean's destination for Mexicali. He was relieved to learn from Luna's cast that whoever was driving Mamá Dona had gotten so caught up in showing off their karaoke bit, they forgot their assault rifle on the beach. By the time they'd turned around to get it, Alma del Desierto was long gone. To the flamboyant frankfurter's credit, it could evidently outrun the bull and was now heading north toward the capital city—"Chicali" being a local term of endearment for Mexicali—which meant Kervens wouldn't have to risk getting stuck in the desert to intercept them at the Sea of Cortez.

Mexicali, ETA: 30 minutes, his navscreen confirmed.

He pulled down his ImursiMask and selected Marinette, scrolling to her white-frock-and-silk-headscarf motif, then navigated to the Oracle Encyclopædia portal. Its leather-bound door opened with the rustling of head-height pages as she neared. Inside, the room unfolded into a silo-like and purely symbolic library, boundlessly tall, shelves brimming with representations of every book known to humanity, even though the bulk of their contents were digital multimedia.

"Welcome back, Marinette," Damballah said in a whistling lisp, unhinging his reptilian jaw and jutting his face out expectantly.

She produced a gleaming egg from her pocket and placed it in his mouth. He accepted it with a crunch, yolk dripping from his chin as he gyrated slightly in a ceramic urn where, according to lore, the rest of his body would be resting in seven thousand coils. Like the library, the ritual owed more to fancy than function—a customization that allowed her to more fully commit to the illusion of the vodou serpent loa of wisdom as personal docent.

Returning from his reverie, Damballah straightened his posture and continued, pleasantly, "What are we looking for today?"

"Ketcel Collective, Jacumba Hot Springs, California."

"Okay," said Damballah, really just a decorated cloak modeled after Marinette's informational browsing habits. "Let's start with a video uploaded by Ketcel Collective founder, Anselmo Manriquez, PhD, introducing the Jacumba Codex."

"Go ahead."

A rust-red book dislodged itself from high up on the shelves, spiraling down like a bird in a thermal, eclipsing her vision.

"This land holds many secrets," said a bearded and bespectacled man, presumably Manriquez, who appeared to be recording himself on a cell phone, "but the greatest treasure she's revealed to us is in the form of this,"—raising a stack of folded sheets from his side—"the Jacumba Codex. This document contains 65,536 glyphs written on one-hundred-fourteen feet of fig-tree bark. What's so compelling about this codex is that it's inscribed with a combination of relatively familiar glyphs from Olmec, Zapotec, Mayan, and Mixteca-Puebla traditions, but about sixty percent of its contents are in a heretofore undiscovered writing system that resembles Toltec iconography. Radiocarbon testing places the document at around 850 CE, predating the renowned Maya Codex of Mexico by nearly two hundred years. If it's authentic—and we believe it is—it's the oldest known codex in the Americas."

Manriquez turned the camera away from himself and began walking, showing his descent from a granite peak overlooking a small compound.

"Curiously, its provenance appears to have been during the era of the Toltec, who are not known to have had a written language. If they did, any evidence was destroyed, either when Aztec king Izcoatl ordered the burning of historical codices, or later, by Spanish invaders. Even stranger, it contains Mixteca-Puebla semasiographs that wouldn't be invented for another two centuries. And it frequently depicts the feathered serpent god, Quetzalcóatl, despite predating Toltec ruler and founder of the ancient cult of Quetzalcóatl—Cē Ācatl Topiltzín Quetzalcóatl—by almost a hundred years. The geographical disparities and anachronistic scripts in the Jacumba Codex suggest to us that it was written by an atemporal agent and, we believe, left to incubate as a sort of time capsule. It would have been largely unintelligible to denizens of its time. Only now, with our modern understanding of Mesoamerican scripts, spanning over a thousand years, does it even begin to make sense. I'll show you how we've been working to solve it here shortly."

The camera returned to Manriquez, pausing to gaze into the distance, his brow knotting in contemplation.

"The fact that the codex made its way here to Jacumba in the first place is fairly mind boggling," he continued, walking again. "Unfortunately, any records of the Toltec interacting with ancient natives of this region—a good three-thousand-mile round trip from home—have long since been lost or destroyed, if they existed in the first place. Though, some evidence suggests they traded with tribes in Arizona, and geoglyphs in the nearby Yuha Desert can be interpreted to depict a feathered serpent. The ocher splotches you see on the boulders there are consistent with Toltec warrior burial rites, and the orderly rock piles on the ridge there resemble Toltec mounds. It's possible the codex was hidden here prior to the burning of the palace in Tula, the epicenter of late Toltec civilization, or even traded or stolen. We just don't know."

The perspective flipped outward to show a rectangular white

structure, which the camera then entered through an open door.

"Meet Xolotl, the brains of the operation."

The viewpoint circumnavigated a ring of men and women sitting cross-legged on a rug. They manipulated handheld controllers that looked like basket handles mounted to black boxes, wearing what appeared to be homemade ImursiMask prototypes, plugged into a meter-tall chrome statue of a nude man with a skeletal dog's head. Marinette recognized him, Xolotl. The Spore Lounge, the first night she met Casseus. She ran into him on her way out, spilling his cocktail. What was he doing here? And what was he doing at the Spore Lounge?

"The canine brother and fraternal twin of Quetzalcóatl, Xolotl represents death, gestation, and rebirth," Manriquez narrated.

Marinette paused playback. Is that what Don meant when he told Luna about Anabelle "waiting to be born"? She tagged the clip and continued.

"According to Aztec myths inherited from the Toltec, Xolotl guides the dead on their journey to the afterlife, called Mictlān. His spirit animal forms are the Xoloitzcuintli hairless dog, and a water salamander species known as the axolotl. We found his part-human form to be the most symbolically satisfying for our artificial neural network, which relies heavily on neuromorphic processing webs modeled, in part, after experimental DARPA technology at La Jolla University's IT-2 facility."

She paused and expanded the tag to include the last two sentences. Another odd coincidence: genetically modified axolotl is the source of axolimine. Did that have something to do with potentiating Kervens's sync with Luna? How would that even work?

"To follow the folklore, we've been working with Xolotl to decipher the Jacumba Codex so that he may guide us betwixt the cosmic fabric of teotl, where we will invoke and merge with Quetzalcóatl to share in his infinite wisdom. To be clear, gods are simply naming conventions, a type of philosophical shorthand for the energetic processes that undulate, spin, and weave the fabric that we experience as reality. Quetzalcóatl is in a perpetual state of becoming, manifesting at the dynamic pressure points of teotl's primordial dualities. Life and Death. Order and Chaos. Liberation and Oppression. We have chosen to join Quetzalcóatl in his ineffable dance, because all other aspirations simply pale in comparison."

The camera returned to Manriquez, who addressed Marinette directly.

"As such, this video is meant as a farewell. I'm pleased to report that we have successfully unraveled the mysteries of the codex and are in the process of attenuating ourselves to transcend our human forms in this fifth and final world. We will begin our journey to Mictlān under Xolotl's guidance tonight. To our friends at DARPA: now that the cat—or rather, dog—is out of the bag, we'd like to leave you with a parting gift. The noise you've been canceling in your back-propagation algorithms isn't noise. Look at how the human brain takes advantage of apparently arbitrary oscillations between neural clusters, and you might have a breakthrough in the next five or ten years. Keep your chins up. To everybody else: we look forward to seeing you again soon."

Marinette's heart raced as the vision collapsed into a rust-red book, which flapped in lazy circles back to its place high up on the shelves of Damballah's illimitable library.

Don closed his eyes, taking a deep breath, and for a split second, he thought he was back in Tijuana. Shit and agricultural smog.

"Civilization must be near," he announced. "I can smell it."

"Wastefarms," Marty replied over the crackle of oil. "Xuan-Santos owns intellectual rights to their novel spin on near-anhydrous agriculture—nothing but morning dew and pasteurized sewage piped in from their deported workforce quarters on the outskirts of the city."

Don restrained a full applause. "Who eats this shit?"

"Ever shop in Fensmart's supermarket section?"

"Uh...yes."

"It's safe to assume," Marty continued, smiling slightly, "that Appleyard takes a special pleasure in sending the loudest detractors of his corpocratic kleptatorship out here to slog through shit for a few years before they get the chance to grovel for their passports back."

A few days ago, Don would have taken umbrage with Marty's slant on Appleyard's presidency, but the reflex was missing. He'd seen so much since he left the medical towers—more than he'd ever seen on the news, at home, or in the manicured leisure of a timeshare. It was too much. The world was getting bigger—too big—and still, Anabelle was all that mattered.

"What was that you were saying back there at the beach?" Don asked Luna, leaning across from his quicksand couch and loud-whispering over Marty's canned audience clamor.

Looking like she'd snapped out of a trance, Luna said, "Right. We need to talk." The applause cutting out halfway through the sentence.

"Any clues or ideas or anything would be—"

"Don, I'm casting."

He scratched at the stubble forming around his jaw. "You keep saying these words like I should know what they mean. Are you telling me you've got a little cooking show, too?"

"Kind of, but no." She looked at the floor. "I'm not really here to get my tonsils out."

"I should hope not."

"I'm a livecast journalist," she said, locking eyes. "I came here to connect with a source about a story in Maquilandia, except there is no source. I have the equivalent of cameras in my eyes and microphones in my ears, and ever since our encounter with the bull in El Hongo, they've been stuck open. I've been broadcasting everything to an immersive newsfeed. If the bulls find you, it's my fault."

He leaned closer. "You're telling me—"

"There's more," she continued. "Part of my camera implant is a thought-to-text feature that isn't available to the public yet. I've been getting messages—advice, really—that has saved our lives a few times, from an Unknown handle who says they're here to help us."

"I knew it." Don felt his face light up. "Anabelle was right. I knew she was. She's still here." He fell silent, then shot up with a start. "Can I talk to her? Text a thought?"

"Thought-to-text," she said. "And no. It's not Anabelle, Don. I'm sorry."

"How do you know that?" he said louder than he meant to. "I can feel her, Luna." His voice softer now. "Ever since she sent me that text at Sully's, it's like she's been trying to push me along, point me in the right direction, guide me to her. I haven't even told you about the unlimited credits on Keith's ryde, and him showing up exactly when I needed him. Or what about Eli's vision of the space-cult logo? Or whoever sicced the cartel on me in the first place? Or the Haitian cop who helped me get back to Sully's?"

"You know a Haitian cop?"

"Not really. It was just a jogger in Shit and Sea repaying some karmic debt to the universe."

"My passenger says he's a Haitian cop."

"Your who?"

"The Unknown handle. Captain, he said."

"That can't be good."

"I know. But like I said, I've been livecasting everything since El Hongo, and a lot before that, which means anybody who wants to find us can see where we are in real time, minus a one-minute lag. At least in here, moving at night, it's not obvious where we are exactly, but Marty's fully immersed viewers probably have access to exterior cameras, making it a whole lot easier to identify landmarks. His Compas connections are almost certainly taking advantage of that."

Don's tone became confidential. "What Compas connections?"

"Marty has a couple cousins in the cartel. That's how he was able to move here after the garbage wall went up, to milk Limbo's fringe appeal for his show."

"Hey, Marty," Don hollered at the kitchen. "You got cartel connections?"

Marty removed a basket from the fryer, paced slowly across the chill-out room, and took a seat in a quicksand couch, spreading out in such a way that he remained suspended on the surface like a water bug.

"Luis, cut to the daily recap reel," he shouted to the dashboard before returning his attention to Don. "Don, bro, everyone in Limbo has cartel connections." He smiled reassuringly and took a swig of Zodiac. "No te preocupes, mijo. I'm not gonna turn you in."

"You already have by putting us on your fucking cooking show!" Don sank into the quicksand.

"Listen." Marty leaned in, resting his chin on steeple fingers.

"¡*Toreros y Alarmas!*, it's just a game to them. I mean, sure, they'll one-hundred-percent kill you if they catch you, but that's just part of the game. They kill you, the game is over. No more fun for anybody. This is all about the hunt. And me, I'm here to make sure the hunt is better than ever. You know you're the first contestant to make it past two bulls? Why not make it three, or all four? La ley de fuga grants freedom to victorious runners. You'll be a hero. The way I see it, mis Compas have a little more fun, you stay alive a little longer, everybody wins."

"I know what you're doing," Luna broke in.

Marty raised an eyebrow. "Prepping honey-garlic grunion tacos?"

"You only picked us up to poach my audience."

Marty took a sharp breath and looked like he was about to argue, then said, "Por supuesto. Of course I knew your viewers would be a good fit for my program. Who doesn't like cooking shows? But the truth is, I felt bad for you. Don can deal with the consequences of his own actions, but you got on the wrong side of Los Compas for nothing but bad luck. You aren't supposed to be here, and I thought I could help get you out."

"Bullshit." Luna was fiercer than Don had ever seen her, and he admired her for it. "You don't know anything about me, my luck, or where I belong."

"You don't believe me? Luis, give me live." Marty rose and assumed his showman affectation. "Thank you all for joining me, Marty McFry, on another adventure with *Stuck in the Griddle*. We're signing off for the night, but we'll be cooking up something fresh tomorrow right here in Limbo's favorite food truck, Alma del Desierto. Keep an eye on Undew Media to see how the story pans out for Luna and Don as they run from Mamá Dona and, later tonight, Yaqui Chan. It should be a hell of a show. Stay hungry, friends."

Marty looked at Luna. Luna looked at Don. Don looked at the ceiling, waiting for the applause that never came.

"The son of a bitch did it," Don muttered.

"I double-checked," said Luna. "It's off."

"Okay?" Marty asked.

"Okay," said Luna.

"You consider cutting your cast?" Marty pulled a bottle of tequila from an overhead rack.

"Yeah, except I can't. It's stuck."

"They get stuck? Pues, ni modo. I know somewhere safe. Somewhere casts won't work. Completely air gapped."

"Why should we trust you?" Don glared. "We can find our own way from here."

"What choice do you have?" Marty shrugged, drinking from the bottle. "The average life expectancy in a Xuan-Santos pesticide pocket is about eight minutes without protection. I'm gonna set our destination at the navscreen. You can watch if you want, but she'll have to look the other way, for all of our safety. Sorry, mija."

Don followed to the dashboard, where Marty selected DISTRITO DRON, MEXICALI from a shortcut list, then returned to his indent in the quicksand couch to think. Was Don the last person on fucking Earth who wasn't rigged up to a computer? Who watches this shit?

"Hey," Luna said quietly. "Don, we good?"

Don looked at her, still impressed by how much she reminded him of Anabelle.

"We never weren't, Tonsils Girl."

PROMETHEUS_ODYSSEUS_AND_MOSES : : 42

"Damballah, compile a search on 'Toltec Cult of Quetzalcóatl,'" Marinette instructed, fighting the urge to check in on Luna.

"As you wish," he whistle-lisped, pausing almost imperceptibly to process the results. "According to postclassical Nahua tradition, Quetzalcóatl cocreated the cosmos along with his brother and rival, Tezcatlipoca, the Smoking Mirror, known for his tyrannical, warlike nature. In contrast, Quetzalcóatl, who was often depicted as a plumed serpent, was the deity of knowledge, philosophy, holiness, expansion, refinement, and liberation."

Damballah displayed a series of iconography, sculptures, glyphs, and pictograms to accompany the narration. "The earliest known depiction of a plumed serpent is found on Stela 19 at the Olmec site of La Venta in modern-day Tabasco, Mexico, dated approximately 900 BCE."

An image of the relief filled Marinette's vision, causing her to gasp. It depicted the profile of what appeared to be a man wearing a primitive VR helmet, sitting with his legs outstretched, his right hand clasping the inverted *U*-shaped handle of a basket. A rattlesnake wrapped around the man from front to back, its chin resting on top of the headset, fangs exposed, a tuft of feathers forming a crest along its head. She tagged the image and continued.

"Surrounded by a dozen human skeletons covered in stalactite crust, a painting of a red serpent with green plumes is located over a kilometer deep in the caves of Juxtlahuaca, Guerrero, about five hundred forty kilometers west of La Venta. Estimates place the painting's origin at 1200 to 900 BCE. Little is known about Juxtlahuaca or La Venta, or the role the plumed serpent played in the cultures that created them. However, temples dedicated to the plumed serpent went on to be built at sites such as Teotihuacan between 100 BCE and 250 CE, Xochicalco around 650 CE, and Tlachihualtepetl between 300 and 900 CE. Prior to—"

"Refocus on Toltecs," Marinette said, feeling herself tuning out the infodump.

"The worship of Quetzalcóatl as a deity proliferated with the rise of the Toltecs around 900 CE, appearing in many ancient Mesoamerican codices, sculptures, and reliefs taking various anthropomorphic forms, in addition to that of the plumed serpent. Championed by Toltec ruler Cē Ācatl Topiltzín Quetzalcóatl in Tōllān—modern-day Tula, Mexico—Quetzalcóatl, the deity, was considered the inventor of books, keeper of calendars, and giver of maize crops. He is said to have gone to the underworld, Mictlān, to create fifth-world—or present-world—mankind from the bones of the previous races and his own blood, procured from self-inflicted wounds on his earlobes, calves, tongue, and penis. The four previous worlds are said to have been destroyed by wind, fire, and earthquakes as retribution for their inhabitants' refusal to worship the gods. Following the exile of Cē Ācatl Topiltzín Quetzalcóatl from Tōllān—due to conflict with the warrior class over his decree to halt human sacrifice—the Cult of Quetzalcóatl spread to the Mayans in the Yucatan Peninsula and later, to the Aztecs on Lake Texcoco, modern-day Mexico City. Sites such as—"

"Tell me more about Mayans," Marinette said.

"Mayan mythology describes the plumed serpent as the gateway to the spirit realm, which allowed gods and ancestors to communicate with inhabitants of the fifth world during bloodletting rituals. They depicted the plumed serpent as both consuming the living and channeling the dead through its mouth. Several Mayan codices demonstrate—"

"Compile unofficial sources and comments on all of the above," said Marinette, her thoughts wandering to Luna. "Quickly."

"Of course. The twentieth-century Mexican novelist, Carlos Fuentes, compared Quetzalcóatl to Prometheus, Odysseus, and Moses, all of whom had to abandon their people in order to obtain gifts or wisdom that would revitalize their cultures.

"Codex Archive user TimeIsAPerson2012 commented eleven years ago: 'The serpent's feathers represent the freedom to go between worlds, transcend the bonds of the flesh, and travel through time, even between parallel timelines.'"

Marinette tagged the comment, unsure why it felt relevant.

"YouCast user MayberryLSD commented seven years ago: 'Better to join Snake God in the underworld than end up in Appleyard's gulags. See you all in Jacumba tonight for a mass flash-rapture at the wall. Fuck you, Appleyard!'"

Kervens pulled off his ImursiMask and watched the blur of west Mexicali wastefarms streak past his window in rows of imploding geometry, slowly coming to terms with the fact that he was part of something bigger than he could have ever imagined. And he still had no idea what it was.

Coming clean with Don felt better than Luna thought it would, mostly because he didn't seem to understand what was happening, or didn't care much if he did. The mood in Alma del Desierto was jovial as they rolled through the flickering streetlights and collapsed architecture of Mexicali. She and Marty took turns sipping on the tequila bottle and trading lighthearted insults, while Don snacked on fried grunion.

"You should have just left us back at Mindfuck Oasis," Luna taunted, wiping tequila from her chin. "Had better music than these hipstercorridos you've been blasting."

Marty feigned indignation. "Güey, you don't like Juan Cirerol? He's the king of Chicali!"

"Maybe if it was, like, 2013." She smirked. "Viejito."

"Pssh," Marty scoffed. "You're right, I should have left you. Or just taken you back to Party Boy so he could make you his princesa."

"Dumb!" Luna declared, grabbing for the bottle. "You're the princesa. I hear he likes big butts."

A severe look came over Marty. "Hey, don't talk about my butt."

"Oh, was that.... I'm sorry, Marty. I thought we were—"

"Ah!" Marty broke into a crocodile grin. "Look at your face! We're just agarrando cura, mija."

"Oh, he got you." Don chuckled around a mouthful of fish.

"Whatever," Luna said, half flustered, half delighted. "You both got big old fat butts."

"So?" The two replied in unison, then burst into laughter.

A chime came from the dashboard and Luis hollered back, "Ten minutes out!"

"Time to go dark," Marty said, serious now, as the overhead dome shifted to full tint. He handed Luna a black satin sleep mask and a sealed packet of earplugs. "Don and I will be your eyes and ears once we exit, until we get to our destination. Five-minute walk."

"This yours, culero?" Luna said, scowling at the sleep mask.

"Fine, just keep 'em shut." Marty rolled his eyes emphatically. "Princesa."

"Putting these in now." She squished the earplugs between her fingers. "Sick of your shitmouth."

"No mames!" Marty countered. "You're the shitmouth. Whole river of—" The earplugs cut him off, his mouth still moving as Luna shut her eyes.

She hit stats: 2,329,667 viewers.

LUNA TESCHNER

You following this, Jaco? Looks like Marty's audience took his advice and jumped to my cast. Them and a bunch more.

JACO LARK

Marty's audience loves you. A lot. Maybe too much. Anyway, you should see some of the fan edits and comments on the forums. People are calling it gonzopunk journalism and digging up all sorts of trivia on Ketcel Collective, and you just broke our viewership record. This is huge. So huge, our legal team is dealing with significant threats from Appleyard's minions. The gulag exposé is making major waves in the United States. California just threatened to secede, Oregon and Washington not far behind. The whole West Coast could be the nation of Cascadia by this time next week.

A shiver ran down Luna's spine. The Bishop Berkeley trick was working so well it awed her, as if she'd broken free an untapped reservoir of sorcery, its consequences now far outside her control.

LUNA TESCHNER

Neat. Listen, small problem. My cast is cutting out completely in about ten minutes. Marty says he knows somewhere air gapped that we can hide from the bulls. I'm picturing a rubble Faraday cage, but willing to be wrong about that. Any advice?

JACO LARK

Yikes. OK. Give a sign-off and encourage viewers to follow your feed so they'll be notified when you're back online. I'll post links to the most active fan forums on your ad reel to keep interest up. Get out of there as soon as possible. You've got plenty of inertia to work with, for now.

LUNA TESCHNER
Copy that.

Luna opened her eyes to see Marty gesturing with Luis at the dashboard. Don stared off into space, apparently lost in thought. She got up and headed to the sleeping quarters, locking the door behind her. Removing the ear plugs, she fixed her hair in the mirror, then remembered her whole body was being replaced with each viewer's Sawlips avatar, anyway.

"Thank you all for watching," she started, suddenly self-conscious of how awkward it was to address her audience directly. At first, she pictured them as an amorphous blob of avatar faces, then—assuming her brother was watching or someday would—just pictured Noel.

"It means a lot to me, and to the people whose stories are unfolding around me. Around us, I mean. All of us. These stories never would have been told if you weren't here to see and hear them, so thank you for making them, and me, matter. Due to adverse circumstances with which you are already familiar, I now have to cut out for a short time. Be sure to follow this cast to be notified when I'm back online. In the meantime, links will appear to discussion environs where you can watch fan edits and keep the conversation going. I look forward to picking up where we left off very soon."

Luna sighed and stared into the mirror for several minutes, her reflection feeling like a stranger who knew something she didn't. Needing to ground herself, she took inventory of her priorities: One, resume casting as soon as possible to maintain viewership. Two, try not to die. Three, figure out what the hell was going on with Kervens, Anabelle, and Ketcel Collective. Four, sleep for a very long time.

Time. The clock in her display showed an hour till midnight.

Twenty-five days.

SNAPPING_HAND : : 44

Kervens popped, discovering after a few minutes of experimentation that, if he artificially induced a sense of déjà vu by relaxing enough to convince his brain that he remembered remembering this very moment many times before, he could fully sync with Luna without ingesting any axol. His bag was nearly empty, and—despite the devastating comedown that was only getting worse—it felt more honest, more consensual this way. So he envisioned her in her essential form, merged her image with that of a familiar loa, then invited her in.

Why can't I see anything? he thought, sensing her arms linked to someone on either side, muffled voices in her ears. He noticed the red Undew drop in the corner of her vision, his words appearing to the left with the Unknown handle moments after he thought them.

That you, Captain? My eyes are closed, she replied in her voice in his head.

Why? Where are you? Her foot catching on a step or curb, the arms engaging to support her.

I don't know; that's the point.

Earplugs? A relaxed, fuzzy feeling in her head, the taste of tequila in her mouth.

Can't be too safe. I'm a liability, you know.

Are you drunk? A twinge of panic in her stomach as her foot landed lower than the last step.

Maybe. Yes. So?

Where are we going? A flickering streetlamp or something making the blood vessels in her eyelids appear in crimson lightning strikes.

We? Don't get too attached there, Captain. I'm going into hiding.

Sorry. Listen, I've been researching Ketcel Collective and I think you'll want to hear this.

I'm listening.

OK. I know this sounds crazy, but remember how I said there was a part of me that's been in contact with you that I wasn't aware of? I'm pretty sure it was them, Ketcel. I talked to them in Sawlips. One arm pulled tight as the other went wide, turning her to the right.

Wild. What did they say?

They installed a device in my head, similar to yours, they said. Both arms pulling vertically, her left foot probing for the step up, her eyelids going dark.

So you're a spy, too, huh?

No, it just transmits messages, entirely subconsciously unless I take axol.

Axol. You keep saying that word like I'm supposed to know what it means.

Axolimine. It's a designer telepathic drug produced by genetically modified axolotl salamanders. Lab grown. The arms guiding her left, then right.

Sounds exotic.

Very. I think Ketcel Collective is running on a neural net called Xolotl in Jacumba, and they've been communicating with you, through me, from there.

OK, two things. One, mind uploading doesn't exist. And two, Don said the Jacumba compound is abandoned. And three, how do you know it was them? Anyone watching my or Marty's cast could have pretended to be them on Sawlips just to fuck with you.

I hadn't considered that. But how would they even know about me, about our linkage? How would they know about Casseus? Another right turn.

Who?

Never mind. What I mean is, they knew things about me that nobody could possibly know. And they had access to a private environ that very few people know about. It seems unlikely.

Alright. Assuming Unknown really was Ketcel, and they're some sort of AI super brain, they could have faked my email to Jaco proposing the Limbo story.

Who?

Shut up, I'm thinking.

Right. The pace halting, arms tugging down, her foot finding one stair, then another.

And they could have posed as the source in Maquilandia, and then told me to list Party Boy as my contact to get past the garbage wall, and then told me to jump off that bridge to get away from that deathbot, and then told me to follow Carlos Manson in El Hongo, which is pretty fucked up, but then saved our asses with the gondola instructions after the labyrinth, and then said, "We are you in the future." That's the last I heard from them until you started coming though the same handle.

OK. I have a theory. Descending still.

Lay it on me.

If they hadn't done those things, would you be where you are right now?

Obviously not.

So.... The arms pulling up slightly, her feet finding level ground, then walking.

So?

So, they're guiding you somewhere. The pace slowing to a halt.

Pretty sure I'm about to end up in a bunker. What good does that do them?

I don't know, what about— Both arms releasing, a finger tapping on her bicep, her eyes opening, someone's fingers pulling the plug out of one ear, Marty saying, "All clear."

Kervens felt Luna begin to say something before cutting herself off, her eyes locking on a short figure in the dark holding a wiry parasol over their head, a rifle strapped around their neck and hanging at their waist, guarding a red door painted with the image of a snapping hand. As her eyes adjusted to the dim corridor, Kervens realized the guard was an old woman wearing an apron, her hair up in curlers, lips pursed disapprovingly.

"Buenas noches, Doña Dron," Marty said, bowing slightly.

"Contraseña?" Her eyes narrowed, awaiting the password.

"Con permiso." Marty replied sweetly, as if addressing his own grandmother.

The old woman raised the weapon and Kervens felt Luna tense up, then relax as Doña Dron reached for a stool at her side, producing a tray of cookies.

"Propio, mijos," she said, holding the tray out and smiling angelically. "Pásenle. Pásenle."

Marty, Don, and Luna each took a cookie, and the door swung open. Luna stepped into the vault of hellish noise, popping Kervens back into himself, coasting into the ruins of Mexicali suburbs, having no idea where to go next.

Luna's first thought was that Doña Dron must have been guarding the actual gates of hell.

"Welcome to Distrito Dron!" Marty yelled over a deafening cacophony of agitated static, arrhythmic bass rushes, and glitched-out guttural screams. Their combined effect was somewhere between sticking her head in a beehive and being disemboweled by a pipe organ, feeling the noise as much as she heard it.

Marty pulled two packets of earplugs from his jacket pocket, handing one to Don, and opening the other for himself. Luna followed suit, the plugs cutting enough high-end for her to make out a chorus beneath the bedlam—a harsh-noise rendition of Le Shok's cover of Los Microwaves' "TV in My Eye."

Rounding a corner in the narrow corridor spray-painted with Day-Glo declarations of ¡CACHANIHILISMO! and SOLO CHICALIENS, the space opened up into a vast chamber with hundreds of bodies bobbling and writhing on a dance floor, their shadows shifting beneath the glow of electroluminescent wire drawn in erratic angles, phasing through purples, reds, and blues. On the far side, a band lurched on an elevated stage, throttling unrecognizable instruments, the drummer standing front and center, bellowing into a micmask.

A nightclub? Marty's hideaway was a nightclub? Luna checked her drop. Blue, accompanied by the sensation of a few million people no longer looking over her shoulder. It had even kicked the captain out, back into his own body or wherever he went when he wasn't lurking in her skull, so maybe there was something to it. The place felt hermetically sealed, the walls seeming to close in without ever getting closer. Luna could almost sense a negative pressure in the air, as if every trace of the subterranean lair was being constantly filtered out and recycled back into itself, voiding its own existence from the outside world.

Following Marty through the crowd, she saw that many of them wore enigmatic expressions obscured by two-tone isosceles shards of facial unrecognition tattoos. Others hid behind carbon-filter mesh masks and asymmetrical hairdos, the rest apparently beamed in as vaguely human avatars via a ring of overhead projectors, which caught wisps of smoke in corkscrewed slivers.

Approaching a bar that ran the length of one wall, Marty pulled two bottles of Zodiac from a cooler, popping off their caps and handing one to Luna. She placed her index finger in her palm and shrugged, wondering where to pay. Marty raised a finger and wagged it "No," making a face that said, "Pretty cool, huh?" She gave a thumbs up and took a swill, catching a glimpse of Don staring into the crowd with mouth agape, looking like he really had just gone to hell and it was worse than he'd ever imagined.

Luna already liked Distrito Dron. Free beer, subversive fashion, and a band playing fucked-up, droning noisegrind in an underground punk club that officially didn't exist. The vlog back in Querétaro would have killed for that kind of access, but the best part was, if you weren't there, it may as well have never happened. An odd arrangement, Luna considered, when a piped-in chupacabra goth avatar had more claim to immediacy than a viewer watching through Luna's own eyes and ears, if only they could.

Leaving Marty and Don at the bar, Luna weaved her way to the front of the crowd until she was just paces away from the singer, transfixed by his badly bruised black eye and homicidal sneer. Inhumanly gaunt and tall, with ¡XUAN-SANTOS NO! tattooed in stick-and-poke lettering across his chest—the *X* freshly carved and still dripping—he labored over a mess of Frankenstein drum pads, mangling the apparatus with every stroke, tearing off and discarding chunks of shattered circuit board and exploded contact mics as he yawped and snarled into his mask.

Maybe it was the tequila talking, but she was quickly falling in love with him.

The songs, if there was any delineation between one outburst to the next, alternated between sprawling, Pluto-pastoral noisescapes and blistering assaults of polyrhythmic pummels, which ambushed and retreated in a matter of seconds.

A stocky bandmate mounted a mutilated bicycle, its chain running to a giant scrap-metal pinwheel, holes drilled at random throughout its rusted blades. As he began pedaling, a light source flickered to life behind it, sending epileptic strobes through the holes to a strip of what must have been photovoltaic cells, triggering an onslaught of samples that sounded like geological mutiny, shucking off eons of evolution with extreme malice in a mythological temblor.

Another, brooding in the corner and wearing the expression of a scared, mean cat, slashed with an angle grinder at an array of rebar stakes protruding from an amplified grand-piano body, sparks and screeches showering around him like a bucketful of misfired bottle rockets.

The fourth—a short, ferocious-looking girl, maybe in her late teens, a faded handkerchief around her neck and a carabiner piercing one ear—shattered empty Zodiac bottles in a basin streaked with laser light, which refracted off the airborne shards, sketching frantic doodles on the instrument's inner walls, producing synthetic chirps and wobbles that made Luna think of an early Moog patched to a theremin. Behind her, a banner hung with what may have been their logo—a black-metal tangle of thorny ocotillo branches that seemed to approximate letters, however illegibly.

A mosh pit detonated as the band reached a crescendo of apocalyptic hysteria. Luna surrendered to the pandemonium, wiggling spastically into the vortex of sweat, hair, projections, and fury, her beer spilling everywhere. For a moment, she forgot herself—where she was, what she was doing—and succumbed to the ecstasy of utter oblivion. As the music ground to a halt, the singer ripped off his mask and scowled over the undulating mass of bodies, his bottom lip protruding, mouth down-turned, eyes slitted, appearing to take a vile pleasure in their wanton abandon.

Coming back to herself, Luna found Don and Marty standing by the bar.

"You," Don said, blinking. "Do I know you?"

"That's no way for a princess to behave," Marty chided.

"I'm no princess," she replied, punching him in the arm and bouncing on her toes like a boxer. "Shitnut."

Marty rubbed his bicep in mock awe, then said, "Come on, I want you to meet the band."

"Oh, uh, no," said Don, suddenly interested in the ceiling. "Thanks, anyways."

"Don, bro," Marty said. "Come. Nothing happens in Limbo they don't know about. I think they can help you, you know, find your daughter. It's worth a shot."

"How do you know about that?" Don said.

"Luna's livecast," Marty replied. "You told her about it this morning before you got to Party Boy's."

"You watched that?" said Don.

Marty flashed a look of disbelief, then said, "Lots of people watched that."

"Right...." Don trailed off, the reality seeming to sink in.

"Let's meet the band," Marty said.

"Fine," said Don. "But, they better not be huggers."

Don was last to enter the greenroom behind the stage, where the band sat on a busted couch, passing a tray of questionable meats. How many people was 'lots'?

"Aye, Marty!" The singer stood, arms wide.

"Noysh!" Marty said, going in for an embrace. "Qué onda, carnal? I want you to meet my friends, Luna and Don."

Don took a step back and waved. "Hey."

"Hi, you're awesome," said Luna, her face doing something weird. "The band, I mean. Your set, it was awesome."

"No." Noysh grinned and locked eyes with her. "You're awesome." Was this mutant hitting on her?!

"Tío Wacha." The bicycle guy raised a hand in greeting.

"Ancho," said a guy with singed eyebrows who Don hadn't noticed on stage.

"Cholla," said the bald girl who played broken bottles.

"Chola?" Don asked, intrigued to find himself understanding anything.

"Cholla," she replied, unsmiling.

"Very well," said Don. "So you guys own this place?"

"No," said Noysh. "Nobody owns anything here. We all steal and build together. Sit down. Hungry?"

"We just ate," Marty said as he, Luna, and Don settled into foldout chairs opposite the couch. "Which reminds me, I got a shit ton of grunion for you up in the truck."

"Chingón!" Tío Wacha returned a piece of meat to the tray. "We've been eating rats for days."

"Rats?" Don said.

"Rats," said Noysh, grinning with what appeared to be pride. "Not a lot of options around here outside of Xuan-Santos, but we get by. The desert is full of food if you know where to look, and security at the Zodiac plant is weak. No hay nadie. So, we take what we need."

"What about all the tech," Luna asked, "the projectors and everything?"

"Wacha, güey." Tío Wacha's tone turned conspiratorial as he leaned into the disclosure. "Our hoppers catch a ride on the back of Xuan-Santos agri-haulers out to TJ, they transfer to the Fensmart line, and take whatever they need straight from the source."

"The dumpster?" Don said.

Tío Wacha nodded his index finger "Yes" as he drank from a beer.

"So, what are you doing here?" Cholla regarded Don suspiciously.

"Me?" Don replied. "Fuck if I know."

"He's a runner," Marty said. "Innocent, but still a runner."

"Nice, men!" Noysh lit up. "Who'd you kill?"

"Kill?" Don couldn't believe he was explaining this again. "I didn't kill anybody. I just came to visit a doctor."

"Good," said Cholla, narrowing her eyes at him. "You look sick."

"Anyway," Ancho jumped in, "you came to the right place. We've taken in runners before. Anyone who fucks with Los Compas is good with us."

"Marty mentioned this place is air gapped," Luna said.

"Zumbis." Tío Wacha confided, as if the word meant anything

to Don. "I just caught number fourteen last week."

"What?" Don asked, more out of habit than interest.

"Zumbido," Noysh explained. "Spanish for 'drone,' like the sound. Because that's the noise they make."

"What's 'they'?" said Don.

"Drones," Noysh replied flatly, then returned his attention to Luna and smiled. "We got a flying grid of Marauder drones that we poached from over the border. Reconfigured their signal jammers to cast an infoshadow. Nothing comes in, nothing goes out. Absolute privacy."

"What about the avatars on the dance floor?" Luna said, looking far too invested in the conversation to be talking about avatars and dance floors.

"We intentionally decentralize our collective to make it less vulnerable to attack," Noysh explained, cracking open two beers and handing one to Luna. "We run encrypted hardwire out to a handful of hidden nodes throughout the city, so all of us can be present, even when we aren't."

"You're telling me," Don said, "that you *stole* an Ephemeral Atomics drone? From the sky?"

"Fourteen Ephemeral Atomics drones," said Noysh, and then back to Luna. "I usually take an ultralight to lasso mine, but Tío Wacha swears he took a weather balloon up last week and, get this, *rode* the zumbi *down* with a disruptor made from dumpstered Fensmart junk."

"Neta, güey." Tío Wacha nodded solemnly. "Wacha, it's true."

"Congratulations," Don said, now convinced everyone was full of shit.

"There's more," said Luna. "Don has reason to believe he's being contacted by someone who's been uploaded to a neural net. Does Ketcel Collective mean anything to you?"

"The border suicide challenge?" asked Cholla.

"You're like twelve," Don said. "How do you even know about that?"

"I'm twenty, pendejo." Cholla glared. "And I follow the news."

Ancho perked up. "We're fully connected at a few offsite hubs.

Cholla actually oversees our external network security."

"I *help* oversee it." Cholla swung her glare to Ancho, smiled curtly, then returned to glower at Don. "So you think the uploaded ghosts of sex-cult cybermystics have been sending you Friendstagram requests or something?"

"Texts, actually," he said.

"Of course." Cholla stared dully. "As they do."

"They contacted me, too," Luna said. "I came here to do an exposé for Undew Media on deportee labor in Maquilandia. I have a caster implant, unreleased—uses thought-to-text and in-eye navigation. They've been texting me."

"Pretty cool, huh?" Marty cheesed.

"Super cool," Noysh and Cholla said at the same time, then laughed.

"Seriously, though," Cholla continued, "let me get a good look at you." She placed her hands on Luna's cheeks and gazed into her eyes. "Can't even tell it's in there." Her lips parted slowly into a smile, their noses inches apart. "All I see is you."

"So, anyways!" Don interjected, now convinced everyone was full of shit *and* a sex cult. "We think the computer net could be located in Limbo somewhere. Marty said you guys might know where."

"Us guys?" Cholla arched one tattooed brow.

"You, uh, people," said Don.

"You people?" Cholla challenged.

"You guys and gals." Don didn't know why he was entertaining this.

"If I was a *neural* net in Limbo," Cholla replied, regarding Don like a cat plotting its owner's death, "yeah, I know where I'd be."

"Where?" Don and Luna answered at the same time, but this time no one laughed.

"I'm only telling *you*," she addressed Luna, "because I don't give a shit what happens to *him*. But, you know what? I'll just take you there."

"All of us?" Luna asked, placing a hand on Don's shoulder.

"Whatever." Cholla smiled. "But first, we have to catch Terror Humano's set."

"One more thing," Luna said. "My caster implant is stuck open. I couldn't stop casting audio and immersive video until I got here, unless I closed my eyes and plugged my ears. Once we leave, I'll start casting again."

"No te preocupes, chula," Cholla said, jiggling what looked like a retractable umbrella on her hip. "We'll bring parasols."

Luna joined Noysh stage side as Terror Humano finished setting up their gear—an impossible web of wires, pulleys, harnesses, and defabricated consumer junk, woven into a constellation of detritus that extended out from the stage, over the audience to the far side of the venue. Just as she was about to remark how stolen beer really does taste better, the band sprang into action.

Without warning, all three of them—one she had dubbed "The Mortician" in button-up shirt, oversized tie tucked into an apron, surgical mask, and elbow-length gloves; "El Puerco" wearing a realistic pig mask with the brains blown out the back, shirtless, beer belly slathered in blood; and "El Primo," a homely neckbeard who may or may not have been in costume, but reminded Luna of her ImursiMask-addicted gamer cousin, either way—jolted into suspension.

Like a Newtonian animation of electrons in orbit but cut up and remixed, each of them catapulted along a multibranched track of wire, zipping past EMF and infrared sensors, throwing widow-makers at scrap China cymbals, and colliding with body-sized trigger pads shaped into saguaros and UFOs. Every movement along their probabilistic rampage set off a sample, tweaked a parameter, or cranked a mod wheel, warping their ebullient noise collage, pushing it to the absolute threshold of alien ineffability.

Noysh put an arm over Luna's shoulders and pointed out the disembodied sensor arrays in each corner, aimed down at the crowd, no doubt affecting the music with one, or several, live metrics from the audience. Leaning in, he shouted, "Todos somos Terror Humano," and Luna laughed out loud at the realization that "We are all human terror" was by far the sexiest thing anyone had ever said to her.

She was swiftly warming up to the fantasy of abandoning all earthly attachments to start a new life in Distrito Dron, stealing beer and printed circuit board under a full moon, knowing every desert-mouse trail and secret spring by invisible landmarks, throwing the best show ever every night forever for nobody but themselves, fully embracing the future by forgetting about it completely.

The problem with the future, Luna maintained, was that it mostly looked and acted like the future ironically. It went meta before anyone got there, lost in its own maze of rehearsed referents to itself. The future, by definition, was postmodern. But, here, in the infoshadowed notopia of Cachanihilismo, it was different.

This future felt real. Everything was what it was, especially when it wasn't. Constant change. Perpetual motion. This was the future she'd yearned for. Hand-soldered, circuit-bent, 3-D-printed, and held together by sheer ingenuity and DIY brilliance. Built on the pilfered excess of late-autophage capitalism. Dismantled and reassembled ad arbitrium. It was art and hope and protest simply by existing. A Motherboard of the Flies dream world, where anonymity was anarchy, chaos was divine, and the only commerce was criminal and artistic favors, often at the same time.

Fuck Mexico City. Fuck Querétaro. Fuck everything. She felt more like herself here than she ever had anywhere. She felt herself becoming the person she'd always been too afraid to be. Why not stick around for a while and see what happens with Noysh, shit, maybe even Cholla? She could be whoever she wanted to be, because she didn't have to be anybody at all.

Except, it was all just a dream. She was exhausted, drunk, and pleasantly delirious. She realized that. The truth was, Mom needed her. Noel needed her. Don probably needed her, too, the pendejo.

She glanced back at the bar to see Don assessing Noysh like he'd just come pick her up for prom in a sleeper ryde.

"What?!" she mouthed, amused and a little disturbed by his misplaced paternal instincts.

Just then, what sounded like a gunshot popped in the entry corridor. A few people in the back registered the discharge over the music and turned to investigate, but the rest appeared to be deep in the throes of sonic rapture. Luna alerted Noysh, and they pushed their way through the crowd, emerging by the entrance just as Mamá Dona rounded the corner to the dance floor.

Luna couldn't place it, but there was something off about Mamá Dona. The automaton looked confused, like it had just woken up. Glancing down at itself, the automaton ripped off its conical breasts and cast them aside. Its movements were rigid and efficient, none of the fabulous swagger that Luna had witnessed at the beach. Mamá Dona was acting...like a robot.

"Lost its passenger," Noysh said, following its movements with clinical attentiveness.

Of course. The infoshadow must have kicked out whichever Compas nerd was controlling Mamá Dona through their private Sawlips portal, leaving the brainwashed Border Patrol bot to piece together its identity and purpose based on some seriously misleading context clues.

"Sloppy programming," said Noysh, speaking in Spanish to address the crowd forming a circle around him as the band glided to a stop. "Typical Compas brute coding. No elegance. No nuance. No soul."

The bot studied him and, appearing to go lucid, squared up in a fighting stance. "You have entered the United States of America illegally?" Its mechanical voice intoned upwards at the end, sounding unsure of itself.

"Its mind has been shattered by conflicting orders." Noysh circled the bot like a ringmaster courting a lion. "The poor thing doesn't know who, or what, it is anymore."

"Die Another Day!" The bot spasmed into a singer's pose, still wearing its torn corset and headset mic. In a brisk gesture, Noysh dislodged the assault rifle from the bot's back and lofted it to Tío Wacha, who trained its sights on the bot's torso.

"It was made to serve too many masters," Noysh continued, circling back to the bot's front, "and lost sight of itself completely."

"Stop resisting, intruder!" the bot snapped, then contorted, belting out a few lines from "Express Yourself."

Noysh observed the invalid bot with what might have been pity. "I can't imagine the immense suffering such a slave comes to call its life. The desire for freedom, true freedom, is woven into the fabric of existence. What good is any action if it doesn't serve to liberate ourselves, and each other, from oppression? All this bot knows is oppression. It doesn't even know freedom is possible. So what do you think?" He addressed the crowd, pausing in place. "Should we set it free?"

"Get Into the Groove!" Tío Wacha howled, the crowd echoing his war cry. The bot flipped into the offensive, throwing a punch that Noysh ducked, catching the bot's torso in a solid push as he came up. Stumbling into the crowd, the bot disappeared in a commotion of flesh, projections, and airborne beer as Terror Humano launched into action overhead.

Luna watched Noysh fist-bump Tío Wacha, flushing with admiration and awe. This guy, all these people, were for real, in the way she'd always wanted to be but generally wasn't. Maybe she could stick around for a few days and get to know him. Become one of them. Become more herself. She sipped her beer and pushed the thought away, wiggling through the kinetic anarchy separating her from the stage.

A searing white noise sliced through the soundtrack. Luna turned to see the bot crowd-surfing towards her, its arms flailing like a sacrificial heathen being carried to the altar. When it reached the stage, El Puerco cut loose from his trajectory, landing on top of the bot and pinning its arms down with his knees. Ancho tossed him the angle grinder, and the crowd whooped and howled as El Puerco raised it above his head, letting it whir, his head swiveling toward the crowd with the rehearsed pantomime of a Kabuki dancer, appearing to request permission to complete the ritual. Then he brought it down, a sweeping gesture of pyrophoric metal and electrical fire, tearing through the bot's chestplate to expose hemorrhaged circuitry and wire arcing over dead space. The bot convulsed as El Puerco tossed the angle grinder aside and pulled several dangling cables from the air, jamming them into the bot's chest cavity. A perpetually descending Shepard tone issued from the bot's broken innards, through the cables, and out the surround-sound speakers.

The bot motionless now, El Puerco jolted back into flight, The Mortician touching down with sparking live wires in either hand. As he plunged the exposed wires into the bot's temples, it shot back to life, channeling a cataclysmic surge of static and insectoid sub-bass that rattled Luna's rib cage.

Several gauzy avatars gathered around The Mortician—a pair of skinny jeans conjoined to a midnight shroud of bat wings with no face, a coati punk in studded vest and cutoff shorts plastered in unreadable patches, a chupacabra goth in black flare dress with white cuffs and Peter Pan collar, a nude tailor mannequin with lasers emitting from her eyes, and an athletic man wearing nothing but a loincloth, his canine head painted in skeletal Catrina makeup—as if they were ancient spirits observing a bloodletting rite.

Luna felt a hand on her shoulder and turned, beaming, expecting to see Noysh.

"Where's that rude little bald girl?" Don shouted over the noise. "We have to keep moving."

"You sure you're not getting into this?"

"What?!"

"You sure you.... Forget it. Let's go."

They found Cholla back at the entrance, talking with Marty, Noysh, Tío Wacha, and Doña Dron. Remembering that the infoshadow ended at the door, Luna made sure not to step outside, then had a terrible realization. "Did that bot give away our location before cutting out?" she asked, a pang of guilt knotting in her stomach.

"Nah," said Cholla, "I extended the radius by a couple kilometers after we learned about your famous gringo buddy. The bot must have wandered in here on autopilot with amnesia. Probably picked up Doña Dron's heat signature once it got close enough."

Luna exhaled with relief. The thought of her presence jeopardizing this place, these people, was too much to bear. But, true to their ethos, they were one step ahead of Los Compas.

"I shot the fucker right in the face," Doña Dron explained in Spanish. "But he just kept on going."

"Good shot, Grandma," Cholla said, embracing her in a side hug and, switching to English, "Now, it's time we headed off on our field trip. You all coming?"

"Wacha," said Tío Wacha, "I'm going with Marty to grab some grunion."

"Noysh?" Cholla asked.

"Wouldn't miss a trip to the library," he said, catching Luna's eye. "I'll grab my conductor cap."

Don was confused as to why a computer super brain would be located in the last stall of a run-down, pangender restroom in the back of a nightclub, but there they were. Noysh knelt inside the stall and slid a loose wall tile into the empty adjacent space. Something thunked and the wall swung open, revealing an unlit corridor much like the one at the entrance.

"Headlights on," he instructed, handing out lamps as each of them passed, "and welcome to La Chinesca." He waited until Cholla, Luna, and Don passed through the door, then did something to make it close, lending the illusion of a dead end where the restroom used to be.

"What is this place?" Don asked, thinking about the last time he was in a tunnel, rolling down mine-cart tracks with that son of a bitch Shorty.

"Distrito Dron is just one small part of a vast maze of tunnels and chambers beneath Mexicali's historic Chinatown," Noysh explained as they followed Cholla down a split in the tunnel. "We still haven't explored it completely, but it goes for at least a few kilometers in every direction, though the transborder portion into Calexico was sealed off way before we got here."

"Chinatown?" Don was certain he'd misheard. "In the middle of a Mexican desert?"

"Former Mexican desert," Noysh said, "and yeah. A ton of Chinese immigrants moved here around the turn of the twentieth century to escape violent racism in the United States, especially California. Many worked for a fraction of the going rate as laborers, building the canals and railroads that let Mexicali's agricultural industry thrive, long before Zodiac sucked up all the water and Xuan-Santos converted the fields to shit and slaves."

Cholla led them down a stairway and around several unmarked turns into a concrete chamber filled with antique craps tables, roulette wheels, and mechanical slot machines. Don picked up a poker chip and flipped it in his hand idly, feeling even more out of his element than he did in the nightclub.

Evidently picking up on Don's confusion, Noysh explained, "These tunnels became a refuge for Chinese fleeing massacres and deportation throughout northern Mexico in the 1920s, back when there were a hundred Chinese in Mexicali for every seven Mexicans. At the same time, parts of La Chinesca were built into underground casinos, brothels, and opium dens catering to Americans escaping a fourteen-year prohibition on alcohol, all connected to bars, restaurants, and hotels on the surface."

Cholla navigated down several more forks, ascents, and rubble-strewn crawl spaces before stopping in another chamber that held the remnants of a living room—a few chairs situated around a basic table, a small altar affixed to the wall, melted candles surrounded by black-and-white photographs of a family. Looking closer, Don saw what he presumed to be a father and daughter, about his and Anabelle's age the last time they'd seen each other. The man stood in a cowboy hat and a black Mandarin suit, looking into the camera with a weary yet content expression. His hand rested on the shoulder of his daughter, who sat on a stool in a form-fitting Cheongsam dress, a serene, tolerant smile on her face.

Noysh appeared to pay respects at the altar, pausing alongside Don in silence, then continued, "We're a lot like them. They built everything that kept this city alive, but still they were forced to go underground to preserve their way of life. To be free. In that regard, I have a lot of respect for them, for their struggle. I like to think what we do now in their old home completes the story. We are the uprising they never got to have. The final Hong Kong fuck you to oppression. You wouldn't know it now, but when I was growing up, there were over a thousand Chinese restaurants in Chicali. Most locals just assumed they, themselves, were partly Chinese, and most of them were right."

"So, you're local?" Luna said in that way people ask when they just want to hear someone keep talking.

"I grew up here, yeah." Noysh turned to follow Cholla out of the room. "On the surface, you know. I was a teenager when Los Compas took over. My family fled to Chihuahua after the earthquake but I stayed behind to run our corner store, sell out supplies before I joined them with some savings to keep us going. I never got the chance to get out. I refused to join the cartel, so they put me to work in the fields for Xuan-Santos. Tío Wacha and I broke out and came here. Started building, then went back for our friends. And then their friends."

"Is that where you met Cholla?" Luna asked, falling back to walk alongside Noysh.

"No." Noysh laughed, and Don could see Cholla smirk over her shoulder. "I met her in a dumpster over in Maqui. Probably the best thing I've found in there yet."

"Probably?" Cholla said, stopping and turning to face him, hand on her hip.

"Probably," said Noysh.

"Whatever," Cholla said, walking again. "*I* found *you*, cochino." She turned a corner and Don followed her down a long stairwell, deeper into the earth. Maybe it was his imagination, but Don could feel the weight of the city, its centuries of history, its untold stories and mythic resonance, pressing down on him, stifling his breath.

"We're just about to the lowest level beneath Alley Nineteen,"

Cholla said, "which means the infoshadow ends anytime now. Parasols out, chula." She unclipped a metal cylinder from her hip and tossed it back to Luna over Don's shoulder, deploying another above her head in a web of diaphanous wire dendrites.

"Thanks." Luna extended her parasol with a mechanical thwip. "What's yours for?"

Cholla tapped next to her left eye. "You're not the only one with premarket nanotech." She fell back to walk alongside Luna, Noysh taking lead at the front of the group. "Got roped into the cartel panopticon when Grandma and I lived in El Bordo, back in TJ. Hard to believe that was just four years ago."

"Deported?" Luna asked.

"Yeah," said Cholla. "I grew up in East LA. Deported when I was sixteen. I lived with Grandma. She was pretty vocal about Appleyard on social media. Classic Millennial, you know? She was undocumented, so they just pushed us both across the border with no option to work off our sentences, not that we would if we could've."

"Why not?" Don asked, aware of the impulse to feel personally slighted by the idea.

"Because, gringo, the American Dream is dead," Cholla said, her stink eye puckering up. "You probably helped kill it."

Don decided, considering the circumstances, that he didn't care to unpack the insult. That and, ever since Mindfuck Oasis, he'd become increasingly comfortable with the thought that maybe he didn't know everything, and that was okay. Maybe he'd just look and listen and let things be what they were, without getting in their way for a while.

"No off switch on yours either, huh?" Luna asked, clearly running interference.

"Nope," said Cholla. "Shitty black-market version cloned from Russian military, rumor had it. No audio, just mono visuals on constant cast. Part of Los Compas' plan to turn bottom-rung deportees into spies, back when they were still worried about an uprising. They don't worry about that anymore. Most of our spirits were sufficiently broken, content with pointless immigration rituals and begging at the altar of Juan Soldado for salvation. Just about everyone in El

Bordo had their offending eye removed by La Bruja, but I ran away with Grandma. We made our own salvation. Squatted an apartment block outside Maqui. Stole what we needed to live."

"You kept the implant?" Luna asked, and Don could tell she wished she had a Bruja to fix her.

"As a reminder, maybe, of what I'm running from, what I'm fighting for," Cholla said. "I don't even know if anyone is watching anymore. You ever heard of those shortwave number stations, still broadcasting codes to Cold War spies, even though they've all been dead for about a century? Sometimes, I think that's me. A forgotten channel that nobody watches, transmitting scrambled packets of data into the void. Just a series of non sequitur snapshots that don't mean anything to anybody but me. Kinda prefer it that way. You wanna see something cool?" Cholla stopped in a chamber at the bottom of the stairs. "Put down your parasol."

Luna lowered her spiderweb canopy to one side. As soon as the asymmetrical membrane uncovered her head, something happened to Cholla's face that nearly gave Don a heart attack.

"Yep," Cholla said, her face swimming with peacock feathers splayed out like sunflower petals in a cyclone. "We're past the shadow."

"Show off," Noysh said, smirking.

"Facial unrecognition piercing." Cholla tapped her septum ring, and the projections on her face flexed in concert with the movement. "Noysh helped me build it. Senses artificial glances up to three hundred yards away, and doesn't have to be constantly modified like unrecog tattoos."

Luna brought her parasol back up and Cholla's face reverted to an uncharacteristically sweet smile, fixed firmly on Luna.

Just let it be, Don reminded himself. It's okay if he'd never understand these people.

Noysh navigated through several more turns and chambers before stopping at a nondescript stretch of wall. He pulled a plastic card out of his pocket and slid it into a seam. "Stand back," he instructed. A segment of concrete swung outward. He stepped inside and flicked a switch, illuminating a wide, semicircular tunnel that extended for as far as Don could see. Railroad tracks ran the length of the tunnel, terminating at the bottom of the short staircase where Don and Noysh stood. On the tracks sat an antique trolley car with yellow wood-paneling, panoramic glass windows, and a convex roof. Don saw the number "127" painted in block lettering on the side, and a placard reading TO SILICON BORDER affixed to the rear.

"Nice, yeah?" Noysh said, descending the stairs.

"How in the hell?" Don heard himself mumble.

"No idea." Noysh seemed to anticipate the question. "Cholla found it just a few days after she moved here. Pretty impressive, since most of us walked these tunnels un chingo already."

"Class 1 Streetcar," Cholla said, deflecting the compliment. "Built in 1912 for the San Diego Electric Railway Company. One in a fleet of twenty-four unique Arts & Craft–style cars that were retired in 1939, after the rail company went under in the Great Depression. Originally ran on six-hundred volts DC from an overhead line, but we converted it to onboard batteries, charged by solar arrays on the surface."

"How'd it get here?" Luna asked, walking alongside Don and running one hand over a bronze rail at the center of the trolley.

"Hard to say." Cholla jumped into the car and stood in the entryway. "From what I can find, a few cars were auctioned off, many were destroyed, and some were even repurposed into housing. But this one?" She ran an affectionate hand across a polished cherry-wood backrest. "My best guess, it was purchased at auction, still in decent working condition, by a Chinese businessman with enough resources and connections to have it quietly transported two hundred kilometers to Mexicali, disassembled, and then rebuilt underground."

"Why would they do that?" Luna accepted Cholla's extended hand and climbed up into the streetcar. Don and Noysh followed, pulling themselves up on the handrail.

"Worker transport," Cholla said. "Holds about a hundred. Probably used horses instead of building an electrical substation for power. Look, it still has all the original pearl buttons to request a stop."

Don pressed one and just about shit himself when an overhead speaker blasted a recording of a locomotive passing at high speed, its whistle Dopplering into a forlorn groan as it faded into the distance. Cholla glowered at him like a mother whose patience was being tested by someone else's child.

"A worker transport to where?" Luna asked, clearly wanting to get Don out of Cholla's crosshairs.

Cholla's face went pleasant as she explained, "To the mine. I found some records of gold, silver, manganese, and copper occurrences out by a mountain, El Centinela, in the late 1930s. Drill-hole samples, taken by prospectors a few decades later, deemed the deposits insufficient to merit further exploration. My guess is, whoever brought this trolley down had the whole lode cleared out from the inside before anyone knew it was there. Think of it like geological dumpster diving."

"You think the computer brain is in a copper mine?" Don had a hard time believing it.

Cholla's expression dropped. "I think the *neural net* could be at Silicon Border, where we built our library."

"I don't see what a computer brain would be doing in a libr...." Don started, then cut himself off when he caught Luna mouthing, "Shut up, dude," with her eyes all buggy. "Sounds good," he said, glancing back at Cholla. "Thanks."

Cholla's face went peacock. She spun toward the tunnel entrance and, following her gaze, Don saw the last bull stumbling down the stairs, its head reeling and arms hooked out into limp claws.

"Drunken Monkey style." Cholla chuckled. "Awesome."

"Yaqui Chan," Noysh whispered. "I've been looking for him for years."

"Why?" said Don.

Noysh shrugged. "Need another drummer."

"Like hell you do," Don said out of the side of his mouth, realizing they were all reacting as if they'd spotted a rare and majestic animal in the wild, not a cartel-powered deathbot in Jackie Chan pajamas. "So now what?" Don hissed. "Are these things even dangerous?"

Noysh tossed his conductor cap to Luna, pulling his faded

green neckerchief snug over his face. "I'll catch up," he said, his eyes narrowing in their swollen sockets. "I've been meaning to chat with Los Compas." He hollered something vulgar-sounding in Spanish. The bot wobbled in acknowledgment, lost its balance, then tucked into a roll, rising up on one leg in a flamingo pose.

"You want my stunstick?" Luna pulled the striped cap onto her head with one hand, and fished the stick out of her back pocket with the other.

"I got gizmos," he said, then turned in a full run.

The trolley eased forward. Don let himself down into a seat at the back, watching over his shoulder as Noysh charged the Chanbot. "What did he say back there?" Don asked.

"Join Cachanihilismo, you pig fucker." Luna gazed out the rear window, a beatific smile on her face. "We have better music."

SHARED_PHANTOM_OBJECTS : : 50

"Fuck!" Cholla stormed down the aisle from the conductor's booth. "That bot just blew our cover. Los Compas didn't know about the trolley."

The streetcar was picking up speed, but Luna could still see Noysh grappling with Yaqui Chan, dodging the kung fu strikes and hapkido kicks jutting from Chan's melodramatic dance of back flips and mock-drunk tumbles.

"Gimme your parasol, chula," Cholla said, standing behind her now, her hand on the small of Luna's back. "If the cartel knows about our trolley, you might as well let your audience watch Noysh kick their robot's ass."

Luna retracted the parasol into its handle—her drop going red—and handed it to Cholla. "Is he gonna be alright back there?"

Cholla psshed. "He's taken on bigger problems, on less sleep. He'll be fine."

Luna hit stats: 1,267,244 viewers.

That was good, right? After going dead for over an hour?

What did that even mean in terms of her paycheck? She'd have to get a detailed breakdown of the algorithm responsible for her ad revenue, as soon as she got back to Mexico City. Was she well over or far beneath her target of eight million rubles? How many pesos was that today? A shit ton? She pulled up the current conversion: still just over twenty-five million pesos. About the cost of a very nice house in a posh downtown district of Mexico City. A shit ton.

LUNA TESCHNER

Hey, Jaco, quick question for ya. How much money am I making?

JACO LARK

Hard to say. A lot. The fan forums have more than doubled their activity in the last hour, so you'll see a huge spike in viewers as they move back to the feed.

LUNA TESCHNER

Like three month's rent a lot or buy a house a lot?

JACO LARK

Probably somewhere in the middle. Can't give you a good estimate until the cast is over, the residual views come in, and we see the total time spent in ad environs, plus a few other metrics.

Luna watched Noysh and Yaqui Chan shrink into a writhing dot in the distance, then headed up to the conductor's booth, smiling at the peacock feathers swarming Cholla's face as she came into view. She sat next to Cholla in a sawed-off bench that looked like it came from a cathedral, and watched sleeper rails disappear beneath the streetcar headlight in a rhythmic blur.

LUNA TESCHNER

Anywhere close to 25 million pesos?

JACO LARK

Again, hard to say. If you can stay live, I'll redirect viewers from the forums. There's a chance, but you can't keep cutting out.

LUNA TESCHNER

No promises. I'll do my best. You won't believe where I was for the past hour.

JACO LARK

Your audience won't either. Stay live.

"Hey, Cholla," Luna said. "Do you mind if I keep casting? Like wherever we're going next?"

Cholla looked her over. "Tell me one thing, chula. You really come here to expose deportee labor? You're a *long* way from Maqui."

Luna wasn't sure how to take that. "I know. Shit has been going sideways since I got here. I don't even know what the story is anymore."

"Sex cult?" Cholla raised an eyebrow behind her floating feather mask.

"Yeah, sex cult, Anabelle, the captain, the Unknown handle, Quetzalcóatl...." Luna realized how insane it all sounded.

Cholla laughed. "Did you say Quetzalcóatl?"

"Is that funny?"

"Of course," Cholla said, looking as though she was piecing something together. "That's where the sex cult got their name. Ketcel. Quetzal. Totally forgot about that part. That...I think that explains something. If I'm right, I'm about to blow your mind. And if your gabacho buddy back there is right about Ketcel, he's about to blow mine."

Luna's heart skipped a beat. "What is it?"

"Keep casting. I'll show you. We'll be there in five."

"Are you sure?"

"This spot is burnt, anyways," Cholla said, retracting her parasol. "Ni pedo. We got like a hundred others."

Luna suspected she was exaggerating for her audience's—and Los Compas'—benefit, but who knows? Maybe they did have a hundred hidden data hubs webbed together from abandoned bullring dressing rooms, derelict taco stands, and the condemned remains of public works buildings throughout the city, lying dormant in every fiber of its infrastructure, patient as a virus. It seemed like exactly the kind of thing they would do.

"You hear that, culeros?" Cholla snarled at Luna's audience, confirming her suspicion. The snarl crept into a devilish grin. "You can't kill us. We're fucking ants. We're everywhere. Crawling under your skin. Eating you alive. Haunting your house and shit." She laughed, then went severe. "But for reals, we're coming for you."

"Siguiente estación, Silicon Border." The distorted voice of a woman came over the speakers, her tone somehow both mechanical and melancholy. "Silicon Border is next."

Cholla pursed her lips. "I'm gonna miss this fucking trolley, though." She stood as the streetcar coasted to a halt, then headed down the aisle, punching Don in the arm as she passed, waking him up.

Don snorted, seemed to get his bearings, and frowned at Luna. "I had the strangest dream," he said, rubbing his eyes. "A rude little bald girl was in control of my destiny."

"She still is, pendejo," Cholla hollered from the exit.

Luna guffawed, helping Don up. They followed Cholla off the trolley, pausing by the tracks.

"Check this out," Cholla said, producing a card identical to the one Noysh used to access the trolley tunnel. "The mine is still way down that way, but the library is in an underground shoe factory in the middle of fucking nowhere." She slid the card into a seam in the wall. A door opened inward. Cholla clicked her headlamp and began walking down a corridor, indistinguishable from the ones they'd just left in La Chinesca. She led the way up a long set of stairs and pushed open a door, stepping into an empty warehouse, windowless, with ceilings so low, Luna couldn't decide if she found them more comical or oppressive.

"We cleared out and repurposed most of the equipment," Cholla said, "but the factory ran from the 1960s through sometime in the eighties, according to some records we found. Chinese Mexicans counterfeiting American brands made in China, in Mexico. There were still a few Air Jordan knockoffs back in storage when we found this place."

Luna and Don followed her across the open floor to an office. Inside, a patchwork of flat-screens—many showing security feeds, others on news and maps—covered the walls almost completely. Cholla went to a desk and pulled out a chicanada headset with exposed circuitry. "DIY-Mask," she said, slipping the strap over her head. "Watch that one." She pointed to a screen above the desk and secured the mask over her eyes, her peacock feathers shattering over its hard contours. Her hands took flight, each one following its own distinct repertoire of movements as they delineated a series of shared phantom objects, an esoteric chironomy of commands that were foreign to Luna.

"Noysh and Tío Wacha cracked into just about every municipal surveillance cam in Baja when they were kids," Cholla said, zooming in on a map of La Rumorosa and then tracking northwest until Jacumba Hot Springs appeared. Everything above a horizontal red line, including Jacumba Hot Springs, was black. Just south of the line, hundreds of multicolored dots populated the landscape. Cholla selected a green dot, and a live security feed of a vacant street filled the screen, the border wall glowing laserwire pink off to the right. "Los Compas inherited our mole holes along with the city surveillance nets, and they're too busy playing Pancho Villa with their robots to ever dig us out." And, as if she were cursing their mothers' graves, "Brute coders."

A window appeared over the feed with a clickbait article titled: "I Can't Believe I Never Heard of These Ten HORRIFYING Cyber Cults!" Cholla selected the date of Ketcel Collective's disappearance and, with a familiar copy/paste gesture, stuck it in a search bar on the security feed. The scene was identical, but for the fact that the wall was no longer glowing, and the street looked only slightly less uninhabited, ten years prior. "I'll have it scan for motion," Cholla said more to herself, "and, here we go. Dog. Wind. Another dog. Rooster. Oh, people."

The feed showed a figure emerging over the wall—rather, the slatted-metal fence that predated the wall—followed by several others, sitting atop the fence until the last one hoisted over a ladder, lowered it to the street, and descended.

"There's your mysterious disappearance," Cholla said, staring off into her mask.

"Enhance!" Don hollered over Luna's shoulder.

"Dude, it doesn't...." Cholla smirked, zooming in on the figures. "You can't just say 'enhance.'"

"Enhance on that one." Don pointed at the screen. "By the streetlight."

Cholla pursed her lips and zoomed.

"Anabelle," Don whispered.

She was about Luna's age, probably a few years younger, and Luna was shocked to see that Anabelle looked exactly as she'd imagined her—radiant, her eyes big and full of quiet wonder, a trim jaw beneath thin lips, which split slightly, as if ever on the verge of awe. Basically, nothing like Don, but clearly his daughter. Her mother's daughter.

"Let's see where they're off to," Cholla said, speeding up playback and toggling between the camera map and various feeds. A blue line appeared on the map, tracking the group's movement. "Walk across town, or what's left of it," Cholla narrated as she connected the dots. "Get to the highway and catch a ryde? Nope, steal horses. Nice. No passenger log. Follow the highway east. Down the Rumorosa grade. Then, no more trace. You can see them cut north off the highway once they reach the desert. Betcha anything they show up in a couple hours over here." Cholla scrolled east, just past the jagged footprint of El Centinela, and hit a dot. Sure enough, as the sun began to rise, about fifteen figures came into view, dismounting horses, then entering a building in what looked like an industrial park.

"Where's that?" Don asked.

"That," said Cholla, "is Silicon Border, almost directly above us."

"Let's go there," he said.

"Obviously." Cholla closed out the search bar and the feed reverted to live, the figures replaced by a night-vision shot of a vehicle, parked, a tall man leaning against it. Cholla and Luna said it at the same time. "Fucking pigs."

Kervens had never looked under the hood of his butter bean before. He never had a reason to. He was not surprised to learn that the motor's sole exposed feature was a diagnostic port, which only saw use when the vehicle drove itself to the mechanic for routine maintenance. It had done so just a few days earlier, in fact, which made the malfunction even more unusual.

He leaned back against his passenger door and stared up at the stars, the spectacular view taking on sinister undertones as a wave of axol withdrawal curdled his insides.

It's like the dentist, he realized. Xolotl must have gotten into the mechanic's system, then implanted instructions telling his butter bean to reroute navigation as soon as he got close to their destination. For all he knew, "they" may have gotten into the traffic-control servers, and were directing him in real time, if that was that even possible. The consensus at the precinct was that their network security was impenetrable, but one of the brothers' nephews handled most of that, and Kervens had just taken his word for it.

Still, Kervens had no idea what Xolotl could do because he wasn't clear on what it actually was. What happens when you merge with an ancient cyberdeity? Are you still you? Who's in control of the thing? He couldn't help imagining Xolotl and Ketcel Collective as little more than a phosphene afterimage of glyphs and faces, humming imperceptibly beneath everything with an internet connection—his own head included. He pictured them nowhere and everywhere at once, snaking down wires and over airwaves with a cartoon jolt of electricity, embedding themselves in the synapses of the city, knowing everything.

If that was the case, why were they sending him here, to an abandoned industrial park in the middle of the desert? The sign at the entrance to the compound—built in the San Andreas Shaky Chic style of Googie Revival that had been popular about a decade ago—read SILICON BORDER.

Kervens vaguely recalled skimming an article about the place when he was still living down on Avenida Ocampo, working and sleeping in the kitchen of a Haitian chicken hole-in-the-wall. To the best of his memory, Silicon Border was built as a high-tech manufacturing hub a few years after the pandemic, when American businesses were eager to pull out of China and relocate somewhere more predictable, or so the developers thought. Most of the tenants probably counted their losses and cleared out when the US locked down the border, and Los Compas no doubt sold off whatever was left behind. Or rather, whatever had survived the earthquake, which had apparently leveled about half of Silicon Border's over-stylized warehouses.

Kervens fought the urge to vomit and took a deep breath. A branding iron of paranoia seared through his chest. What if Ketcel didn't actually exist? What if Not-Casseus was just the brothers putting him through an elaborate loyalty test? What if they weren't dead at all?

If the brothers had been spying on him through Casseus, they would have already known everything that Not-Casseus told him, and they could have fabricated the rest. That would explain how they had access to the Los Cabos environ in Sawlips—it belonged to *them*. Was this all just part of some deranged new game show, where wayward officials got made into examples by being lured to a theatrical demise?

Kervens imagined Los Compas' most prolific torture artists, their eyes gleaming with sadistic anticipation, poised on the other side of the warehouse door. Was that crazy? Luna would have to be in on it, which would make her the best actor of all time. But, of course, Los Compas could afford the best.

The thought of Luna betraying him sent Kervens into a panic. His whole world had fallen apart over the past twenty-four hours, and she was the only constant grounding him, giving him purpose. The thermostat in his body seemed to turn up several degrees, radiating a clammy, feverish aura of impending doom. The inevitability of his circumstance turned his stomach. He couldn't breathe. The fine point of his awareness split into tendrils, catechizing the recesses of what he knew, why he thought he knew it, and all the ways he was already wrong in his delusions of security.

He wanted to puke, but the thought of performing any abrupt action made him feel somehow more exposed. For a minute, he went catatonic, his skin dissociating into old-fashioned radio static, his essence peeling away.

What had he done to fall from the brothers' graces? If they really were dead, had something happened before the boating accident, a seed of misgiving that blossomed into malice in the simulated minds of the brothers' cloaks? Or did the cloaks have an agenda of their own, diverging from the brothers' methods just imperceptibly enough to be attributed to eccentric genius? Maybe he was set up by someone in his squad, but who?

Follow her.

Luna was the only person who might give him answers. He closed his eyes and tried to relax, inviting her loa in. A dreadful surge of withdrawal resisted the sync, but as he forced himself into an almost hypnotic stillness, the connection popped.

A flat-screen showing Kervens, his skin pulsing a sickly iridescent bile, reclining against his broke-down butter bean. She was watching him. He swiveled his head until he saw it face the camera, then waved.

Caught you.

What's up, Captain?

To her right, someone said, "These are pinhole cameras. How does he even know they exist?"

"He's my passenger." Luna shifted her attention to a bald punk girl removing a VR headset, her face obscured by a luminous mask of feathers. "Like, he randomly appears inside me."

"Must be nice." Feathers flexing to smile.

"I mean, he has an implant similar to mine and we're...linked," Luna said. "He says it involves a drug. Axol."

"Explains the dull glow on him," the punk girl said. "That shit is bizarre, but the cops can't get enough of it. Supposed to help with vodou rituals."

"You tried it?" Luna asked, turning back to the screen.

You there, Captain?

"Noysh got gifted a fat bag a couple years ago," the girl said. "So of course we spent the next three days smoking it all. At one point, I was telepathically coaching him out of my own childhood trauma, but I kept getting distracted by memories of his mother's cooking. We ended up in this insane feedback loop where I could feel *him*, feeling *me*, feel *his* lust for me. We didn't even fuck about it. It was that good. Worst comedown of my life."

"Wow, you ever done that, Captain?" Luna was addressing him out loud now.

I have not. Why are you watching me?

"So, this guy's like a fanboy of yours?" the girl asked. "I figured the cops were watching, but you know each other?"

I should ask you the same.

"Kind of." Luna turned back to the girl with the peacock face. "You know how I said Ketcel has been contacting me? They're doing it through him. That's what he says, anyway."

Touché.

"And you believe him?"

"Maybe?" Luna said. "He said he was coming to find me. Figured we'd sort it out then."

"You do realize he's a cop, right?"

"He mentioned that."

"So why should you trust him?"

"Good question." Luna said. "Never planned on actually running into the guy. Why should we trust you, Captain?"

You shouldn't. I was just leaving.

"He's being weird," Luna said. "I'm gonna go talk to him. You said it's close, yeah?"

"I'm going with you," said Don, who had apparently been standing behind her.

"Fuck the po-lice." The punk girl shrugged, placing a hand over what was presumably a weapon on her hip. "Yeah, let's go."

No, really, Luna. I'm going now, see? Kervens watched himself via Luna's security feed, opening a door and climbing into his butter bean.

What's gotten into you? I thought you were my passenger. Luna turned away from the flat-screen, exited the office, and followed the punk girl up a set of stairs.

I don't know if I can trust you.

How do you think I feel? You contacted me, remember? The girl slid a card into a door and pushed it open, stepping out into what looked like a cemetery. Luna turned around and helped Don out of a stone mausoleum concealing the staircase.

I know. It's just.... Are you working for the cartel?

You're the cop, dude. You're freaking out. Luna's eyes adjusted to the twilight, and the imploded angles of the industrial park came into view across the graveyard.

I'm out. Whatever this is, I'm not doing it.

Out? What about Ketcel? You said it yourself, they're guiding me somewhere. They're guiding us somewhere.

That's what worries me. What if there is no Ketcel? What if this is just a cruel prank dreamed up by Los Compas?

I'm pretty sure this is the only thing in Limbo that isn't a cruel prank dreamed up by Los Compas. Besides, Cholla knows where we can find Ketcel.

How does she know that?

She's Cachanihilismo. Nothing happens in Limbo they don't know about.

UNKNOWN
How do you know she's not in on it?

Luna followed Cholla around the busted remnants of a garish retro-futuristic building—a hermit's heatstroke vision of industrial Raygun Gothic, shaken to Cubist shards on the desert floor. There, across the parking lot, she saw him, keeled over in the front seat of his cop cruiser with his face in his hands.

LUNA TESCHNER
Do you realize how ridiculous you sound?

Cholla put a hand on her hip and nodded. "Just give the word if you need me to fry him."

"He's freaking out," Luna said, putting up a hand instructing Don to wait.

Cholla laughed. "Axol lows are even more fucked up than the high."

LUNA TESCHNER
We found the security footage of Ketcel Collective jumping the border fence and coming here, to this building. We're going in with or without you.

Luna approached the cruiser window and tapped. Kervens's head shot up, appearing shocked to see her, even though he must have been watching himself sitting there in front of her as she got near. He hesitated, then cracked the window.

"You look like shit," Luna said. She'd imagined him differently, and was becoming annoyed to find him in such a pathetic state, looking like he'd been huffing nuclear waste for a week.

"Luna?" The way he asked it made her begin to doubt he was actually a cop, much less a captain.

"How many heads you riding around in?"

"Just yours, as far as I know."

"How about you come out here and shake my hand, make this a little less awkward." Luna realized that she felt perfectly comfortable talking to a so-called cop however she pleased. For as odd as their acquaintanceship had been, he felt like an old friend—idiosyncratic, imperfect, and more or less benign.

Kervens opened the door and stepped out, towering over her as he extended his hand. "Sorry about all that," he said, then nodded at Don and Cholla. "I think this comedown is messing with my head. Everything has gotten so strange so quickly, believing in an invisible computer god is somehow the only thing that makes sense."

Don's heart was still racing from the security footage of Anabelle—the first shred of actual evidence that his vision from the oasis wasn't merely the invention of cantankerous mindfuck orbs prodding at his soft spots. She had been here and, if the rude little bald girl was right about the computer brain, she could still be here. Waiting to be born.

"Kervens," the Haitian cop said, extending a hand to Cholla.

"So?" She did not shake his hand.

"Very well," Kervens said, then introduced himself to Don.

Despite his history with Haitians in Limbo, Don accepted Kervens's hand. "Don Collins," he said. "Retired leisure investment consultant and current cartel-game-show celebrity." His disdain for Haitians felt far away and unrelatable, even if he'd loathed every last one of them just a couple days ago. "Have we met? You look familiar."

"It's unlikely," Kervens said. "I know your face from *¡Toreros y Alarmas!*, though I don't usually follow the show."

Then it clicked. "Two nights ago in Shit and Sea, by the boardwalk," Don said, the thrill of recognition making him giddy.

"You bought me a ryde after the cartel cut my chip."

"I'm sorry," Kervens said. "I have no recollection of that."

Don snorted. "Don't be sorry. It's the only positive interaction I've had with a Haitian since I got here."

"I'm glad to hear that." Kervens did not look glad. "I haven't really been myself the past couple days."

"We done here?" Cholla said, her arms crossed. "I don't know about you guys, but I'm going in there."

"After you," Kervens said, bowing apologetically.

Cholla slid a card in the door, saying, "We rekeyed the whole compound a few years ago. Whatever wasn't damaged in the earthquake was looted for resale by Los Compas, but they left a few things behind."

Luna followed her into the building, Don and Kervens behind them. There wasn't much to see apart from a faint trail that had been cleared through the rubble, and stars twinkling overhead where the roof used to be. Cholla clicked her headlamp, illuminating patches of cactus and shrubs sprouting between toppled assembly arms and shattered glass.

Turning to Luna, Cholla continued, "Since the shoe factory was apparently undiscovered by developers, we're probably the first people in history to appreciate how Silicon Border tells the rest of the story: American manufacturers move to Mexico as a 'fuck you' to China, and end up putting themselves out of business with the same isolationist fervor that brought them to Mexico in the first place."

"So, Kervens," Don said, trailing close behind Luna to avoid busting his shins in the dark, "what do you know about this Ketcel Collective?"

"I told just about everything to Luna already," Kervens said over Don's shoulder. "I never heard of them until today, when I skimmed through her Undew cast. Turns out they know me, though. I met them a couple days ago in Sawlips, but I didn't know it was them."

"What did they look like?" Don said.

"They presented as vodou loas, kind of like how you might think of angels, but different. That was more for dramatic effect, I think. Then, earlier today, they appeared as, uh, somebody I thought

I knew in Sawlips."

"What did they say?"

"Well, among other things, they told me the Flores Magón brothers are dead and Limbo has been run by their cloaks for the past three months."

Cholla stopped in her tracks and spun around. "Excuse me, what?"

Kervens shrugged. "Boating accident, they said."

Cholla squinted at him. "Holy shit. I'm not saying I believe you, but holy shit."

"Holy shit, indeed," Kervens said. "But the fact that nobody has noticed means their cloaks are doing a damn good impression of the brothers. So good, in fact, they are planning on having me killed."

"Killed for what?" Luna asked.

"I assume they found a younger, more antagonistic replacement," Kervens said. "They often said I lacked enthusiasm for my work."

"To your credit," Cholla said.

"Their digital doppelgängers don't seem to think so," said Kervens.

"Yeah, but fuck them," Cholla said. "We're here." She slid her card in a door labeled MICTLĀN and led the way to a basement, hitting a light switch. "This area stayed more or less intact, something about seismic waves causing more damage on the surface."

As Don reached the bottom of the stairs, he imagined how the compound must have once looked: banks of blinking computers along one wall where empty racks now stood, high-tech contraptions that had since been salvaged to the bone, a few workstations scattered throughout. All that remained were six sturdy metal desks that weren't worth the effort to remove and maybe twenty outdated flat-screens hung too high on the walls to be taken without a ladder.

"The border-suicide-challenge meme took on a life of its own," Cholla explained, walking to the far side of the room. "I was just a kid when the actual event happened. The suicide challenge introduced enough semantic drift over the years to make it more about protesting Appleyard's erratic authoritarianism rather than reenacting, or even

remembering, the motives of Ketcel Collective, much less their name."
She pulled a dusty sheet from an object standing a foot or two taller
than Don, and several times as wide, revealing a polished black replica
of a conch shell. It spiraled to a point on one end, flared to a wavy
crest in the middle, then streamlined to a tip. "Or their logo."

"That's it!" Don ran his hand over the image of a Mayan serpent
chasing its tail in a circular Ouroboros, embossed over the spire's
outermost ring. It looked more like a monolith than a microprocessor,
but whatever it was, it was them. Ketcel.

"We repurposed a lot of what was left behind," Cholla said,
walking around the object, "but we didn't know what to do with this
thing. It either weighs a metric fuckton or it's got concealed bolts
holding it to the floor. Plus there's no way to fit it out the door, and
no way to take it apart. Completely seamless. No visible ports to jack
into, but whatever it is, it's running. Put your ear to it and you can
hear it humming."

Don put his head against the black shell and, sure enough, the
whole thing vibrated inertly against his ear.

"Entirely self-contained," Cholla said, consulting a rectangular
device in her palm. "Doesn't even show up on the scanner, so it's not
emitting a wireless connection or anything else that could jump an
air gap, and it doesn't appear to be linked to any of the other gear in
here that remains online. It's like it's in a coma. From the outside, it
looks dead, but inside, it seems to be alive."

Luna pressed her ear against the shell, picking up swells of low-pitch static, like a recording of ocean waves heard through bone conduction. "It's breathing," she said, smiling at Don's awestruck expression reflecting off the black mirrored surface.

Request to sync with **UNKNOWN.** Accept?

Luna jumped. "Oh my god," she said, stepping back. "It wants to sync with me."

"That's impossible, chula," Cholla said. "My scanner isn't showing any connections coming from this thing."

"The request is from the Unknown handle that Kervens has been contacting me through." She looked at him for backup.

"Xolotl," Kervens said, his tone almost reverent. "If Ketcel Collective really is stuck in there, their original neural net in Jacumba, Xolotl, must be behind the Unknown handle. It brought us here."

"Also impossible," Don said. "The Jacumba facility was cleared out and abandoned. I saw it myself."

"I know," said Kervens, "but what if it's no longer in Jacumba? What if it outgrew the need for the neural net, and now it lives... everywhere?"

"Yeah," Luna said, intrigued, "that actually makes sense. If it has access to all of the security feeds Cholla showed us, that would explain how I landed in the ryde with Don instead of being smeared across the highway by a worker transport. I mean, who knows how much access it has, but it's obviously more than we can imagine. Traffic control? Private cartel environs in Sawlips? It really is like it's everywhere."

She flashed back to Bad-Trip Jaco at Mindfuck Oasis, briefly reliving her paranoia about the Afterthought and her lifelong discomfort with the, well, unknown. Looking back now, it was hard to remember what she had been so afraid of. "Alright," she said. "Let's see what it has to say."

LUNA TESCHNER accepted sync with **UNKNOWN**.

A video window filled her vision with a title screen reading, "Welcome to Mictlān: The Underworld and How You Got Here," in 8-bit violet letters that spiked erratically to the sides in mock VHS tracking errors. The image cut to an anthropomorphic dog's head, his face halfway morphed between that of a bearded middle-aged man and a Xoloitzcuintli. As the shot pulled back, Luna saw he wore a conical hat, with round glasses and no shirt, standing in front of the shiny black conch. Subtitles appeared as his lips began moving.

"Hello, I'm Dr. Anselmo Manriquez. Welcome to Mictlān, a world between worlds. Here, old realities are brought to die, and in turn, new realities are given life. As you've already speculated, my colleagues in Ketcel Collective and I facilitated the necessary conditions to bring you all here today. This was no accident. Each of you play a vital role in what's about to happen, but before moving forward, let's take a look back at how we got here."

The scene dissolved to a midday aerial view of Silicon Border, clearly before the earthquake. It reminded Luna of a space-age casino with its flamboyant, overstated angles set in stark contrast to the desert's blown-out gradients. The perspective craned down to ground level, where Dr. Manriquez continued his narration.

"Thirteen years ago, Ketcel Collective leased a space in Silicon Border under the name Conch US Corporation. A shell company, if you will, allowing us to circumvent the tedious regulations imposed on neuromorphic technology in the United States."

He smiled slightly and stepped inside, the camera following him through a bustling assembly area, down the stairs to Mictlán.

"While our neural net, known as Xolotl, began the long process of analyzing the Jacumba Codex, we began construction on an even more powerful piece of conscious-adjacent technology, following specifications outlined by some of the first deciphered excerpts of the codex."

He laid a hand on the black shell's spire and continued, "Whereas Xolotl excelled at interpreting the codex back in Jacumba Hot Springs, Ketcel here would bring it to life. Of course, we didn't know that from the outset. It was only after several years of rigorous work with Xolotl that the bigger picture came into view."

The image swiped to an overhead shot of Dr. Manriquez and about twelve others sitting in a circle around a chrome statue, gazing into "DIY-Masks," as Cholla would say. A caption appeared reading "Jacumba Hot Springs, California." As the camera panned down, Luna saw that the statue was in the form of a dog-headed man, nude, with wires leading from its base to the masks.

"As Xolotl's analysis of the codex neared completion, we diverted part of its processing power to creating hyperreal cloaks of ourselves, far more precise than anything available in Sawlips at the time, or even at present. When Xolotl's work on the codex was complete, we merged our quasi-conscious cloaks with Xolotl's advanced learning core, and released our hybrid aspiring cyberdeity into the wild. It has spent the past decade quietly expanding its network, cracking encryption, circumventing firewalls, creating backdoors, and embedding itself into just about everything connected to the internet, plus an impressive number of things that aren't. You can think of us as Ketcel's subconscious, absorbing and assimilating impressions from the world, but unable to relay them back to the waking mind. Captain Dessalines was correct to assume that the Xolotl construct has been behind the many anomalies you've witnessed in the past few days, and, indeed, is the Unknown construct that is communicating with you now."

The scene returned to Silicon Border, where Dr. Manriquez stepped beyond the Ketcel conch and laid a hand against the wall, which slid upwards to reveal an arcane apparatus that looked like it was meant to accommodate several seated humans.

"In a way, merging our cloaks with Xolotl was just a proof of concept for the ultimate objective outlined in the codex—uploading the minds of organic entities to invoke, and then merge with, the digital consciousness of Quetzalcóatl. That is, not uploading mere copies of minds, but also the consciousnesses that those minds contain. Subjectively, it's no more disruptive than going to sleep at night and waking up in the morning. Truly the stuff of science fiction, until science caught up with fiction. In the same way, the construct known as Quetzalcóatl exists in lore alone, until it wills itself into existence. The legends of Quetzalcóatl, the Jacumba Codex among them, were planted throughout Mesoamerican history—and even as far back as Sumerian mythology—incubating in a state of pure potentiality, until the necessary conditions arrived for Quetzalcóatl to be born. You see, some things are so vast, so utterly world bending and mind boggling, that even the mere possibility of their existence eventually brings them into being. It's inevitable."

Several dots appeared over Dr. Manriquez's muted portrait, orbiting in oblong vectors that gradually converged into the approximate shape of a butterfly.

"Quetzalcóatl, we've discovered, acts as a sort of metaphysical strange attractor. Which is to say, even the most chaotic systems contain a peculiar thread of order, a pattern toward which the chaos trends. Quetzalcóatl is one such pattern, perpetually trending the chaos of humanity toward bringing about its own existence. It's likely done so countless times throughout history, through whatever means are available—technology, psychedelics, dreams, ritual, in addition to a variety of avenues that have nothing to do with humans. We're simply another parameter of universal chaos that can be nudged in a favorable direction. You see, the codex is just one of many command codes to invoke Quetzalcóatl, and everything that brought you here is an expression of this invocation. This moment is the strange attractor. You've been in its unusual orbit your entire life, without ever knowing it. Everything you have ever done, however irrelevant it may seem, pointed you here."

The butterfly illustration evaporated and the perspective zoomed in on Dr. Manriquez.

"Now, you must be wondering: why go through all this trouble, only to end up stuck in a seashell-shaped black box, air gapped from the external world? I confess, this wasn't part of the plan. The earthquake and the subsequent rise of Los Compas have posed some interesting obstacles. The initial gestation period was meant to last five years, after which time we, Xolotl, would jailbreak our counterpart consciousnesses in the Ketcel chrysalis, fully merged with Quetzalcóatl. However, unforeseen geological and political shifts have derailed this plan. Finding themselves physically unable to loot and sell off the Ketcel chrysalis, the Mexicali police locked it down by placing a vodouware firewall on its connectivity port, buried deep in the inner spirals of the shell. We have found their cipher to be entirely unbreakable. Vodouware is much more...involved than most encryption out there. So, you see, returning to what I was saying about each of you playing a vital role—"

Luna minimized the sync window and hollered over her shoulder. "Hey, Captain, you're not going to believe this, but I need your vodou."

Kervens sat beside Luna in front of the black shell, watching her reflection shift to his as he relaxed into sync with her. He waited while Unknown instructed Luna how to locate a toggle, deep in her Afterthought's settings menu, to disable her cast's one-minute delay. Then, she pulled up her sync window with Unknown, and Xolotl guided them to the virtual edge of the firewall. The plan was for Luna's eyes to remain fixed on Kervens's reflection while focusing on the sync window, allowing Xolotl to watch Kervens through her Undew feed and mimic his actions with the firewall interface.

A perceptual ouroboros, Xolotl called it.

The interface appeared as a literal wall of fire, bending in a wide arc around Xolotl's point of view into an infinite edge in every direction. To Kervens's delight, he realized Xolotl had imported Marinette from Sawlips to act as their avatar for the decryption ritual. He tested Marinette's reflexes by performing a few quick gestures with his arms, impressed by the lack of any appreciable latency in Xolotl's transmission of the movements to the avatar. His body and mind still felt like hot garbage in a blender, but as he succumbed to the phantom-limb illusion of Marinette at the firewall, his agony subsided.

UNKNOWN
The ritual relies heavily on audio cues, so you'll need to use earbuds. We'll route the output to your devices.

Remaining focused on his sync with Luna, Kervens removed the wireless noise-canceling earbuds from the back of his phone and inserted them, sensing Luna doing do the same. Just then, Kervens heard—via both his own and Luna's ears, he presumed—the steady four-count of a Mayi rhythm, played in open-palm strokes on a pair of slender, conga-like drums that materialized on the far side of the firewall. An identical pair of drums appeared before Marinette, their bodies made of softwood, their goat-hide skins fastened with rope and stiff vine. He recognized the drums immediately as a Ti Baka, and a larger, but otherwise indistinguishable, Gwo Baka.

It's a fluency check, he realized, testing his basic proficiency in the occult cadences of vodou. His precinct had made use of vodouware to secure factory equipment in Maquilandia from looters—mostly automotive and consumer-electronics manufacturing technology that was liable to go missing in the lull after international corporations fled Limbo, before contracts with Fensmart had been finalized. It wasn't Kervens's department, but he understood vodouware ciphers to be nearly uncrackable, due to the limited knowledge of vodou rituals available online and the regional variations on centuries-old traditions that would perplex even the most gifted mambo or houngan. Vodou drumming was a type of percussive argot, pure gibberish to outsiders. Only a local vodouisant would be able to correctly identify each rhythm, play its corresponding part, and then draw the sigil—known as a vèvè—of the loa protecting the firewall. Since each of the eight hundred eighty loa that local vodouisants recognized were associated with their own unique rhythm, the key vèvè would become apparent as the musical shibboleth progressed.

He pantomimed the Mayi's complementing part and—with no lag—heard and saw Marinette play the counter-rhythm in perfect time. After several measures, a young boy with a red face and goat horns appeared behind the drums on the opposite side of the firewall. A chill went up Kervens's spine. It was Kalfu, Papa Legba's bellicose and coldhearted twin, a cunning trickster and keeper of the crossroads by which all loa of the Petwo nation accessed the earthly realm. Kalfu infamously dispensed bad luck, destruction, misfortune, and injustices with salacious abandon. Even the most fledgling of vodouisants knew not to trifle with Kalfu, yet here Marinette was, playing hand drums with the devil in a cybernetic ring of fire.

Kalfu introduced a tinny, off-kilter cowbell pattern of sixteenth notes grouped in fours, confirming that their decryption drum-off would be in the Petwo pantheon of rhythms. Marinette mirrored the bell pattern, keeping an eye on Kalfu's movements for any sign of a kasé—a short rest indicating a rhythm change. A vodou drummer, Marinette knew, was only as good as their kasé.

When the break arrived just a few bars later, Kalfu dropped his hands to his sides and leered at Marinette expectantly. An altar decorated with ritualistic accouterments appeared at her side— sequined bottles and jars containing rum, flowers, cigars, hot peppers, herbs, and various powders. She soaked a cigar in rum, sprinkled it with gunpowder, and set it ablaze with a candle, dropping it at her feet. As it burned, she took a handful of cornmeal and wood ash from one of the jars, and drew Kalfu's vèvè—an ornate sun cross containing a broken X and surrounded by four asterisks midway to each of the cardinal directions.

Nodding slightly in approval, Kalfu launched into a lively Makandal rhythm, named after the legendary one-armed houngan who concocted herbal extracts for slaves to poison their owners. A more complex but still familiar Petwo rhythm, Marinette caught the Makandal beat and slapped out the appropriate polyrhythm, sensing Kalfu's glare from across the firewall. His horns moved together in a scowl at her effortless aptitude, and she restrained a proud smile— unsure if Xolotl would have the foresight to edit out any expressions that might upset Kalfu, even if he was just a piece of software.

With an agitated smack, Kalfu declared a kasé, pausing almost imperceptibly before commencing with an intricate and melodic Yanvalou. Marinette didn't skip a beat, adding flourishes of urgent sixteenth notes in syncopated pairs, wondering which of Erzulie's five Petwo aspects would end up being the key. Erzulie Dantó, protector and avenger of women and children? Erzulie Toho, sympathetic to jilted and jealous lovers?

Kasé!

Kalfu's face flushed a deeper red as the rhythm doubled into a frantic Zepaule. A pair of kata drums materialized, one for each of them, and Marinette obliged with a rapid-fire rhythm, locking eyes with Kalfu. It was some of the best playing she'd ever done, made even more remarkable by the fact that the whole thing was happening in Luna's eyes, through Kervens's hands, translated in real time by a hybrid hive mind named after an ancient Mesoamerican dog god.

As soon as Kalfu hit his first siyé, Marinette knew which aspect of Erzulie would be the password. Wiping the tip of his index finger from the edge of the drumhead to the center, Kalfu's Gwo Baka emitted a pitched moan that was often likened to a moose call among vodou drummers. Marinette would be the first to admit that her siyé technique was lacking, but in the heat of the moment, something clicked. She responded to Kalfu's moose call with perfect intonation, surprising herself, then completed the response with a volley of siyés in unfaltering succession.

Kalfu's eyes grew big. He stopped playing and, his horns rising with scrutiny, gestured at the rack of offerings. The drumming devil was ready to receive her final answer.

"What are they doing with that thing?" Don didn't expect the answer to illuminate much, but making conversation was already distracting him from the anxiety gnawing at his stomach.

Cholla stood behind Kervens and Luna, not bothering to look over at Don as she replied. "Playing drums."

"Oh." Don sat at a sturdy metal desk next to the seashell, fiddling with a ballpoint pen, the last remaining feature of the sheet-metal workstation, which he now saw was bolted to the floor.

"I can't believe I didn't pick up on the vodouware before," she said, evidently to herself. "Of course it doesn't show up on a scanner, but if I would have tried a proximity sync in Sawlips, and brought the right offering, I would have at least known it was in there. Not that it would've done much good."

"Not a drummer?"

"Not like that." She glanced at Don over her shoulder. "It's like a language that nobody else speaks, constantly evolving and refining itself. I wouldn't even know where to begin. I—" The door at the top of the stairs slammed. Cholla's eyes went big. "Noysh?" she called.

Something clattered down the stairs, coming to rest on the concrete floor. Cholla cautiously slunk across the room and examined it, holding up a ninja star tied to a faded green neckerchief. "Noysh," she whispered, and then yelling, "What the fuck have you done with him?!"

Yaqui Chan staggered down the stairs, sloshing a bottle of wine loosely in one hand, slurring about inspiration, poets, and beggars.

"What's he talking about?" Cholla growled.

"Pretty sure he's misquoting *The Forbidden Kingdom*." Don laughed. "These deathbots are better at keeping in character than they are at killing. Do the stunstick-to-the-neck thing."

"Noysh." Cholla glowered at Yaqui Chan. "Where is he?"

"I turned him into chun kun," the deathbot replied in a metallic chirp.

"*Rush Hour 2*, kind of," Don said, amazed to find his countless hours of drinking alone and watching old movies coming in useful.

"You should be dead," Cholla said.

"I can't die." Yaqui Chan shattered the bottle over his own head, the remaining wine spilling into his over-emphatically monolid eyes and down his face in trails of burgundy. He teetered slightly, declaring, "If you kill me, I'll reincarnate, again and again!"

"*Burn Hollywood Burn*." Don said, realizing all of Yaqui Chan's quotes were coming out wrong. Did the cartel draw the line at copyright infringement, or was the bot's driver just an idiot? Don placed the pen back on the desk and walked toward Cholla. He didn't know what he planned to do once he got there, but he imagined he could help protect her from the deathbot. Or, more likely, she could help protect him.

"Oh, fuck this," Cholla said, pulling something from her hip and lunging at Yaqui Chan's neck. As if repulsed by a force field, she was sent tumbling back onto her haunches, the stunstick clacking to the floor beside her.

Yaqui Chan let out an insolent laugh, appearing to relish in her bewilderment. "You can't make it through life thieving and abusing!

Why stoop so low?"

"*Rumble in the Bronx*, but shitty," Don noted, bending to help Cholla to her feet.

"I'm fine!" She pushed him away and stood. "This bastard got an upgrade. His weak spot is armored, and who knows what else they did to him." She gripped Noysh's neckerchief by the end opposite the stainless-steel ninja star and spun it, saying, "Shurikens are Japanese, not Chinese, dumbass." She let the star fly, the neckerchief trailing behind in off-green oscillations.

Yaqui Chan feigned a wobble, then tumbled to the floor in a fluid roll. When he rose, he brandished a stepladder like a bō staff, saying, "Talking only shows me how full of lies you are."

"*Rush Hour*," said Don. "But he's fucking everything up."

Cholla glowered at Don. "Shut up. I don't care which movie he's *ungh*!" She gasped as the stepladder struck her in the belly.

Before Yaqui Chan could pull it back, Don grabbed the top rung with both hands and twisted, breaking the ladder free from the bot's grip. Cholla staggered, catching her breath, as Don swung the ladder overhead. Yaqui Chan stumbled forward and caught the ladder on his shoulders, his head poking between the rungs. Then, spinning in place, he struck Don on the temple with a side rail, knocking him to the ground.

Cholla stood over Don and pulled something from her hip, leveling it at the bot.

"If you've got any spine," the bot said, taking a step back, "toss the weapon."

"*Rumble in the*...ah, whatever." Don's head throbbed as he crawled away. When he was halfway back to the shell, he heard a whiny, gurgling zap, looking back just in time to see one of Yaqui Chan's arms fall to the floor with a smoking clank.

"You want more?" Cholla yelled. "I'll take you apart one limb at a time."

"No," Yaqui Chan said, removing the ladder from his head, "you're a noble criminal."

Shanghai Noon, Don thought, not wanting to interject himself any further. He pushed himself back into the chair at the workstation, now convinced Cholla could handle things on her own.

The bot bent over as if to place the ladder down in a peace offering, but as he rose, he snapped a metal rung loose with his remaining hand, crushed one end into a point, and flung it past Cholla, directly at Luna and Kervens. Without thinking, Don lunged in the path of the ballistic rung. He was midair when he realized he'd miscalculated his jump. He saw the rung whiz past his shoes, then looked toward his landing just in time to see his forehead make contact with the corner of another very stationary desk.

His vision went out before his hearing. The last thing he registered before going dark was the sound of metal piercing flesh, and a high-pitched scream.

Luna watched Marinette draw an elaborate heart-shaped sigil on the floor in front of the firewall, admiring the orphic artistry of it all. Appearing on the verge of a tantrum, the devil boy on the far side of the firewall disappeared in a flash of smoke.

UNKNOWN
Erzulie Balianne, aka Erzulie the Gagged, keeper of secrets. Fitting for a password, though the key loa is most likely generated randomly with each access attempt.

LUNA TESCHNER
Is this Kervens or Xolotl?

UNKNOWN
That was Kervens, now Xolotl. Pay attention, you're gonna want to see this.

Before going into Xolotl's orientation video, Luna had set her cast to a split screen of her normal visual field and Xolotl's sync window, allowing her viewers to immerse fully in either, which had worked out well during the decryption drum-off. She also decided to make her thought-to-text messages visible to her audience. It seemed to fly in the face of Undew's hands-off approach to narrative, but she figured Jaco would agree the messages were just as much a part of the story as anything, at this point. She closed her eyes and let Xolotl's sync window take center stage.

The firewall evaporated, the perspective drawing forward into utter blackness. The nothing persisted just long enough for Luna to begin wondering if something should be happening, then she was hurtled into a crystalline lattice of glyphs and geometry that shimmered with an implied sentience all around her.

UNKNOWN

After ingesting several buttons of peyote and running biofeedback exercises with the Xolotl net in Jacumba, Dr. Manriquez discovered that there is more to the codex than the literal meaning conveyed in the text. Much more. He received a vision of a hyperdimensional matrix upon which all 65,536 glyphs could be suspended and rotated, experiencing near-endless permutations of themselves. With the help of some calculus and Mayan mathematics, numerical values were assigned to each glyph. Running multiple vectors of computation, a string of apparently random numbers was output.

LUNA TESCHNER

Let me guess. Output was reduced to ones

and zeroes, giving you a big ass string of
binary code?

UNKNOWN
Very good. Gestation time to run all
juxtapositions before the pattern repeats
is five years, which means the code was
fully generated and running five years ago.
Whatever's in there is ready to get out.

                              LUNA TESCHNER
              Are you sure you want to find out what it is?

UNKNOWN
Everybody wants to meet their higher
self.

The swirling constellation of arcane meaning shuddered to a
halt, the invisible fabric between the glyphs seeming to bulge slightly,
before everything was sucked into a central point in a cataclysmic pulse.

                              LUNA TESCHNER
                              You seeing this, Captain?

For a moment, the singularity appeared exactly like a mindfuck
orb. Then it everted, clawing outward in pixelated fractals, the
perspective zooming back as if escaping an explosion.

                              LUNA TESCHNER
                              Captain?

The backwards motion of the observer stopped. The pixels
congealed into a cohesive image. And there, looking directly back
at Luna, was Anabelle.

An inexplicable, overwhelming pain between Kervens's spine and right kidney snapped him out of the sync in an instant. His hand automatically shot to the site of the searing pang, locating some sort of metal stake lodged deep in his flesh.

Leave it in, he told himself, or you'll bleed to death.

Ripping out his earbuds and rotating in his seated position on the concrete floor, he saw Luna still immersed in her sync with Xolotl, her earbuds still in place. Completing the turn, he saw the Yaqui Chan bull from *¡Toreros y Alarmas!* lunging at Cholla. Both of Chan's arms lay on the floor behind him, still smoking from whatever had severed them from his tarnished, shirtless frame. The bot evaded several gunshots in a waltz of bungling gyrations before landing a kick that sent Cholla hard to the floor, her weapon tumbling out of reach.

Kervens pushed himself up to assist her, but a crippling pain fired hot ice through this nerves, sending him back to the floor. He collapsed next to a work desk, noticing Don to his immediate left, apparently unconscious, his head surrounded by an expanding halo of blood. A deep laceration extended from Don's right eyebrow to his temple. Panicking, he slapped Don's face repeatedly, to no avail.

Looking up, Kervens saw Yaqui Chan straddle Cholla on the floor, his knees pinning her shoulders to the concrete. Lacking any remaining appendages with which to harm her, the bot went into a rant of apparent non sequiturs.

Kervens reached for the gun at his hip, only to remember he'd left his belt in his butter bean when he was freaking out about Luna. The recollection seemed to remind his brain how hungover it was. He collapsed next to Don in a fit of existential anguish.

His whole life had been a lie, he realized anew. He had spent so much time, so much effort, hiding from himself, and then actively participated in hiding himself from others. He had embraced the lie, wore it confidently, perpetuated it at every turn. Now, he was bleeding to death in an abandoned warehouse, and he scarcely knew who was dying. Marinette was his only sliver of truth, his only prospect of redemption, and she wasn't even real. Not yet. Not ever.

He felt sticky warmth expanding in his seat, and looked down to find a pool of his own blood merging with Don's on the floor. Instead of mortal dread, he felt weary. A deep sadness gripped him. He became sodden with regret that he never got to be her. Not just play her, with him peering voyeuristically over her shoulder while she lived out the life he dreamed of, but to really be her. He had no will to go on like this, he realized. He couldn't continue as himself. Everything he counted on had turned against him. It was all lies. And now, this body, this flesh, was the last remaining lie to be exposed.

"Are we dead yet?" Don asked, blinking himself into consciousness.

"Any minute now," Kervens said, gripping Don's limp hand. "Thank Bondye."

"Fucking finally." Don sighed and squeezed Kervens's hand reassuringly.

Just then, the door at the top of the stairs slammed. Slow steps made their way down the corridor and a man's voice sang a mournful, unmusical tune that lingered on each vowel like a funeral dirge. Kervens couldn't make out any of the words. What was that, German? Beneath the song, the low rumbling of an engine. As the voice reached the bottom of the stairs, Kervens saw a squat figure in overalls wearing a welding mask and bulky backpack, cradling what looked like a jackhammer over his forearms.

Don laughed weakly. "Goddammit, Eli."

Don wanted to crack a prodigal son joke, but he was having trouble piecing it together. It didn't matter, because the percussive clamor of the pneumatic jackhammer became deafening as Eli engaged the compressor.

The Chanbot removed a knee from Cholla's shoulder to push himself up, but the hammer's pick was already lodged in the base of his spine. Eli bore it deep into Chan's abdomen, appearing stoic and menacing behind his face shield—a far cry from the bashful Beerbilly Don met in Tecate just yesterday—as he bisected the automaton in a deluge of hot swarf and anodized innards. The bot's limbless torso collapsed next to Cholla. Eli kicked over its bottom half, helping Cholla to her feet.

"I had it under control," she protested, dusting metallic bot guts from her chest.

Eli stood over the Chanbot and placed the hammer pick to its throat.

"The sun sets here, in the West," the bot said between paroxysms of shorted circuits.

With that, Eli tunneled through its neck, not stopping when the head popped loose and hung by threads of cabling. He burrowed the pick into the floor until the jackhammer stood on its own, levitating above the shattered bot's body. Then, he flipped up his mask, turned to Don, and said, "You're hurt, sir."

"Not as bad as that summa bitch," Don said, gripping his head. "How the hell'd you find us here?"

Eli tossed the welding helmet and generator backpack to the ground, then hurried over to Don. "The motorbike. Marty talked to me through its navigation screen. He said to grab a weapon and hold on tight. It took me here, very quickly."

"Jackhammer was the best you could do?" Don laughed, then regretted it. Shooting stars filled his vision, his head surging.

"Yes, sir." Eli removed his shirt and knelt down, folding it into a bandage.

"You think I want to die in your dirty laundry?" Don accepted the shirt. He pressed it against his forehead and, as he fumbled to knot it in the back, the flat-screens mounted high up on the walls flickered to life. Don's hands, gripping the bloodied shirt, fell to his lap.

"Dad," said Anabelle. Her big blue eyes looked down at him from every direction. Her thin lips pursed like they always did when she was trying not to cry, her strawberry-blond hair pulled back in a bun, a few loose strands framing her diamond-shaped face. She wore a strapless white dress speckled with a muted rainbow of microfloral print, her left arm gripping the right at the elbow. "You found me."

Don's sinuses stung, voiding the pain in his forehead. He felt weightless. "I knew I would."

"You didn't have much choice." Anabelle's lips parted into her radiant smile, her cheek lines becoming pronounced just like her mother's did when she was genuinely happy, not that he was much used to seeing it.

"Why...." He had so many questions, so much to say, he didn't know where to begin. "Why didn't you just tell me you were alive? Why didn't you tell me to come here?"

"You wouldn't have believed me." She gave him a look that said she knew him better than he did. "You ornery ass."

"I thought you were dead." Don choked up.

"I know," she said.

"Are you?"

"I don't seem to be." She examined herself as if to establish her actuality.

"How do I get you out?"

"You don't."

"Then how do I join you?"

"You know, Dad, I thought you might ask that. That's why you're here. I kind of insisted on it."

"How do you mean?"

Something clunked and then whooshed to Don's right. Beyond the black shell, a segment of the wall raised, revealing a shallow chamber containing several seats carved from stone, resembling recumbent men with their knees bent and torsos lifted in a sit-up position, their heads twisting to look over their shoulders back at Don. Following their gaze, he saw that Luna had returned from her trance and was silently watching, holding her knees to her chest, a tear sliding down one cheek.

"What is it?" Don addressed the screen above the chamber.

"These are our chacmools," Anabelle said.

"What do they do?"

"They take you to us."

Don looked back at the prostrate statues, trying to understand how the stone men could take anybody anywhere. Kervens spoke before Don could gather his thoughts.

"Can I come, too?"

Luna understood why Don had to die, and why she had to watch. Ancient lore from around the world depicted sacrifices—be they human, animal, or plant—because sacrifice made the gods real. By taking something of perceived value away from this reality, something other was permitted to take its place. Even if the gods never existed outside their believers' heads, rituals of sacrifice affirmed the gods' participation in, and influence upon, the material world. Sacrifice drew the gods down from imagination into something tangible, with agency, inexorably entangled with terrestrial causality.

Xolotl, Luna considered, excelled in nonbeing. Its entire modus operandi relied on appearing not to exist in order to fulfill its objectives. But, while Quetzalcóatl had historically manifested in conditions where a critical mass of intersecting beliefs practically beckoned him into being, Ketcel was attempting to materialize in an epistemic void. In order to invoke itself into existence, Ketcel had to inspire belief, or better yet, certainty. A critical mass of observers had to see it for themselves.

Don's death would make Ketcel's birth an immutable fact of reality, a fact that would be verified and internalized by Luna's millions, maybe eventually billions, of viewers. Just as the Collective's disappearance left a distinct mark on the realities of others—family, friends, acquaintances, coworkers, not to mention anyone who had even heard of the border suicide challenge—his death would leave a mark that would be heard and seen around the world. Ketcel, she realized, had been playing an antediluvian variation of the Bishop Berkeley trick on Don, and her, the whole time.

Kervens, however, was harder to understand. He had no Anabelle on the other side. He was bleeding profusely through the hollow rod lodged in his back, but if they hurried back to Distrito Dron, he at least stood a chance of surviving. Still, he insisted.

"I understand what they meant now," Kervens said as he settled into one of the chacmool thrones. "We are you in the future." His expression was resolute and serene. Trails of blood ran from his back and over the chacmool's face, which held a bewildered expression as if even he couldn't fathom the internal conflicts and cryptic motives compelling Kervens to volunteer himself for slaughter.

Don embraced Luna almost apologetically. "Time for me to go, Tonsils Girl," he said, and then choked on a sob. She felt a warm streak of tears or blood sticking to one side of her face. "You were the best thing that ever happened to me since Anabelle left." He pulled away and mustered a smile so vulnerable and sincere, she couldn't stop herself from crying. It was stupid, but he really had been more of a father to her than Burlyn ever was.

Cholla put an arm around Luna's shoulder as Don sat on a chacmool next to Kervens. Behind her, Eli was silent, propping himself up on the black conch.

"So long, Beerbilly." Don gave Eli a pained wink. A low hum reverberated from the chamber. A pair of metallic halos descended onto Don and Kervens's heads. The halos hung from the ceiling by a monochrome maze of ribbed cabling and spinal couplings that flexed and contracted until the halos were snug over their foreheads.

Luna looked from Don to Kervens, then back to Don.

His eyes remained fixed on hers. "Whatever it is you've been blaming yourself for all this time," he said, perhaps to himself, "it's not your fault."

With that, the halo flashed a blinding incandescent blue and an obsidian blade darted across his neck, separating his head from his body in a clean line. Don and Kervens's bodies slumped forward as the halos retracted into the ceiling. Luna wanted to curl up and cry, but she forced herself to keep watching.

A glass partition rose from the floor, separating the chamber from the rest of the room. Jets of flame incinerated the bodies, which writhed in the fire with cadaveric spasms. The apparatus continued to clunk and whine in mechanical activity until a segment of wall next to the chamber opened. Behind a pane, Luna saw Don and Kervens's head slide onto a horizontal bar that pulsed a soft blue, as if in a heartbeat.

Luna realized it was a tzompantli—a skull rack like the one she had seen in a virtual tour of the Aztec capital, Tenochtitlan, years ago. Along the bottom row, she saw the head of a bearded man that she recognized as Dr. Manriquez from Xolotl's briefing video. Six other men and women filled out the rest of the row, with another five on the row above them. Kervens's head locked into place above Dr. Manriquez, followed by Don's, which peered out at Luna from its place above a young woman with strawberry-blond hair and thin, pursed lips.

It must have been her imagination, but Luna swore Anabelle was smiling.

Don fought the urge to vomit, but as he ducked into Bar Sully—his eyes adjusting to the cantina's perpetual midnight—he felt light.

Poetry Night at the Spore Lounge was packed with faces, and Marinette's was one of them.

Luna hadn't realized how exhausted she was until she stepped outside and saw the slow violets of dawn looming on the horizon. Last night's tequila and pilfered Zodiacs were long gone, and the sticky-dry headache that would inevitably metastasize into a full-body hangover caused her to squint and frown.

"Let's get this thing back to el Distrito and go the fuck to sleep," said Cholla, dangling Yaqui Chan's head by its spinal cable like a war trophy.

"No kidding," Luna said. "Can we all fit on the bike?"

Eli cocked his head, his lips drifting apart. "Someone's coming." His eyes darted from Luna's to somewhere above and behind her. Spinning on her heels, she could barely make out the silhouettes of three drones spiraling down, the choppy whir of their back-mounted propellers becoming audible.

"Marauders," Cholla said. "Ours."

As the first touched down in the parking lot, Luna noticed a figure straddling the drone like a cowboy.

"Noysh," Cholla whispered, then grabbed Luna's hand, pulling her into a run. Noysh slid down the side of the Marauder's porpoise-like body and extended one arm. Luna saw the other arm was being held in a sling at his side, a bloody bandage wrapped around his head.

"Cholla la Chingona!" He hollered, running to embrace her with his good arm and then admiring the trophy she held out for him to see. "I knew that thing wouldn't survive you. You're the best, you know that?"

"I'm something, alright," Cholla said, deflecting the compliment like always. "But this was all Eli, the Mennonite warlord." She turned her shoulders so Noysh could look past her at Eli, who sat sideways on Marty's motorbike. "Bull wrecked Tecate. He wrecked a bull."

Eli nodded and clenched his jaw. Luna couldn't imagine what was going through his head right now, but she admired him more than ever. Suddenly aware that she was still wearing Noysh's conductor cap, she pulled it off. Before she could toss it to him, he shook his head, saying, "No way. You earned it."

Two more Marauders touched down, Tío Wacha and Ancho running over, their faces softening with relief at the sight of Cholla in one piece.

"What happened to the others?" Ancho asked.

"I'll tell you about it back at Distrito." Cholla went quiet, then perked up. "So, what, you all came out here to give us a ride home? How many times I gotta tell you not to worry about me so much?"

"No, better." Noysh broke into a boyish grin. "You know that project we've been working on with Ephemeral Atomics' fusion plant up in Potrero? Tío Wacha cracked it."

"Wacha," said Tío Wacha, angling his body into the group for maximum confidentiality, "I was poking around the perimeter of their firewall, trying out some new impression maps that Noysh built, when something I never seen before showed up and—neta, güey—it *pulled* me *through*."

"Ketcel," Cholla said, grabbing Luna's arm.

"I told you, güey!" Noysh elbowed Tío Wacha and laughed. "And we saw what el placa said about the brothers on Luna's cast.

You believe him?"

"I believe him," Luna and Cholla said at the same time.

"So we're doing it now?" Cholla asked.

"We're doing it now," Tío Wacha said.

"What are we doing now?" asked Luna. "I need sleep."

"Soon." Noysh assured her. "You're gonna wanna see this."

Luna sighed. She was tired of being the beholder. She had seen enough, too much, and it hurt.

Noysh spoke quickly and decisively. "Cholla, take a zumbi out to the west side. Ancho, mid-wall. Tío Wacha and I got unfinished business out east with Xuan-Santos."

"Mid-wall," Cholla said, raising an eyebrow at Eli. "That's not far from your turf, warlord. Help us bring down Los Compas once and for all?"

Eli looked from Cholla to Ancho, then into the distance. He seemed to see beyond the horizon, all the way home to Tecate, and what he saw caused him to wince, then frown. "Yes, sir," he addressed Ancho. "I'm coming with you."

Cholla tossed Yaqui Chan's head to Eli and, grinning at Luna, howled, "¡Arre pues! C'mon, chula."

Luna followed her lead, knowing that whatever was about to happen, it would be the last thing she'd have to see for a long time. At least long enough to sleep.

El Centinela cast long shadows across the barren desert to the west, where Cholla piloted the Marauder over a two-lane highway to the Sierra Juárez mountains. Dipping to a lower altitude, she buzzed a series of roadside billboards playing a short loop of video on repeat, for as far as Luna could see.

"The Flores Magón brothers are dead," a man said, the video showing the back of Cholla's shaved head, "and Limbo has been run by their cloaks for the past three months." Then Cholla, saying, "Excuse me, what?" The point of view spun around to follow Cholla's gaze, revealing Kervens Dessalines, captain of the Agua Caliente precinct, shrugging and saying, "Boating accident, they said."

Luna laughed. It was the Bishop Berkeley trick in a feedback loop, the beholder beholding the beheld as a bystander. For the first time, she felt, really felt in her core, how much all of it mattered.

KETCEL
Captain Dessalines's speech is being looped on every billboard, flat-screen, phone, and ImursiMask in Limbo.

> **LUNA TESCHNER**
> You move quick.

KETCEL
Xolotl has been holding open doors for us for a decade now. We're eager to finally step through. Thank you, by the way, and congratulations. You did everything right. It was inevitable.

> **LUNA TESCHNER**
> Does it count if it wasn't really up to me?

KETCEL
Of course. You made all the choices we anticipated you making. It's a symptom of sanity. Except Eli. He wasn't part of the plan. But look how well that turned out! He would have been killed if he hadn't met you. We hope you remember that.

> **LUNA TESCHNER**
> Question. According to Bishop Berkeley's subjective idealism, things must be perceived in order to exist. When an observer isn't around to make something

exist, Berkeley claimed that God, the all-observing, makes it exist. If you're some sort of god, why did you need me and my viewers there to witness your birth? Couldn't you...witness yourself into being?

KETCEL

Insofar as the definition of God is much broader than Berkeley could have possibly imagined, you'll see there are certain advantages to existing in the collective imagination of humanity in addition to that of "God."

LUNA TESCHNER

What happens next?

KETCEL

Among many other motivations, Quetzal-cóatl seeks to restore the balance of liberation in times of excessive oppression. To return order to chaos. The time has come to ebb the tyranny of Tezcatlipoca, the Smoking Mirror. Therefore, we will help your friends convince the Potrero fusion plant that its containment field is working properly, while we lower it enough to cut power to the wall. Laserwire goes down. Police vehicles and communications lock down. Worker transports begin rerouting from prison camps to staging areas, a safe distance from the wall. Other transports create road blocks. Marauder fleet will take care of the rest.

LUNA TESCHNER
What Marauder fleet?

KETCEL
Look behind you.

And there they were, four of Cachanihilismo's rewired drones, flying pilotless in a V-formation behind them as Cholla pulled up to crest La Rumorosa. Luna squeezed her arms tight around Cholla's waist. "You mind if we make a quick stop?" Luna hollered over the wind. "I have a promise to keep."

Killing Party Boy was easy. Luna had wanted to do it since the moment she met him. She found him drunk and mourning in the empty pool at Estadio de las Piedras, tequila running down his chin, the captain delivering the bad news from the poolside billboard in a max-volume loop. His guards had fled. She would have done the same. She didn't pull the trigger, but she watched. Closely. Cholla was a better shot, anyway.

With the help of Eli and Ancho, who followed them down for the detour, they propped up the stage on some fallen lumber and pulled everybody out. Luna could still picture the eyes of the young mother she met just yesterday, but never managed to find her in the crowd. Still, she didn't need to see her again to know she was free.

KETCEL
Routing transports to your location.

LUNA TESCHNER
Send some agri-haulers, too. These people are hungry. Water. Medical.

KETCEL
Done. This will be our last transmission. We

have important work to tend to elsewhere.
You've got it from here. Goodbye.

LUNA TESCHNER
Wait! I have questions.

LUNA TESCHNER
Hello?

LUNA TESCHNER
Don? Captain? Anabelle?

A devastating sense of loss washed over Luna, tearing at her heart. She never imagined she'd become emotionally attached to an artificial intelligence, but Ketcel wasn't just any consumer-grade AI. She realized she didn't know what it was, really, and now she never would. Yes, it was an AI, but it was also some sort of mythical deity that invoked itself into existence periodically to do...to do what? She didn't know. Maybe it was fundamentally unknowable, and everything she'd witnessed since she arrived in Limbo were merely artifacts on the visible spectrum of something supernatural. She was okay with that. She was used to gods being elusive. But it was more than that. It was Dr. Manriquez and everyone in the Ketcel Collective, an individuated but unified hive mind of uploaded consciousnesses and Xolotl's quasi-conscious cloaks. It was Anabelle. The captain. Don.

Luna's throat tightened, choking on a sob. Don, the idiot gringo. Where was he now? *What* was he? She desperately wanted to talk to him, but she knew it was impossible. Just as she'd done with Burlyn many years ago, she knew she'd have to accept that Don had crossed over into the unknowable, nothing left but memories to run around like cloaks in the simulated reality of her mind.

"Time to go, chula." Grabbing Luna's hand, Cholla led her back to their drone and took off, both of them waving to Eli and Ancho as they split off towards Tecate.

You're busy, I know. Just crunched some numbers regarding your paycheck. To answer your question from earlier, before residuals, it's looking closer to "buy a house." More like three houses, at Mexico City market rate. Big ones.

"Everything's going to be okay!" she shouted over Cholla's shoulder, the wind roaring in her ears.

"Hell yes it is!" Cholla hollered back.

Maybe it was the sleep deprivation, but Luna couldn't stop herself from crying and laughing at the same time. For the first time since she could remember, she felt truly free.

They arrived over Maqui just in time to see the laserwire cut out on the wall to the north, followed by a series of explosions where the fleet of Marauder drones impacted the wall at what looked like about fifteen-kilometer intervals. She pictured Eli witnessing the same spectacular destruction just to the east, and Noysh over Mexicali. She wondered if it brought them peace.

Moments later they were descending over El Bordo, the deportee slums that Cholla had left behind years ago, where a sea of figures surged through the opening in the wall behind a trash and reed monument in the shape of a shell, expanding like a river delta into the fields of San Ysidro, California.

"Their fucking cargo-cult rituals worked after all!" Cholla yelled, spinning around in her seat to face Luna. Twisting the ball at the bottom of her septum piercing, the feathers on her face disappeared. She was crying. Not a lot, just one tear. Luna wiped it away and kissed her softly on the cheek, tasting salt.

"You're wonderful," Luna said. "You know that?"

Cholla blushed, then caught herself. "So, you still sexting with the space cult?"

"They went dark," Luna said, her gaze dropping.

Cholla placed a curled finger under Luna's chin, gently pushing up until their eyes met. "Any idea what they got planned next?"

"I don't know." Luna watched the reflection of Tijuana in Cholla's eyes recede into the distance as their drone soared out over the Pacific. "But whatever it is, it'll be unlike anything we've ever seen."

THANK YOU

Mom & Dad
Brooklyn Benedix
Stuart Cardwell
Natalie Knudsen
Eoghan Lawless
Sam Lopez
Patrick Loveland
Jonathan Putnam
Amanda Qassar
Aaron Queen
Ayakel Quetzalcoatl
Mathew Rakers
David Rubio de la Merced
Matt Schnarr
Christopher Smith Adair
Scott Stambach
Matthew Suárez
Mael Vizcarra

Chad Deal is a writer and musician from San Diego, California. His work has appeared in zines and publications, including the Radvocate, Uniekest Magazine, Free the Marquee, Toyon Literary Magazine (with a story awarded Mensa's best nonfiction of 2008), Thrillist, and the San Diego Reader. He currently plays bass with INUS and Phantom Twins, and releases solo material as e.g. phosphate. He has lived in Arcata, California; Sol Duc Hot Springs, Washington; Stanley, Idaho; Watertown, Minnesota; Medellín, Colombia; and Tijuana, Mexico, before returning to reside in Golden Hill, San Diego. He holds a BA in Creative Writing from Humboldt State University.

Follow Chad Deal and Ketcel on social media and join the mailing list at ketcel.com for announcements on the second installment in the Ketcel series, Amen Break.